Praise for Russel D. McLean

"A dark and bloody excursion into Glasgow gangland . . . Edgy from page one."   *Sunday Times Crime Club*

"Chillingly plausible . . . a wonderfully dark and disturbing tale of misplaced loyalty and betrayal; a beautifully paced, action-packed thriller of a book."   **James Oswald**

"An uncompromising work of Glasgow noir, brutal and driven . . . at its heart is a woman torn between loyalty to her criminal family and a desire for a better life. Complicated and conflicted but achingly real, you'll be rooting for her all the way."   **Eva Dolan**

"This tense, violent thriller heads towards its climactic confrontation at a relentless pace, while posing tough questions about undercover work and family loyalty."
   Alastair Mabbott, *Sunday Herald*

"McLean has an ability to write about families that is uncanny when it comes to shaking the family tree to see what drops out."   *Crimespree*

"Conflict, blood on the floor and heightened emotions all conjugate well to deliver a high-octane read with ounces of 'noir' to spare."   **Maxim Jakubowski**, *Love reading*

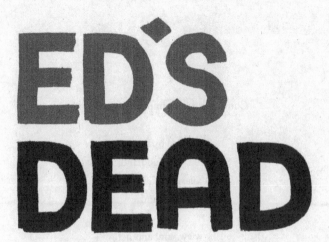

ED'S DEAD

RUSSEL D. MCLEAN

CONTRABAND

Contraband is an imprint of Saraband

Published by Saraband
Suite 202, 98 Woodlands Road
Glasgow, G3 6HB
Scotland

www.saraband.net

ISBN: 9781910192696
ISBNe: 9781910192702

10 9 8 7 6   5 4 3 2 1

Typeset by Iolaire Typography Ltd.
Printed and bound in Great Britain by Clays Ltd, St Ives plc.

For booksellers everywhere.

Especially those who haven't killed anyone.

PART ONE

THE BODY

One

The two-year anniversary of my friend's disappearance.

Not that she was taken. She went of her own free will. Given everything that happened, who could blame her?

The papers and the bloggers and the telly claimed she disappeared with a fake ID and a bundle of cash. The cash had been illegally obtained by her boyfriend, who just happened to be an undercover cop.

At least one part of that makes sense.

The other doesn't.

Then again, what do I know?

Me and Kat, we knew each other, but in the end I guess we didn't really. We'd drunk with some of the same friends, and I was there the night she met her boyfriend – the one who turned out to be an undercover copper looking to get to know her family a little better – but honestly, I couldn't say much about who she really was other than she liked all kinds of white wine with the exception of Chardonnay. We bonded over that. There are shakier ways to maintain a friendship.

Oh, and she had pretty good taste in men. I mean, if you leave aside the undercover guy who went crazy, killed her family and tried to run off into the sunset. But other than that, he seemed pretty decent towards her. And besides, they weren't together when he did all that. He'd already dumped her so that he could get closer to her uncle, the target of his operation.

3

Some people have exciting lives.

I just live day to day.

This one, he's a reporter. I can tell just by looking at him. He's got the walk, and then there's the gleam in his eyes when he clocks me alone at the table. Christ, did he know I'd be here, or did he just get lucky?

Probably just popped in for a quick espresso. I have enough troubles in my life without imagining the press are stalking me every time I go into a coffee shop.

I ignore him as best I can. Stare straight ahead. Make it clear I'm waiting for someone. But he's got the scent of blood. And maybe he doesn't see the second cup, or maybe he thinks someone left it there. But he's like a predator who's spied an animal abandoned by the herd.

I should tell him where to get off before he even opens his mouth. But that's not who I am. Never have been.

Good old Jen. Quiet wee girl. Always polite. Not that much of a wild side. Why would she need one, after all?

The reporter says, 'You knew Kat Scobie.' It could be a question, but the way he says it, I know it's a statement. He doesn't need to ask. This one, he likes to rake around for scandal. I'm getting to know how various reporters are: the different species and the different attitudes and expectations.

One TV interview. I didn't think it would hurt anyone. I thought I could clear up some misconceptions.

Now I'm a target. The story should be cold, but they don't seem to care. Maybe because Kat was young, beautiful and supposedly the only innocent person in a family of criminals. After what happened to them, there's no need to add 'alleged' now.

They can't find her, and no one directly involved is saying anything. So they turn to idiots like me who think maybe they're doing the right thing talking on camera about what a nice girl Kat was.

If I'd known I'd have to put up with this kind of nonsense, I'd never have done it.

I look to the window. People are walking past, shoulders hunched against the rain. I try and spot Ed. Hope that this reporter gets the hint I'm not here alone, and more, that I don't want to talk to him.

'You did, didn't you? You knew Kat Scobie. Come on, it's not like it's a secret. You said on national TV.' Just the slightest hint of aggro there. Not too obvious. Hidden below a kind of reasonable tone, like all he's doing is telling me the truth.

'I knew her. Barely.' Oh, Jen, why are you talking? What are you doing? Get up and leave. Or tell him to sod off. Don't engage. That's the worst bloody thing you can do.

'But you knew her?'

'I just want to drink my coffee in peace.' Assertion. Finally. Probably too little too late.

Right enough, he doesn't take the hint. Sits across from me. In the chair where Ed had been sitting not five minutes ago. This guy's thin, with black hair brushed back from the temples and oiled in a way that he probably thinks makes him slick, but only succeeds in giving him the slight air of sex offender.

I try not to let my distaste show too much.

He doesn't notice the second cup on the table.

Or he just doesn't care.

Take your pick.

'It's almost two years now since she disappeared. Have you heard anything from her?'

'We weren't that close.'

'No emails, texts?'

'Like I said . . .' My focus moves to just behind his left shoulder. I wonder if he'll notice.

'I hear you, but . . .' He stops talking. His head turns in the direction of my gaze.

He sees Ed, stands up. Ed looks over at him, then at me. Then back at the reporter. 'You and me, pal,' he says.

He likes to think he's tough. Scrawny bag of bones, really, but the lank hair and the way he dresses, you can't be entirely sure. What he makes me think of is one of those bad boys in Hollywood films. In his head, he's Johnny Depp. Sometimes I convince myself that he's right.

The reporter doesn't look too certain about what he should do.

Ed's soaked from the rain outside. His black curls stick against his head. The man would stand in a typhoon just for a two-minute smoke. But right now, he looks like he's walked in from the set of some horror movie, and I'm thankful for that. An air of intimidation does wonders for him.

'What's your name?'

'Dan McCarthy, *Evening News*.'

'Right, Dan,' Ed says, 'this is how it is . . .'

I smile and drink my coffee as Ed leads Dan outside. I watch through the windows. Nothing happens. No one gets beat up. People walk past on Sauchiehall Street, none of them batting an eyelid at the confrontation because it's so calm none of them notice. The two of them stand in the rain and Ed does all the talking and then he nods like that's it, and comes back in and sits across the table from me.

I keep looking out the window.

Dan looks at me, and then looks away again when he sees Ed's still watching him. He turns up his collar, runs into the rain.

'What did you say to him?'

Ed grins.

One of the baristas walks past. Girl in her late teens, maybe early twenties, who would look good in anything, even the uniforms these places make them wear: shapeless black trousers, ill-fitting polo shorts, those daft caps that I guess are better than hairnets. Ed notices. Stops looking at me.

Like I'm no longer in the room.

I guess I should be used to that by now.

From knight in shining armour to heel in one dick move.

That's Ed all over.

* * *

Ed makes me think we're going home. Back to mine. But when we get in the rear seat of the taxi, he gives an address in the East End – Bridgeton – and then settles next to me.

I say nothing.

Of course I do. Pointless arguing with Ed when he gets a plan bubbling. Not like he'd hit me or something if I stood my ground, but more that he wears you down with his constant talking. He's all talk. It's his secret weapon. If he wanted to be a salesman, he'd be incredible. He has this ability to talk anyone into almost anything.

I say *almost* anything, and I mean it. That threesome he suggested last year with a girl he met at a bar – Heidi, that was her name – is never going to happen, no matter how much he pleads and wheedles and begs.

The driver hesitates when he hears the address. 'You sure, pal?'

'I'm sure. Look, there's a wee bit extra in it for you if you wait, aye? Just got some business to–'

'Naw, naw.'

'Come on.'

'Look, I don't–'

'Nothing illegal,' Ed says. 'Honest. Just a wee favour for a friend, dropping him off something.'

'Aye?'

'Look, and then we're heading to Partick, right?'

'Partick?'

'Up near the Hyndland end,' Ed says, and what he's doing now

7

is turning on the charm. There's a slickness in his voice that's easy to fall for. Doesn't just work on women. Men, they tend to believe anything he says too.

'Aye, well.'

'Easy money for you,' Ed says.

'Anything happens,' the driver says, 'on your head and all.'

'I can always get another cab,' Ed says. 'I'm a big tipper.'

The driver doesn't say anything this time. I hear him sigh, but he drives anyway.

I look at Ed. He looks back at me and smiles. The kind of reassuring smile you might give a nervous child. It's too late to object now. I don't want to know why we're going out to the East End, but what I know for sure is that there's something dodgy about this little errand.

I've always known about this side of Ed. He tends to do things without thinking too hard about the long-term consequences. 'Live in the moment,' he says whenever anyone questions his choices. He likes a wee smoke, and not always just tobacco. Sometimes he takes a little pill at the start of an evening. He's tried to persuade me it's a good idea, but the only time I did ecstasy, I was eighteen and trying to fit in, and all I'll say is 'never again'.

Maybe it works for some people. Not me.

I feel nauseous just thinking about it.

The driver makes double quick time to the address Ed gave him. Where we end up feels abandoned, even by the standards of the poorer parts of the East End. Away from the main streets – the pound shops, the offies with bulletproof glass – we enter into what feels like the Badlands. Some of the houses are big, but look like people long ago gave up on caring for them. When we stop outside the address Ed gave the driver, the brakes work only hesitantly.

Ed pulls an envelope out of his jacket. 'Be a doll,' he says, 'just knock on the door and ask for Chris. Give him this.'

8

I don't even ask 'why me?' – just shoot him a look.

'Look,' he says, 'I go to the door myself, Chris is going to want to talk and the boy can talk those hind legs off that donkey, you know what I'm saying?' His eyes go wide. A trick that works on me every time. I've always been a sucker for hazel-browns, and his are big and expressive when he wants them to be.

I sigh.

He smiles.

I take the envelope. 'You owe me,' I say.

'Love you,' he says like a reflex, and steals a quick kiss. I try my best not to respond.

I can see the driver watching us in the rear view. Maybe thinking he should say something, but then deciding what happens between two people in the back his cab isn't any of his business. Not unless one of us is hurting the other. And maybe not even then.

It's not raining any more, but the wind's picking up a howl as I step out of the taxi. Stupid idea. Should have just refused. But it's too late now.

I can imagine my friend Caroline telling me to stop being a door-mat and stand up for myself. But I'm one of life's pleasers, really. I don't want trouble. I want everyone to be happy. Maybe there's a touch of martyrdom to what I do, but in the end, what can I do about it?

Nothing much.

Just hand over the envelope. Don't think about what's inside. Get this over and done with. Get back on with the rest of your life.

The front garden is overgrown. The remains of a concrete path highlights the way to the front door, but is obscured by weeds that sprout through the gaps and cracks between the stone. Glass crunches underfoot, but I don't look down, not wanting to know if I'm stepping on bottles or the remnants of needles.

I reach the front door. No bell. I have to knock. I do so as loud as I can, thinking that this is the last time Ed tricks me into being his lackey. There are boundaries in any relationship. At least for normal people.

This can't go on.

There's a talk I've been meaning to have with him, and it can't wait any more. If it was just limited to incidents like him going all Alpha male with that journalist, or just a general showing off and being a bit of a Jack the Lad, then I wouldn't really care. But when you combine all of that with his selfish bullshit, then something has to give.

No more doormat, Jen. Stand up for yourself.

The door opens. Hesitantly. A face pops out. Not what you'd call handsome. Bad skin with signs of old breakouts and a thick pair of glasses held together with sticky tape. Looking at him, he could be any age between thirty and fifty. He twitches every so often, his right eye doing most of the winking, but it's clear this isn't a flirt or anything; just an involuntary movement. Nerves, maybe.

'Aye, aye,' he says. 'Help you?'

'You're Chris?' He nods. 'My name's Jen . . . I know Ed.'

'Oh, aye. Aye, aye.' A stutter? An affectation? Just plain whacked out on something? Could be any of these things.

I hand him the envelope. 'I have this for you.'

He looks behind me at the taxi. 'Your man's there?'

'We need to get moving.'

'No time for the little man, aye?' Chris says, shakes his head. 'Better be all in here.' He holds up the padded envelope. Doesn't take much to guess what's inside.

'I should–'

'He didn't tell you whether he wanted to make another order or nothing?'

'No.'

'Good. Until he's paid up in full, you know? Aye, aye.' He stares off again at something I think only he can see.

I back away.

'Good to meet you, aye, aye,' Chris says. Then he produces

something out of thin air. A little flourish. His wee magic trick. It's a card. He holds it out. I take it, not wanting it but not knowing what else to do. 'In case you ever need anything.'

'Thanks,' I say, not sure what else I can say. I stuff the card into my jeans pocket.

'Have a good night, aye?'

I nod, then beat it back to the taxi.

'I'm serious,' he shouts after me. 'No judgement here. Just service.'

I don't want to think about the kind of service he means. Just want to get back in the taxi. Get home.

Have that final conversation with Ed.

Finish with this nonsense once and for all.

Two

For the ride back across town, I sit a person's-width away from Ed. He doesn't seem to notice, keeps reaching across to touch my leg with his long guitar player's fingers. The fact I flinch probably makes him all the more eager.

In the front seat, the cabbie keeps glancing at us in the mirror. Not like he's expecting a floor show, exactly. More like he's waiting for the barney to kick off.

And it should. I have something to say to Ed. Something I've been meaning to say for a while. Tonight, it's a confirmation of everything for me, of how I feel, of what he does to me.

And still . . . the same old mistakes.

We're barely in the front door when he's pawing at me. I'm not in the mood, still thinking about the barista, still thinking about what was in the envelope and who the hell Chris actually was. As I unlock my door on the second floor, I'm thinking about saying he might want to go back to his place for the night. I'm also thinking that I might just finally call it off. I don't care any more that he stood up for me at the café. That was about his ego more than me, getting to play the big man, the tough guy. That's the kind of thing that does it for him, one of the reasons he's horny now (that, and the barista, of course).

I try to shrug him off, but he persists and by the time the door's open, I'm into it, my body betraying me, ignoring the rational protestations of my brain.

as been. Back in the early days, I told myself it was fate
...ng. We were two objects destined to collide. Even if he
had his issues, I couldn't control myself around him.

In the cold light of day, I mostly think what a mistake it is to let
him into my bed. Or anywhere else, for that matter.

We fall into the front room and he pulls down my panties and
undoes his trousers, and we do it there, still semi clothed. As ever,
he doesn't look right at me, but at some spot just a few inches to
the side of my head, like he's seen something else, or else he's not
thinking about me at all.

And I know he's thinking about the waitress and I should slap
him and tell him to get out and oh, God, what he does to me is
electric and . . .

He rolls off me, and I catch my breath.

'You're still on the pill?'

I nod dumbly. I know he has condoms, and I know I keep
condoms in the bedroom drawer and yet what he does to me
means my mind isn't my own. I guess it's my concession to risk.
And it's a big one.

'Who was he?'

'Who?'

'That guy I gave the envelope to. Chris.'

Even in the dark, I know he's grinning in the way that means
he thinks I'm being thick. Naïve would be a kind way of putting
it. 'He's just . . .Chris.'

'A dealer?'

'Yes and no. You want something, you go to Chris.'

'Drugs? Women? Guns?'

'Yes, yes, and . . .probably. Look, he's one of those guys who
knows guys who know guys. But he's cool. I mean, look, all you
did was give him an envelope. Not a hanging offence.'

'And you didn't do it yourself because . . .?'

13

'Like I said, he'd have talked my ear off. Seriously

I adjust myself, go to the bathroom and lock the d
there in the dark before pulling the cord for the light ar
look at myself in the mirror.

'Jesus, Jen,' I say, voice barely above a whisper. And unlike
Ed, I look my reflection right in the eye. 'What the bloody hell
happened to, "this isn't working"?'

* * *

It's not the alarm that wakes me. It's something pressing against
me, pushing against my buttocks, rubbing against them. Something hard. And unfortunately familiar. An arm snakes its way up
from my stomach to my breasts.

But the electricity is gone. All that energy last night that made
me forget why I was so angry with him, it's finally dissipated.
Maybe it was all adrenaline, the thrill of knowing that whatever I
handed over to that guy, it was somehow wrong. Sex and naughti-
ness, the two tangled up: the danger instinct and the sex instinct.

But this morning is different. Something about the light
sneaking through the window or maybe the dream I had about
his shagging that barista girl doggy style in his kitchen, looking at
me the whole time and winking like it was the most natural thing
in the world, and what the hell was I yelling at him about?

The girl was grinning, of course, and looking at me, too, like
she was in on the joke and I was the only person in the world who
didn't get it.

Sisterhood.

Solidarity.

Aye, when it came Ed, such things went out the window. I
should know. I'm pretty sure I was the other girl for at least five
minutes.

I push him away.

14

'I'm not in the mood.'

'You're always in the mood.'

He's insistent. His fingers try and play me, like one of his precious guitars. He may have risen to the occasion, but I haven't.

I get out of bed.

Screw it.

'I'm not in the mood.'

'Okay,' he says, 'Okay.' He gets out of bed too. Stands before me. Erect and unashamed. To make the point clearer, he touches himself, seemingly absent-mindedly. 'Sure I can't change your –'

'Just leave,' I say. Not quite the speech I wanted to give, but a start. Better than usual.

He shrugs like it's my loss, struts off to the bathroom.

I pull on some clothes while he's showering – oh, God, please let that be all he's doing – and go into the kitchen. Shove a couple of slices of bread in the toaster. Look at the clock. I have maybe two hours before I need to leave. Fair enough.

I'm buttering the toast when he comes out of the bathroom. I can feel the swagger before I even turn around. I act like I don't even notice, but when Ed struts into a room like that it's because he wants you to ask why.

'I think you need to go,' I say.

'Aye,' he says. Although he's not even dressed. Just has one of my towels wrapped around him. There's still the sheen of water in his hair, and a few droplets falling free. 'I've got what I needed.'

I turn around.

'What?'

'Well, a man has needs.'

'Jesus! In my shower?'

He shrugs.

'Not my fault. I was trying not to think about it, and then I saw that bag. The one hanging on the back of the door handle in there.'

'What?'

'With the girl on it.'

Takes me a minute to realise what he's talking about. The canvas bag I bought on a trip to Venice. The one with the artwork on it. A girl lounging in the Piazza: long legs, dark glasses, blond hair, red lips.

Stylised art, though. Nowhere near what anyone would . . . I mean . . .surely . . . ?

He grins. Suggestively. Pushing it. The way he always does.

Too far.

For the last time.

I whip the toast off the counter and throw it at his head. Should have been a plate or a mug, but I don't have time to think about it. Toast was the closest thing to hand.

He waits a moment, then wipes the butter off his forehead and stands. 'Guess I'll be going then.'

'Aye,' I say, calmly as I can. 'And don't come back.'

That gets me another smile. One that says he'll be back, that I can't stay mad at him forever.

'I mean it.'

He doesn't say anything, goes through to the bedroom.

I wait in the kitchen. Stand there for a bit, fuming, and then decide I need to do something, so I pick up the toast, throw it in the bin. I think I might get that bag too. Much as I love it, I don't think I'll ever look at it again without thinking of him.

When he comes out of the bedroom, pulling up the zip on his jeans, he winks before leaving.

I lock the door behind him.

Go into the bathroom.

The word 'relief' doesn't cover what I feel when I see the bag hanging on the wall. For all his faults, I didn't think he would leave any evidence of his pleasuring himself, but even if the woman on the bag remains unsullied, the idea that he'd think so

16

little of me to wank over a stylised drawing of a woman on canvas says everything about him.

Ed.

Jesus.

I think about the reporter for some reason. The confrontation they had. And then I think, what am I hiding from? If the eejit wants to pay me money for talking about a girl I knew but didn't know, then more fool him.

Might make me feel better, anyway, knowing I have something coming my way.

Three

'Worst boyfriend ever,' Caroline says as she turns the key in her locker.

I'm sitting at the table, nursing my pre-shift coffee and I tell her that it's over between me and Ed. Of course, I haven't mentioned the bag.

I can do nothing but agree with her.

'You're better off,' she says. 'Believe me.' She grabs a cup of coffee herself, sits down across from me. We're both working the ten-thirty to seven shift, and this means we have a bit of time before we need to be on the shop floor.

'And the journalist?'

I shake my head. 'Stupid idea, yeah?'

'Wait till you see this month's wages.' She grins.

I don't say anything. No, it was a stupid idea. I'd feel like a fraud. I'd obsess over what I told him. I'd worry about what would happen if someone who worked for her family took what I said out of context.

No, best just to stay away from all that. Keep living the quiet life.

'So,' I say, 'you finished the book yet?'

She's been working her way through a book on Russian history for almost a month now. Taking her time. Absorbing it. Between that and her art classes, she's got a pretty full life outside the shop, and part of me's a little jealous.

I don't do a huge amount that's self-improving. A few years back I took a proof-reading course, thinking maybe I'd rather go into publishing than bookselling, but I got bored after a while and jacked it in. Same with my novel. Same as with most things that were worthwhile.

What does that say about me?

I've stuck with Ed for years, but the things that were good for me, I gave up in months, sometimes even days.

'Not yet,' she says, smiling. 'Worst bookseller ever, eh?'

I smile. We're both in on the joke. She's a notoriously slow reader, but her knowledge more than makes up for it. She has this ability to know things about books she hasn't even read. A bookselling sixth sense.

I look up at the clock. Sigh. We're a minute late back to the shop floor.

'Look,' Caroline says, 'tonight after work, we go for a drink and say fuck Ed. Or, we don't. We don't mention the bastard at all. Deal?'

I nod. 'Deal.'

'Come on, then,' she says. 'Let's go sell literature to the masses.'

* * *

People have this idea that bookselling is all about standing behind a counter, making nice displays and chatting with old ladies about the latest book from Jeffrey Archer or Dan Brown or whatever. The reasoning is that it's an easy job. Stressless. The kind of thing you could do as a hobby.

I wonder if that was ever true, once upon a time.

Most days, you try not to murder people. They expect you to know everything, even when the customer can't describe a book. They demand you have every book in the world available in your limited shelf space. And let's not mention how heavy books can be when over-packed in delivery boxes. On top of everything else, the physical aspect is the part that most people really don't consider.

I spend most of the shift today booking in a delivery in the stock room. I enjoy the work. It's hypnotic in its regularity. Distracting. And it gets me away from people. Today of all days, the first person to ask me about that 'blue book that was somewhere in the window maybe a year ago' is going to get a punch in the face. Jesus, I sound like Ed.

I've never been a violent person, but as I howf the boxes onto the shop floor for shelving, I think about what it would be like to just give Ed a good old-fashioned punch in the face. Not a slap. No, nothing so gentle. A real, honest-to-goodness fist in the pus. Maybe break his nose. That would be satisfying, although he'd trade on having a broken nose, try and make out to girls like that wee barista that it made him rakish and a little dangerous.

He is a little dangerous, of course. With friends like Chris, you have to be. One of the reasons I kind of fell for him in the first place. Of course, it's more an attitude with him than anything. The people he knows are scary, but Ed's so far from walking the walk, it's laughable when you think about it.

Pity he's so good at talking the talk, of course.

'Jen?'

Just think of the devil, and his minions shall appear.

I put down the box I was carrying over to the history section. Here, at the rear of the main floor, we're pretty well hidden from everyone else. Not the way I like it. There's something about Big Dave that puts me on edge. It's not just the way he always looks like he's angling his neck to get the best view down my top, but more it's the way that he gives the impression he's one wrong word away from snapping someone's neck. He's a big lad. You ask him, he'd say cuddly, but most everyone else would say fat.

That's what happens when you spend your days sitting on the sofa playing computer games.

I've never known what he does for a living. Must do something to be able to afford to live how he does. An inheritance, maybe. Or something computer related. To give him his due, he knows computers. At least I assume he does, from all the crap he keeps around his flat. Wires, cables, boxes, everything.

'Look, Dave,' I say, 'If Ed sent you . . .'

'Nah,' he says. 'That's not it.'

He doesn't know. So I lay it out. 'It's over,' I say. 'Between me and Ed.'

'Oh,' he says. 'Aye?'

'Aye.'

'You still have his number, though?'

'So do you.'

'Except he's not picking it up.'

Because he's crying over the fact I kicked him out? Not bloody likely.

'I don't know where he is,' I say. 'And I don't care.'

'Aye, okay,' says Dave. He moves in closer. Is he going for a hug? Oh, Jesus, no! 'I don't think you do.'

I control my breathing. I step back.

'He's a dick,' Dave says. 'I know that. But he's cool too, aye?' Ed always claimed that Dave has something of a man crush on him. Looks that way most of the time. Dave holds Ed up as some kind of idol. Probably to do with Ed's lady-killing ways. Dave doesn't know how to talk to women, not really. He's not threatening about it, just so stumblingly awkward that you could never imagine going to bed with him.

'No,' I say, 'I don't.'

Dave nods. 'Okay, okay. Look, if you see him, I know you'll have other things on your mind, but really, if you could tell him about these calls, because I'm getting creeped.'

21

'Okay,' I say. 'I'll see if I remember.'

He grins. 'Thanks,' he says. 'Guess it means you won't be coming around much anymore.'

'Guess so.'

'It's cool,' he says. 'Been nice knowing you.'

'Aye, you too,' I say, starting to look around the store as though I'm seeing things that need my attention.

'I'll let you get on with it.'

As he slinks back into the shop, I wonder why a guy like that would hang out with someone like Ed. Even more, I wonder why it happens the other way round too.

Some things about men, I guess I'll never understand.

'Excuse me?' An old woman pulls me out of my thoughts. She's waving a book in my face. Black cover. Tagline that says: *What would you do if . . .?*

'Can I help?'

'I'd like to make a complaint about this book.'

I should be able to spot them a mile off. This is why I didn't want to come out on the floor. I try not to let my irritation show, and smile as sweetly as I can. 'What about it?'

'Have you seen the first line? Disgraceful!'

* * *

'What was it?'

After work, on the subway, heading to the West End. We have to lean in to speak. The sound of the carriages as they creak through the tunnels is almost deafening.

'What?'

'The line she objected to?'

I shake my head. 'You really want to know?'

'Uh-huh.'

I take a deep breath. Not something I want to shout out loud.

22

Knowing my luck, the train will come to a halt and then everyone will hear me when I say it.

Now or never, though: '*I sucked twelve cocks in Magaluf.*'

Thank God, no one else seems to hear me.

Caroline doubles over.

I let her laugh.

When she's done, she can't stop grinning. 'Of all the books for her to pick up,' she says.

'Could have been worse.'

'Aye?'

'Don't know if you looked in the fiction section. I think Andy's been ordering books again without anyone else knowing. Found a book called *The Fuck Up* in there.'

'No way.'

I nod. 'Across the cover. Plain as day.'

'Must have been further on in the alphabet if the old biddy didn't see it.'

'Maybe she'll be back tomorrow.'

'Thank God you're on a day off.'

'Aye.'

'So let's get royally drunk, shall we?'

The train enters Hillhead station. Wobbles to a halt.

Royally drunk sounds good to me. A night of abandon. My first night in a long time without wondering what the hell Ed's going to do next to embarrass me.

Throw caution to the wind.

What's the worst that could happen, after all?

Four

I'm somewhere around halfway to drunk. My mood seems to affect how fast the Prosecco hits me. Like it's got to get past all the pent-up anger before it can do anything. Most evenings, I'd be under the table by now.

Adrenaline?

Extreme Boyfriend Dumping can do that to a girl.

Caroline looks at me and shakes her head. 'Come on,' she says. 'Loosen up.' She's not looking at me directly, so I crick my neck to see where her focus has drifted.

Maybe I could have guessed. The waiter. Slicked-back hair and those baby-blue eyes. He's maybe nineteen or twenty, whereas Caroline and I are in our early thirties. But that doesn't stop her from ogling. Have to admit, I don't mind an eyeful either.

But then I think about Ed, his thing for younger women.

Drink more Prosecco. Down the glass I just filled. Still no effect. I'm going to regret this in the morning.

Live for the moment.

Regret nothing.

'You should ask for his number,' I say.

'You should be the one asking,' she says. 'Fuck Ed out of your system, maybe.'

I smile and nod, but really, I'm not that bothered. It's not about sex. But I don't know that I can explain that to Caroline. 'I'd rather drink Ed out of my system, if it's all the same with you.'

She shrugs, and we drink.

The conversation wears on for a while. We quit talking about men, talk about work and books. 'You ever going to write that novel?' she says.

I shrug.

'You totally should.'

'I don't . . .' The sentence trails before I give it a chance to begin. Which in itself explains why I never finished.

'What's stopping you?'

I don't know how to respond. My plan had always been to write. Even got myself an agent for a while on the back of some well-received short stories in magazines and websites coupled with a synopsis of the Great Book itself, or at least how I envisioned it. But that plan went the way of the dodo when I found I was unable to deliver. Despite my detailed plans and notes and synopses, I couldn't get past chapter three.

Five thousand words.

Your great novel, right there.

Not surprisingly, the agent in question gently suggested we part company. I didn't tell anyone, and now when people ask, I hum and haw around the issue. Shame and embarrassment: two great traits I'm pretty sure all Scottish people share.

I look at Caroline, and I'm maybe drunk enough to say something when that waiter walks past, and my hand flies up in the air to attract his attention. 'Another bottle, please!'

* * *

The world spins too fast.

I'll regret this in the morning, but all the same, right now I'm walking on feet that feel like the bubbles in the Prosecco, lifting me off the ground.

There's a lightness to the night that I don't expect.

I know why. It's because Ed's gone. For good.

Even if – no, even *when* – he comes crawling back, I know that I'll be able to resist him. Sod his games. His . . .his *shit*.

Feeling naughty, halfway down a long street that's nothing but old residential buildings, mostly occupied by middle- and old-aged folks with the occasional burst of students, I throw my hands up into the air. 'Fuck you, Ed!' I yell. My voice echoes among the buildings, bouncing off brickwork.

A light comes on.

I giggle like a naughty toddler and then run down the street before anyone can come outside and tell me to shut up.

Some women, this time of night, they'd be afraid to walk home alone. I've always been pragmatic about the idea. Stick to well-lit streets and places you know. Wear sensible shoes. Only do it when you're drunk enough to feel confident, but not so drunk you couldn't kick someone in the nuts.

Caroline thinks I'm insane. Maybe I am. But part of it is the idea that you can't give in. The fear gives them control.

I'm thinking I'm only ten minutes' walk from the flat and I know this part of the city intimately. Put me in the East End or on the South Side, maybe I'd think twice, but here in the leafy West End, I know the statistics. Bad things happen, sure, but the way I was brought up, my dad taught me sometimes you can take all the precautions in the world and still you'll get hurt.

That's life.

Just how it is.

This evening, like almost every other, I get back to the flat without seeing anyone, except a few people gathered outside the Quarter Gill bar, just a few streets away from me. They're smoking, more interested in their conversation than they are in me, but there's one guy with cropped white hair and the faint crease of a scar under one eye who looks at me, and creases his lips into the kind of smile he thinks is friendly. I don't return any kind of look and I walk faster.

More paranoia?

Just the everyday kind, I guess.

At the top of my street, I look back. But there's no one there.

No one.

Fine. I'm okay with that.

I take a deep breath and walk to my front door. It takes me two goes to get the key in the lock, but finally I'm inside. I trot up to the second level and prepare to struggle with the front door to my flat.

But there's no need.

The door is already open.

Five

When I was young, I had this fear about monsters in the cupboard. I got it from watching some TV show when I was wee. That's how things go, sometimes: you get scared of something because you're told you should be.

The idea that when I'm not looking, someone or something could suddenly slip inside somewhere I was familiar with scared me. Worse than strangers on the street. Or terror attacks. Or planes dropping out of the sky. It was, every time it kicked in, worse than pretty much anything else I could think of. Rationality didn't enter into the equation. The idea embedded itself in the back of my brain, refused to leave.

And every so often it would resurface, become the only thing in my head.

Like now.

I look at the door, hanging ajar, for a long time, thinking about whether I closed it before I left. I really can't remember. My brain says *of course you did*, but it still sounds uncertain, as though there really was the possibility that today I had made a mistake I'd never made before. Made sense, in a way. After all, the morning hadn't exactly been normal. All the crap with Ed could have resulted in me forgetting to close the door properly on my way out.

Which is fine. Because the main door to the building was closed. No one could get in without a key.

Except Mrs McDowell upstairs sometimes forgot to lock the rear entrance when she took the bins out.

No, no. That's the worst-case scenario. And anyway, why would someone randomly enter a building on the off-chance a door had been unlocked? Maybe I just had a moment, and now everything's fine. Lesson learned. I'll spend the next few days being paranoid, but that's okay.

Aye, that's it. Leaving the door open is the kind of mistake I can laugh off later when I'm sober and when I've gone through the hell of the hangover.

Except I'm suddenly feeling very sober. The sensation of walking on prosecco bubbles is now a distant and slightly embarrassing memory.

Could be an upside. Might shock me through the hangover too.

My neck prickles. Same as when I believed in the cupboard monsters. Things that you can't describe or really visualise, but you just know are lurking somewhere in there, among the shadows, ready to grab you and kill you.

'Don't be stupid.'

Saying it out loud grounds me again. Makes me feel confident. Maybe even a little embarrassed. I'm thirty-three. Not a child. A bloody grown-up.

So, Jen, if you're an adult, then act like it.

I walk forward, push the door open further. There are no lights on.

'Hello?'

No response.

So that's good.

I walk inside, go into each room, turning on the lights each time. My heart. I keep moving slowly and deliberately.

In the bathroom, I can't think of anywhere an intruder could be hiding. They'd have to be super-skinny to fit inside the tallboy, and even if they could, they'd have to remove the shelves first. All the same, I open the door just to check.

As I suspected, there's no one there.

Stupid, stupid, stupid. Even though no one's here to witness it, I know I'll be thinking of this as one of my most embarrassing moments. Top ten, more than likely. The kind of night that comes back to you when you least expect it and you can't do anything but cringe at the memory.

In the kitchen, I check the pantry at the rear. It's empty too. Except maybe for the weevils I'm pretty sure have been mating in the half-open packs of flour I seem to accumulate.

I walk past the knife rack. Bought it after a brief period where I thought I'd try cooking something more ambitious. Lasted about three days but resulted in several books by Nigel Slater, Jamie Oliver and Nigella that remain with spines unbroken next to the block.

This is paranoia. Unless it's not.

I take the biggest knife in there. The one the advertisements claimed could cut through an old boot if it needed to. A tin can too, if I remember correctly.

Figure it's a pretty good defence if someone's going to come at me.

Not that there's anyone there, Jen. Keep telling yourself that.

The bedroom's a bust, even under the bed itself. Nothing and no one hiding there. I've read enough Thomas Harris to know how these twisted serial killers think. There's always one place you don't think of.

Not me.

I'm not that dumb

I'm breathing easier.

My heart's slowing.

The embarrassment is beginning to win over the fear. I don't know which is worse.

The living room's the same. Nowhere to hide, anyway. I didn't have to look to know that. But I do, anyway.

I stand in front of the fireplace, look in the mirror that hangs above it. I'm pale and my makeup is beginning to look a little worse for wear. I think I should clean it off, but already I can feel my head starting to pound. I was sobered up fast by the shock, but now the hangover's hitting earlier than I would have liked.

'It's okay,' I say. 'It's okay.'

I breathe.

Listen to the quiet of the night.

And that's when I hear the noise. Out in the hall. The sound of something moving, shuffling. And I know there's nothing out there.

And then I think:

The cupboard.

Of all things.

The one place I didn't think of.

In the hall. The walk-in cupboard I thought about converting into a small office one day. When I moved all the crap that had accumulated, of course. The boxes, the old clothes, the ancient computers and the boxes of old university papers.

One day meant never. As it always did. Like the David Nicholls' novel. Like growing up. Like getting a job that really paid the bills.

The cupboard.

The last place in the flat where I would think someone – or something – could hide.

'Just the floorboards contracting,' I say, still looking in the mirror, trying to form an expression that says, *I know what I'm talking about.*

It's true: this building is old enough that at night there are all kinds of odd noises that you could mistake for an intruder. Just the kind of thing that happens when temperatures drop and old wood is exposed. Old buildings creak. They have draughts. All

31

the things that I was warned about when I moved into the place, and all the things I didn't mind because the flat felt like home the moment I walked across the door.

Five years ago.

And now, in two seconds, my home feels alien and terrifying. As though it's been hiding some terrible secret from me.

'Just look,' I say to my reflection, but she really doesn't seem convinced. 'There's nothing there and when you see that, you'll laugh.'

The girl in the mirror frowns. The wrinkles in her forehead form a little too easily.

Aye, of all the times to notice something like that.

I hold up the knife. The girl in the mirror smiles. It's half-hearted, but it's something.

The weight of the knife in my hands is awkward. I try to balance it properly. Remember a self-defence class I attended a few years back with Caroline. We were taught the best thing to do is run. But there are situations where that isn't possible.

Like when, Jen?

Like when you don't need to defend yourself because you're imagining that there's an intruder in your house.

I think about what they told us about the knife, about the most secure grip you can have that stops someone from twisting it out of your hand. But it doesn't feel right. It's counterintuitive to hold the blade point down, facing away from me. And what if I'm getting it wrong? I'd treated it like a game. When would someone like me ever have to defend themselves using a knife?

Goes to show you never can tell.

I hold the blade with the point facing out, simply ready to stab anyone who comes near me. I might not take them down, but maybe I'll give them something to think about.

I walk back out into the hall.

I notice for the first time that there's light spilling from inside the hall cupboard. Normally, I have the light off. Sure – like I did with the front door, I could have simply forgotten, but this time I'm sure my memory's not playing tricks on me. I definitely turned that light off. I haven't been in the cupboard in days. I would have noticed before now.

This is no longer paranoia. Childhood fears begin to feel justified.

My heart starts doing its business again.

My throat constricts.

'Anybody in there?' I say, and the words rasp out more harshly than I expect. I almost cough at the end of the sentence.

Nothing.

'Last chance.'

I think about calling the police. But what if I'm wrong? What if there's nothing in the cupboard? The chances of them arresting me for wasting their time are slim, but all the same, the horror of being so completely stupid would burn for days. I'd feel like people could see it written all over my face every time we talked, like somehow they'd heard about the girl who got so freaked out she called the police to investigate a cupboard with a light inside.

'Last. Chance.'

Okay, okay.

Then I hear it: something moving in there.

Something?

No. No. Someone.

The door opens.

I panic.

A shape. Taller than me, definitely male. That kind of build: looming, threatening.

I act on instinct.

The knife feels solid in my grip. Reassuringly so. That rubberised handle feels natural, like the adverts promised.

I should have used it before now.

I push it forward and up to protect myself from the psycho in the wardrobe. He'll get the point.

'The fu–?'

The shape doesn't stop. In fact, it falls forward. Arms out. Slamming against me as though to push me away. But how can I, when he's falling on top of me?

My arms stays where it is, thrust out at waist height.

The shape of the man has a familiar smell. One I know, but I can't place because my brain is screaming at me to get out. To move. To escape.

But I can't.

His weight falls against me. I can't push back. My knees go and I'm falling.

I hit the floor hard. The handle of the knife presses bruisingly against my torso, just below my breasts.

Jesus, it hurts.

I let go of the knife, and use both hands to push him off. Roll away.

Lie on my back. Feel where the handle impacted. I'll be black and blue, but otherwise, I think it's okay. If I broke a rib, I'm sure I'd know about it.

The man – the shape – doesn't seem to be moving. I can hear him breathing, though.

I turn my head and get a good look at him.

'What the bloody hell are you doing here?'

Six

Ed gargles.

Blood comes out his mouth.

His hands are somewhere near his chest, gripping at something.

I'm not holding the knife any more.

Because what I've done is left it in him. The sharp end going in and up right below his ribcage. That's why he can't speak. Probably punctured his lung. Something like that.

'Jesus,' I say, and somehow it doesn't seem strong enough.

Ed makes another sound, but it's not words any more, just a strange, strangled noise that keens a little, like a wounded cat.

I get up and kneel beside him. His eyes are wide and panicked. But he's alive. He's alive. 'Okay,' I say. 'Okay, it's going to be fine. It's going to be fine.'

What do I do?

'I'll call an ambulance,' I tell him. 'It'll be fine.'

He grips at the handle of the knife with both hands.

'I don't think that's a good–'

But he's not listening. He tugs at the knife.

Rips it out.

The blood comes out of him in a thick tide, soaking his clothes. He drops the knife and starts to shake.

I put my hands on the wound. Applying pressure. Isn't that what they always do? Why didn't I take the first aid course they offered me? Like they would have taught us how to handle something like this.

Bloody seeps between my fingers. Pressure makes the bleeding worse.

Ed howls and bucks beneath me.

I've fantasised about killing him, but the reality is ugly and brutal. The blood is thick and warm and the noises he makes are guttural, sickening sounds.

And then he stops.

One last gasp.

The blood slows.

I stand up. Look at my hands. Covered in Ed's blood.

I look at him.

His eyes are.

He doesn't move after.

I watch him for maybe another five seconds.

Ed.

Ed. Ed. Ed.

My mind is all over the place. I feel this pressure in my chest. Like I want to scream. Sometimes, when I'm dreaming, that works enough to wake me up. But I can't do it. The best I can do is squeak.

Besides, I know this isn't a dream. Much as I want it to be.

I take deep breaths. Stand up.

My legs are unsteady. I keep swallowing to keep from crying.

I look down at Ed, but I don't touch him.

He looks strange. If you didn't see the knife, see the blood, you would think maybe he'd just gone to sleep. Stumbled in drunk, decided just to snooze where he fell. Certainly not an unusual sight. I made the mistake of giving him a spare key. Sometimes he's been nearby and decided just to pop in. Those occasions when he's been too drunk to even think about sneaking in beside me – not to sleep, never to sleep – he's collapsed in the hall.

I could kick him now, like I did on those mornings. Try to get him to move that way.

His face is oddly relaxed. When I stabbed him, his face took on an odd elasticity of fear and surprise. I expected it to stay that way in death, a kind of clue that he died in pain. But it's not true. Everything about him has suddenly relaxed.

There's a smell in the air that I didn't expect. The relaxation has also reached his bowels.

I look at the phone on the antique dresser I use as a telephone table.

999.

Three very simple digits.

'What service do you require?'

'Police.'

'Can you state the nature of the emergency?'

'I just stabbed my boyfriend – my ex-boyfriend, let's make that clear – in the chest with a knife that was advertised as being able to cut through leather boots and tin cans. I know he masturbated over a canvas bag when I was just in the other room, but that's got nothing to do with why he's dead. It just kind of happened.'

Sure, they're going to believe that.

I can't bring myself to do it. I can't work out what I'm going to say. Besides, if he's dead, is this really an emergency?

I spend a long time thinking about it. The thoughts aren't something I remember later, like part of my brain decided to delete the internal debate. Perhaps because there were some aspects I'm better off not remembering.

But now I'm done, I have a plan.

I take the phone off the hook.

The number I dial is more than three digits.

Seven

By the time Dave arrives, I've changed my clothes. What I was wearing when I stabbed Ed is now piled up in the bath and soaking through. Now I'm wearing an old pair of jeans and a heavy jumper I usually reserve for the winter. It's the kind of heavy wool that feels like a hug. What I need now.

Dave looks wired. His eyes are red-rimmed, and I suspect he's been smoking a little something. How he drove down here without being stopped is beyond me. Guess the police have better things to do than troll the West End for drivers who might have had a little toke before getting behind the wheel.

When Dave sees Ed's body he just looks down and says, 'Whoa,' like some Californian surfer dude. 'He's really dead?'

'Yup.'

'And you . . .?' He gestures at the knife, which is still on the floor beside Ed.

'Uh-huh.'

'You doing okay?'

I shrug.

'The fuck did you stab him for?' Dave's walking round the body now, not taking his eyes off it, like maybe he'll see something I missed. A breath, perhaps. A movement of the hands.

But I know Ed's not going to move. He can't. He's dead.

And you killed him, Jen, don't forget that. You're the one stuck a knife through him and then didn't do a thing when he pulled it

38

back out. What? Don't tell me you didn't know that last bit was a really bad idea.

Dave squats next to the body. He's wearing rubber gloves. 'What did he do?'

'Why the gloves?'

'What did he do?'

'Why are you wearing gloves?'

'You asked me for help,' he says. 'I thought they might be sensible.'

'Why?'

'Are you going to call the police?'

I don't answer.

He nods. 'I didn't think so.'

'I thought you might–'

'What did he do?'

'He was in the cupboard,' I say.

'What?'

'He was in the cupboard. He broke in. Well . . .he had spare keys. I forgot to ask for them back. But he knew he wasn't supposed to come back here. I asked him to leave. That's still breaking and entering, right?'

'When did you forget to ask him for the keys? I mean, how long's he had them?'

'This morning.'

'Huh?'

'When we broke up.'

'Oh.' Dave looks pretty calm, all things considered. Part of that's probably the drugs. He's one of those people you just have to assume is always high. But part of it's also just that Dave is Dave. He's the walking definition of Stoned. Lives for weed. One of the reasons he liked having Ed as a flatmate: Ed was Dave's connection. I guess he wasn't much more than that, the way Dave's come with rubber gloves.

39

Does he have a hacksaw in the boot of his car, maybe?

The idea makes me want to laugh. But it turns into a weird kind of shudder.

Dave looks up at me. He bites his lower lip and scrunches his forehead. He looks about to say something and then changes his mind.

'I just want this to be over,' I say. 'If I call the police they won't believe me that this was an accident. Given everything that happened with me and Ed, if they start asking around, I know what people are going to think and there's no way I could prove otherwise.'

'It wasn't otherwise, was it?'

'No,' I say. 'No. No.'

'Okay,' he says. 'Okay.' He stands up, looks at the cupboard. The door is still open. The light is still on. Dave steps over Ed's corpse and into the cupboard. 'He was in here?'

'Aye.'

He doesn't say anything for a moment. He just stands there, looking around as though the answer as to why Ed would hide in the cupboard will come to him in a moment. 'Come here,' he says.

I stand beside him. The corpse is behind us now. Some part of my brain imagines it starting to move, standing upright, reaching out to grab us and snap our necks in retaliation for what we've done.

We?

Me.

My stomach flips. I swallow to keep from vomiting. Think about something I read in a forensic thriller once. Maybe it was a Patricia Cornwell. About how smiling helps the gag reflex. What I do is probably more a grimace. Maybe it's just a placebo, but it helps.

'What do you see?'

40

I look around. 'Junk.' A sad way of describing things that remind me of various points in my life. Old shoes, even old printers and computers I didn't know how to dispose of. Some boxes filled with photographs that stop somewhere around the time I started to do everything on digital camera and upload to Facebook.

'Anything unusual?'

'I . . .' I don't think so. Until my eyes fall on two leather gym bags I know don't belong to me. They're old. They have the Head logo on them, and they've cracked a little with wear and age.

'I don't recognise those.'

Dave nods. Picks up the bags. Hefts them to check the weight. He carries them, stepping over Ed's corpse, through to the living room. Suddenly he doesn't look like the friendly stoner I thought I knew. There's a different purpose to him. A kind of seriousness I would never have imagined he was capable of.

I follow. There's something a little dreamlike about it all, as though my feet aren't really impacting on the floor and my body isn't quite here.

We sit down on the sofa. Dave doesn't open the bags right away. Instead he clicks on Sky and turns to the BBC's twenty-four hours news channel. 'Things I hate,' he says. 'Silence.'

I'm tempted to say something like, 'Even when there's a dead body in the next room?' but the joke withers before I even part my lips. I don't think I want to speak again. I want to go to bed, hide under the covers. Like Ebenezer Scrooge confronting the ghost of Marley, I want all of this to be a hallucination brought on by eating cheese before bedtime.

But that's not going to happen.

This is real. I can't escape it. I could pinch my arms until they turn blue, but I won't wake up.

Dave picks up the first bag, unzips it and tips out the contents onto the floor. The bundles land with a heavy cascade of noise on the floorboards. I thank goodness there's no one living in the downstairs flat right now. All the noise tonight, I'd have been calling the police.

'Holy shiteballs,' he says.

'Uh-huh.'

What else can I say?

Bundles of money. Wrapped up tight. I've only seen hundred pound notes on rare occasions. The shop don't usually accept them because the chances are they're fake. But I've never seen so many in one place before.

I pick up one of the bricks.

'What is this?'

'What does it look like?'

'I mean, where did it come from?'

Dave nods, sagely. 'I knew the dude had money,' he says. 'Like, a lot of money he wasn't supposed to have. He was stashing it here. I guess because he figured you'd never go looking in that cupboard.'

'It was kind of my own dumping ground. Always meant to have a clear out, but . . .' I think about when my dad died, how me and Mum decided to clear out the loft which was filled with all the things in life he thought might be useful again one day. Most of what we found could be easily discarded. But maybe I got something of that from him, the way I couldn't really bear to throw anything out when I was done with it. Even old clothes that no longer quite fit found their way into the cupboard. You know, just in case.

'Then you dumped him.'

I look at Dave. He looks back at me, and I can see he's trying to figure out a way to explain it so I'll understand what he's getting at. 'You dumped him,' he says, 'and he knew he couldn't leave this lying around the flat anymore.'

'So he waited until I went out . . .'

42

'And then he came in to get it.'

'Except I came back and surprised him.'

'That's all she wrote.'

I look at all the money.

Dave empties the second bag.

No money this time.

Still, the contents smack heavy onto the floor.

'Well, fuck,' Dave says, after a few moments of contemplative silence.

Eight

Money and drugs.

I had no idea. Honestly. None. Much as I knew he was into dealing, I didn't think he'd ever involve me. Especially without my knowledge.

How long had he been storing stuff at my place? Was he ever going to tell me?

The money was the kicker. The way Ed acted, he was always close to broke and only just able to afford going out or getting in a taxi to come see me. Sometimes, he'd phone up pleading poverty and I'd go trotting round to his with a couple of packed Sainsbury's bags like the dutiful girlfriend, even wind up cooking for him and Dave.

Dave, I knew, wasn't lying when he pled poverty. Spent all his cash on dope, and didn't think much further ahead than the next toke.

All this money.

Jesus.

'How much do you think there is?' We've gathered all the bricks of cash into neat little piles. The bags of drugs are still scattered. I'm trying my best not to think about them.

'Dunno,' he says. 'Like, maybe sixty or seventy thousand.' He seems unusually focussed. The soft-bellied pot-head replaced by someone who seems to be taking everything in with a reverence and thoughtfulness that is, frankly, unnerving. His eyes are clear, and every movement considered.

'Yeah?'

He looks at the drugs. 'Maybe a mil . . . If you take what we could make with . . .well . . .' He doesn't know how to finish the sentence. He knows how I feel about drugs. Even the soft stuff. He's always tried the old 'it's the same as alcohol' argument with me, but it doesn't wash. It's not the same. It can't be.

I make things easy as I can for him. ' . . .With what we can sell.'

'Aye.'

I nod. I stand up. 'And what about . . .?' I can't even bring myself to say his name out loud. 'I mean, do we call the police?'

'You called me.'

'And?'

'And not the police.'

'I told you. I wasn't thinking straight.'

'And now?'

'I don't know.'

He nods. Stays sitting on the couch, leans back and exhales. 'Wish you'd let me spark up.'

'My flat. My rules.'

'Aye.' He nods in the direction of Ed. 'I see what happens when a man breaks them, right enough.'

That does it. The casualness of his comment sets me off. My legs stop working completely and I collapse. There are tears on my face. I feel like I'm floating out of my body, like I'm looking at it from a distance from a few feet behind. The world is unsteady, like everything's made of melting ice cream.

Dave's got me before I hit the ground. It's comforting to be held by him. He has a slight odour. A hint of sweat, but it's not unpleasant. Makes me think a little of my dad for some reason. He holds me so that I don't collapse completely. 'I'm sorry,' he says. 'I'm sorry. I'm sorry.'

He gets me to my feet. He walks me out past Ed's corpse, and makes sure that I don't look at it. 'I'll take care of it,' he says. 'I'll take care of it.'

45

He takes me to the bedroom.

I lie down on the bed.

Close my eyes.

I'm safe with Dave.

I'm safe with Dave.

* * *

When I wake up, I look at the bedside clock. Green numbers glow – 09:43.

I stretch and think maybe it was nothing more than a bad dream. But I don't want to know, so I stay beneath the covers for a while, thinking that if I don't move then I don't need to look and see what really happened last night.

I can smell bacon.

Why can I smell bacon?

The door creaks. Dave's head pokes through. 'I made breakfast.'

Breakfast?

He sees the look on my face, and he smiles. 'It's fine,' he says. 'Everything is fine.'

* * *

There's no body.

There's no body.

Dave's in the kitchen. Bacon and coffee. The spit of fat in the frying pan. Everything domestic. Normal. I didn't know better, Dave's acting like we just spent the night together.

But I can't see a body.

There's not even a stain on the floorboards.

I walk through to the kitchen, wrapped in my dressing gown. Dave turns round. He says, 'Sit down.' Not quite a command, but close enough. He's a gentle giant. And I don't know that he's got any sleep.

I do as he says. I don't say anything. He turns back to the bacon and the fat and the sizzle.

When he serves up the bacon on floury white rolls, he says, 'You need to eat something.'

'Uh-huh.'

'It wasn't a dream.'

I nod.

'Ed's dead.'

The words sound vaguely unreal. I don't have any reaction to them. There is no sense of guilt, no sudden flashback to the look in Ed's eyes when he realised I'd stuck a blade into him. All I feel is a little numb spot where my heart should be.

I don't know if that's good or bad.

Should I have called the police?

Where's Ed?

If he's dead, then where's Ed?

I suppress a giggle.

Dave hands me the tomato sauce. I squeeze it out onto the bacon.

'You keep the cash,' he says. 'I'll take the stash.' It sounds a little weird, like a line from a movie, something nobody says in real life.

'Do what you want with it,' I tell him. My voice is flat, like I'm recovering from a cold.

He grins as he sits at the head of the table and looks down at me. 'Oh, I know what you're thinking. That what I'm going to do is smoke it or something. Naw. The hard shite, that's not for me. I figure, though, I can sell it.'

'What if someone comes for it?'

'Who? Look, if Ed owed someone or was holding from them, they're not going to know it was here. It's obvious this was his

47

hiding place, right? Somewhere he thought no one else would think to look?'

'Not even me.' None of this feels right. I figure maybe if I eat the bacon, I'll be okay.

'So the way I see it, whoever it is, they're going to think Ed's missing with the cash, and they'll be looking all over for him, but they won't be coming to you.'

'He's not missing.' Except he is. Where's the body? Where's Ed?

'He will be. Missing, that is.'

'Where is he now?'

Nausea. A sharp pang in my stomach. The bacon threatens to return. I force it to stay down. I'm not going to humiliate myself.

Dave takes a sharp breath through gritted teeth, then lets out a little whistling sound. It's pretty clear that he's uncomfortable saying this. 'Look, maybe–'

'What did you do with his body?'

'He's in the boot of my car.'

'Oh.' Dave has a mini. 'That's got to be a squeeze.' The words are mine, but I don't believe I'm speaking them. Like hearing someone else who sounds like me. The voice is calm. Collected. Maybe even rational. I should be panicking now, running around the room screaming, and instead I'm making jokes.

'Works easier when you've taken him apart.'

'What?'

'While you were asleep, I did what needed to be done.'

I put down the bacon roll. 'Jesus.' Shock. It has to be shock.

'Last night, we agreed calling the police was a bad idea.'

'Yes, but–'

'But if you're not going to call the police, you can't just have a body hanging around in your hallway stinking the place out. You were already shaken up. Someone had to put their thinking cap on, make a decision.'

48

'Oh, Christ.'

Dave says, 'You're working today?'

'No, no. Day off.'

'Then we're going to take a trip.'

'Where?'

'I figured Loch Lomond.'

'Oh.'

'One of those wee secluded places on the edge of the water.'

'Right.'

'Some bricks, a little shove, no one will ever know.'

'They won't?'

'Except the fish. The fish might know. And who are they going to tell?'

All I can do is nod, like I'm agreeing with every word he says. Maybe I'm still asleep. Maybe I'm still dreaming. None of this can be happening.

'Come on,' he says. 'Finish your bacon. Maybe this afternoon, a wee bit of retail therapy? Help you figure things out? See that this is the only way things could ever have gone. And don't worry about what you buy, I guess. Not like you won't have the cash, aye?'

He smiles.

I don't.

Maybe when I get rid of the body, everything will be fine. Maybe I'll even be able to forget what happened.

I guess there's only one way to find out.

Nine

We get ready to drive out to the loch. I've thrown on some clothes, not really thinking about what I look like. No makeup either. What's the point? Dave looks at me, shrugs and says, 'Well, then,' but no more than that.

I ask him to open the boot when we get to the car. Do I really need to see? He shakes his head. 'Not here,' he says. 'No fucking way.'

I almost argue, and then I look up. I see the windows all around, on both sides of the street. I notice the sun. The other people walking, people with no idea of what happened the night before, whose lives are carrying on with the same routines, the universal worries that everyone shares about jobs, money, family.

And then I think about what's in the boot.

Little plastic bundles filled with bloodied flesh.

I get in the passenger's side, and wait for him to get in the driver's seat. 'Cheer up,' he says. 'Could be worse.'

'How?'

'You could be going to jail.'

He has a point.

As we drive down through Hyndland and onto Great Western, I lean my face against the window and watch the world go by. The stereo's on, playing '60s collections on the MP3 player. Stoner anthems, mostly. Something about bogarting a joint he tells me was on the soundtrack to *Easy Rider*. Like I care. Like I've ever seen the film.

The city passes.

We hit the motorway. I watch the countryside flash by.

'Teeth,' I say.

'What?'

I can't stop thinking about how he got the body in the boot. 'Teeth. You can identify someone by their teeth. I know the chances are he'll just sink, but if someone does find him . . .'

'I know what I'm doing.'

'Aye? How many bodies have you disposed of?'

'None yet. But there's Google.'

I laugh. A little too hard.

He doesn't.

At some point, I fall asleep. When I wake up, my head feels tender and I realise I've been bouncing against the window the whole drive.

We're surrounded by trees on all sides. Thick-trunked branches and leaves obscuring the sky. The road we're on seems like little more than a track, marked out by pebbles that crunch under the wheels of the car.

'Where are we going?'

'Place I know.'

'Place you know?'

I stretch. Look over at Dave. His eyes are red-raw, and I think he could do with some eye drops. How long now since he's gone without a toke? I don't think I've ever known him to go longer than a few minutes.

'Did you get any sleep?'

'I don't sleep.'

'Everyone sleeps.'

'Sometimes I nap.'

'Aye?'

'It's wasted time,' he says.

I almost laugh. Guy like Dave, who spends most of life playing

Grand Theft Auto on the Xbox between joints, and he's telling me about wasted time.

We keep driving. I can see gaps in the trees and notice the river's on our left. There are no other cars. Anyone comes towards us, we'll have to pull off the road to let them pass.

'Seriously,' I say.

'No one comes down here,' he says. 'Or not enough that we need to worry.'

There's a bag at my feet. I didn't see it before. I think it rolled out from under the seat. A little plastic bag, the top tied tight. I pick it up, suddenly curious. There's red liquid inside, and . . .

I drop the bag.

'Jesus,' Dave says. 'I forgot that was there.'

'What was . . .?'

'You asked about the teeth,' he says.

The bag is between my feet now. I stare at it.

'Should also be some fingertips in there.'

'What the–?'

'Look, I told you I'd fix this. Those things, we dump them somewhere else once we've dropped the rest of him into the water.'

'Oh, Christ.'

'Don't think about it, Jenny,' he says. 'Don't think about it because you know that you killed him. We're in this together.'

I look over at him. He's focussed on the road, but I have to ask myself why he's going to all this trouble to help me. What did I ever do for him?

* * *

Where we pull over, it's a small drop to the water below. We leave the car, locked, and he walks me through trees and undergrowth until we're at the edge and looking out across the water. It's a

52

calm day, and the water seems solid: a giant mirror reflecting the sky.

I look down.

Dave says, 'It's deep.'

'Uh-huh.'

'We chuck him in, and walk away. I made sure the bags will sink.'

'Uh-huh.'

'He's not coming back up.'

I look at the water. Calm. Peaceful.

Dave puts a hand on my shoulder. 'Not you,' he says. 'You didn't do anything wrong. All we're doing here is preventing a miscarriage of justice.'

I look at him. 'Didn't cross my mind,' I say.

He smiles. 'Come on,' he says. 'We have work to do.'

Ten

Looking at the neat little packages in the boot of the car, I can't believe that they're actually Ed. Not until I pick one up, feel the flesh give way beneath my grip, get the sensation of the blood sopping through the black plastic.

'It's okay,' Dave says. 'It's fine.'

We carry Ed piece by piece from the car at the roadside down to the edge of the river. They are heavier than I expect, and Dave explains that he packed in stones and bricks to the packages. I don't ask where he got them from or how he had time to even think coherently about cutting up the body and dumping it. His answer will be the same one he always gives, anyway: *internet* or *Google.*

I drop a hand. An arm. What I think might be a thigh. They drop, wrapped in plastic, and disturb the serenity of the water below. And then they're gone. Swallowed up. As though they never existed.

Dave has the last package. Even with the stones disguising the shape, I can still guess at what it is.

'Is that . . .?'

'Head.'

'Oh.'

He looks at him, cradling the package to his chest like it's a baby, and then he makes this little movement and I think that he's somehow offering me the head, as though I might want to do this final act, let the last piece of Ed get swallowed up by the water.

I raise my hands and turn away. I drop to my knees, collapse onto my side and lie in the wild grass.

Dave comes over, kneels beside me. 'It's over,' he says. 'It's done.'

* * *

When we get back, I tell Dave I'm fine to go into the house on my own. He tries to say something, but I get out the car and slam the door, making it clear that I don't want to talk to him any more. To his credit, he takes the hint and drives off.

I watch from the front door until he turns off the road, and then I go inside.

As I walk up the stairs, each step makes me heavier with tiredness. There's a lump in my stomach that makes me think of the bricks that weigh pieces of Ed down at the bottom of the loch.

My front door is closed. And locked. I check and double check. I unlock it carefully.

Inside, I check the cupboard, check every room. I go to the kitchen and down several glasses of water, pouring the tap continuously. When I'm done, I head into the bedroom and fall on top of the covers.

I close my eyes.

There's no gap between sleeping and waking.

And there are no dreams either.

When I eventually wake up, the first thing I think is that it's over.

Truth is, it's only just beginning.

Eleven

The phone wakes me up. Loud and insistent.

I get up and stumble into the hall. I pick it up, groggy, say, 'Hello?'

'Jen, where the fuck are you?'

'What?' My eyes are barely able to open. I try and blink a few times and regain focus, swivel my head to look at the clock on the cooker through in the kitchen.

'Where. The. Fuck. Are. You?' Caroline. Angry. Urgent.

'At home. That's why I'm on the phone.'

'You're supposed to be here.'

'No I'm–' I glance through to the kitchen, see the time on the cooker. It's light for late evening, surely.

My brain kicks into gear. It's long past night time. I've slept right through to morning. 'Oh. Crap.'

'Oh, aye. Robin's on the warpath.'

'I'll bet.'

'Suzy called him in when you didn't show.'

'Right.'

'He's not happy.'

'Right.'

'Are you ill?'

'I'm coming in.'

'I can say you're ill.'

'I'm coming in.' One of the things Dave said: act like everything's normal. The man talked some crap, but this was one of the few times he actually made sense. All the money I knew was in my cupboard, I had to try and act like it was business as usual.

Which means turning up to work.

I hang up the phone and change my clothes as fast as possible. I run out the door, texting Robin as I do. Chances are he won't check his personal phone, but at least he can't later say I didn't make the effort.

* * *

When I arrive at the shop, it's as though I've just run a marathon. Ten minutes on the subway, then another ten of running. Maybe I'm not as fit as I thought. Maybe it's just being woken so abruptly. I have this dizzy sensation, like I could just collapse at any moment. Given the sleep I got, it can't be simple tiredness.

I do my best to sneak through, make sure Robin's not on the shop floor. Caroline – behind the front till – tells me that he's in the cash office. 'You okay?' she says. 'I mean you really don't look well.'

'I'm fine. I'm fine.'

I go downstairs. Underneath the shop, there's a rabbit warren of corridors. The staff room's at the far end. You have to pass every other room to get there. It's almost impossible to pass any room without someone noticing you. All the same, as I pass the cash office, I try to keep quiet, hoping against hope that Robin won't realise anyone's there.

Some chance. The man has ears like a bloody bat.

'Jen? You mind coming in a second?'

I take a deep breath and push at the door. It's unlocked. Generally Robin only locks it when the safe's open. In this case, he's just looking through some printouts. He likes printouts. Has that kind of mind: sees the world in charts and numbers and statistics.

'You're late,' he says, as I come in. He's not sitting at the desk. He's standing beside the printer. He doesn't sit down much. I think he has a fear that it might affect his productivity.

'I'm sorry.'

'It's not like you.'

'It's been a tough few days.' Like he cares.

He looks at me, with head cocked to one side. I can almost sense his brain trying to work out how best to respond. He's been on a mandated sensitivity training course in the last few months, and since then he's been just a little off when dealing with people, as though constantly afraid of saying the wrong thing. 'Is there . . .something you want to talk about?'

'No.'

'I . . .' but he doesn't finish the sentence.

I look at him. 'What?'

He takes a breath. 'You know, sometimes you hear things, and, well, the thing is, Jen . . . I know about Ed.'

My heart stops. I expect two coppers to step in from behind and place their hands on my shoulders. *Jennifer Carter, you are under arrest on suspicion of the murder and dismemberment of Edward . . .*

But nothing happens.

'I know you broke up with him.' In a shop like ours, it's hard to keep secrets. We're a small team. Word gets around. Even when people don't say anything.

'Right.'

'Sometimes these things can disrupt our work. It's only natural.'

'Uh-huh.'

'So what I'm saying is I'm willing to give you some leeway because of your hitherto excellent attendance record, attitude and performance. Particularly over Christmas last year when you stepped up.'

Stepped up. I ran the bloody place practically by myself while our assistant manager was ill and Robin was off helping out at some shop who were in even worse trouble than us.

Not that I'm going to say that.

'If you want some time . . .'

'No,' I say. 'This won't happen again. And I just want to work.'

'Okay,' he says, and his voice is soft, like he's afraid if he speaks too loud or too fast, he might set off an explosive device somewhere. 'But anything you need, please just let me know.'

'I will,' I say. 'I will.' Desperate to get away from the conversation, to find some mind-numbing task to distract me, to regain some sense that the world hasn't been completely knocked off its axis.

* * *

End of the shift, Caroline says she'll walk to the subway with me. I don't want the company, but I know I need to act as normal as possible. So I say, sure, why not?

'So, what, you just slept in?'

We're heading down towards St Enoch station. Maybe ten minutes' walk from the store. Argyle Street is busy, as usual. There's a food market on in the pedestrianised area. The smell of bratwurst and paella fills the air, just about masking the smell of traffic fumes. A group of people claiming to be Peruvian play pan pipes to tinny backing tapes.

'It happens.'

'Not to you.'

I'm keeping as fast a pace as I can. We weave in and out of pedestrians as we walk. Caroline jostles to keep as close in step with me as she can. I want to tell her to piss off, but I know she's only doing it because she cares.

Jesus, if she only knew.

'Look, the last few days . . .'

'You weren't that drunk . . . were you? Two-day hangover?' She laughs. 'Bloody hell!'

I smile and nod, as though I've been caught out. 'I had some Bacardi back at the flat, I was feeling like the party ended too quickly and, well . . .'

'Well indeed.' She shakes her head. 'Telling you – that waiter, the one with the bum . . .'

At the subway, I go through the barrier with my Smartcard. I wait for Caroline, who's still not got around to getting one, still pays full price for her tickets every day.

We head down to the platform and wait for the wee orange train to pull up. As it does, I have this crazy urge to run to the tunnel opening and throw myself onto the tracks. Mind you, the Glasgow trains always look so paltry when you think about the ones in London, Paris or New York, I have to wonder whether I'd do myself that much damage.

Okay, it would be enough.

But it would inconvenience everyone waiting to get home.

Politeness can be a pain in the arse, sometimes.

* * *

Caroline gets off the stop before mine. I tell her I'll be in the next day and she laughs as she gets off. Her parting shot is, 'Don't give him another chance. Even if he comes begging.'

I just nod.

Try and fight the giggles that suddenly gather in my chest.

A whole group of people get on. There's enough seats, but all the same this old man shuffles into the seat beside me. He looks at me as he sits down. I think to myself that maybe he could leave a space between us. That's etiquette, surely. But he doesn't. He sits down right next to me like the carriage is hoaching.

The train lurches off. Everyone sways. The old man's hand brushes my thigh.

And stays there.

I look at him.

He looks back at me. Under the brim of his bunnet, his grey eyes are clear. He knows what he's doing.

'Get your hand off my leg.'

'Sorry, love. An accident.'

'Get your hand off my leg,' I say. Any other day, I'd have stood up and walked away as though the situation was my fault. Or, if I was in a particularly dour mood, just accepted what was happening and silently prayed for it to be over. But today, I feel different.

'Get your fucking hand off my fucking leg.' I maintain eye contact with him. There's a slight hesitation in his features, as though he's suddenly seen something in my face that he didn't expect. He reaches up and grabs one of the poles that people use to keep their balance when there's standing room only. He shuffles away. Mutters something under his breath. Definitely a word beginning with 'C'.

A woman in her fifties is sitting across from me. Her blonde hair is verging on grey, and she has deep lines in her face. She smiles at me. 'Good on you, hen,' she says. 'Shows the bastards what's what, aye?'

I just smile back.

What else can I do?

* * *

Over the next few days, life goes back to normal.

More or less.

I keep expecting to have nightmares about Ed. But I don't. I don't dream at all. Is that surprising? I'm not sure. How can I keep my calm? Why don't I break down?

This isn't shock.

It's something else. Maybe something in me I never knew was there.

People at work say I'm looking better than I have in a long time: that my attitude's improved. I deal with the customers well. I don't find myself worn down by stupid questions or by the occasional condescending prick.

Some evenings, when I get home, I bring out the money and start to count it. Note by note.

I never finish. Always pack it away before I'm finished, as though afraid that by even acknowledging its existence, I'll somehow reveal to the world what I've done.

Four nights.

Life goes on. Nothing happens. I begin to think that everything we're taught about our actions having consequences is nonsense, that sometimes things happen and life just continues. The world doesn't open up and swallow you whole.

And then there's the knock at the door.

Loud. Confident. Direct.

The kind of knock you think the police might have. Right before they slam through with the battering ram.

Twelve

I answer, and I'm confronted by a man in dark suit with salt and pepper hair and the kind of face that's seen a lot of bad things in life. Even if he tried to smile, he'd probably just look sad. Wistful, actually, might be a better word.

There's a woman behind him who's maybe a few years younger, with blonde hair and the kind of face you might expect a primary school teacher to have: the kind of soft features that you'd just want to open up to. She's dressed in a similar dark trouser suit and a white blouse.

The man shows me his ID.

'Detective Inspector Crawford, Police Scotland,' he says. 'This is my colleague, Detective Sergeant Hendricks. Do you mind if we come in?'

I almost sick up on his shoes. But I manage to remain calm and say, 'Of course not,' my voice rasping with the sudden effort of not showing my surprise.

A burp gathers in my chest. I swallow it back down. Although at least that way I can blame whatever I had for dinner.

Neither of them slaps on the cuffs. Instead they follow me into the living room and Crawford gestures to the sofa, asking if he can sit down. I nod my consent, but stay standing.

Why?

Am I going to run?

Where would I run?

What good would it do?

All that rubbish about actions not having consequences was just a delusion.

'We just need to ask you some questions,' he says.

'Fairly routine,' Hendricks says.

'Good,' I say. 'Long as you're not here because I murdered someone.' I laugh, and then stop laughing almost instantly.

Yeah, great move.

Brilliant.

The two detectives look at each other.

My heart stops.

This is it. Goodbye, Partick. Hello, Cornton Vale.

'No,' Crawford says, a little slowly, like he's not sure how to react.

My heart takes that as permission to start again at three times the speed it was going before. He thinks it was a joke in poor taste, but at least he just thinks it was a joke.

Hendricks says, 'Do you know Edward Matthieson?'

I swallow. 'I . . . I did. Know him, I mean.'

'You did?'

'We were . . . I mean he was . . . We broke up.'

Hendricks confirms what I mean: 'You were involved?'

I smile, grateful to her for pulling me out of the hole. We share a look. She's probably thinking female solidarity. She doesn't know why I'm so happy she put words in my mouth. I was maybe three syllables away from turning myself in. And I can't go through that. Not now.

'Unfortunately,' I say.

My smile's too big. Too insincere. I don't need to see it to know. My cheeks sting with the effort. My eyes are probably too wide.

I can only imagine what I look like to the two detectives: mad? Or guilty?

I take a breath and say, 'What's he done now?'

'We don't know,' Hendricks says. 'He's been missing for several days.'

'Oh?'

Crawford says, 'He meets his mother every Tuesday for lunch.'

I nod. I didn't know that. Odd how you don't think about these things. Just because Ed never talked about family doesn't mean he never had one. He could have a wife and three kids tucked away, for all I knew about his private life. Oddly, even though I knew someone had to have given birth to him, that would have been less strange to me than his having a mother. A mother he met for lunch every Tuesday.

'This week, he didn't show up.'

'And now it's Thursday,' I say, finishing the thought.

Hendricks nods. Crawford doesn't say anything. He's a man of few words. Something about him seems oddly subdued. That sadness I noticed earlier has an odd anger to it, I think. As though he thinks this particular chat is beneath him in some way: he'd rather be somewhere else, dealing with things that matter.

Is this a prelude to something? All the police shows on TV, this is how the climactic scenes unfold: an innocuous conversation that leads to a sudden arrest. The Columbo method. I need to try and keep calm. I stay standing. Most people are nervous when the police come to their house, right? That's what I keep thinking, that most people will feel guilt even when they haven't done anything.

'He's a missing person,' Hendricks says. 'Officially.'

'He's a grown man.'

'Missing in unusual circumstances. His credit and bank cards haven't been used. His flatmate doesn't know where he is . . .'

'Dave?'

'Yes,' Crawford says. 'David Miller.'

Hendricks says, 'He gave us your address. Mr Matthieson's mother didn't know he was dating anyone.'

'I didn't know he had a mother.' I think about what I've just said. 'I mean . . . I knew he had a mother. I just didn't . . .'

Crawford waves that off. He's making notes. Scribbling in his notebook, looking up at me only when he has something to say.

Hendricks says, 'We just need to ask if you know where we might find him.'

Crawford adds, 'When you last saw him?'

I pretend to think about it. 'It's been a few days,' I say. 'Nearly a week, actually.'

Hendricks says, 'Can I ask why you ended the relationship?'

I take a breath. 'He was . . . I mean, I feel bad saying it in case something happened, but . . .he was a bit of a dick.'

Hendricks gives me a tight-lipped smile. Sisterly solidarity? We've all had bad relationships. Although I'm tempted to put Ed in a class all of his own.

Looking at his notes, Crawford says, 'Can you be any more specific?'

'We just weren't a good fit,' I say. Then, after a moment. 'He wasn't what you'd call faithful.'

Crawford says, 'Was he seeing anyone else that you know of at the time of the breakup?'

Hendricks jumps in, the voice of reason. 'We know this must be difficult to talk about.'

'I don't know,' I say. 'He wasn't the having an affair type as much as he was one night stand and apologise later type, you know? And there were other things, just a whole raft of . . .' My voice is getting tight and faster. I let myself trail off.

'I'm sorry,' Crawford says, in a flat tone. 'We have to ask.'

'I told him to go,' I say. 'He went.'

The detectives stand. 'If you think of anything,' Crawford says, reaching into his inside pocket to pull out a card. He hands it to me. 'Call us. Day, night, whenever. Someone will be able to talk to you.' He sounds like he'd rather have his teeth pulled than keep investigating this particular case. Fine by me. Don't look too deeply, Inspector. Just keep up the good work. Let me live with my guilt, which I'm sure is punishment enough.

'Thank you,' I say. 'I hope he's okay.'

'We're sure he will be,' Hendricks says. 'Everything we're learning about him, despite what his mother says, seems to indicate he's not the most reliable of people. Maybe just went on a bender or something.'

'Maybe,' I said. 'Sounds like him. I'd look at massage parlours or something.' Saying too much. Sounding too eager to help. No, no. Bad move. They'll know. They'll know.

Crawford hesitates as they're about to leave. The final part of the Columbo technique: the dramatic remembrance of important information. 'Maybe this is a sensitive question,' he says. 'And you're not in any trouble here. But you wouldn't know anything about whether he was into drugs? Dealing, maybe?'

I shake my head. 'It's possible,' I say. 'But never around me.'

They head to the door.

As they leave, Crawford says, 'Thank you for your time.' Hendricks just makes eye contact.

I stand in the door and watch as they head down the stairwell. Then I head back inside and got to the living room window, watch as they cross the street and get into a dark blue car. I try not to make it look like I'm watching them, and stomp around the living room a little as though I'm looking for something. Just in case they wonder why I'm looking out.

Then I hear an engine start and I go back to the window to watch them leave.

There's a weight in my chest.

They didn't get me this time. But who's to say they won't be back for me again? Who's to say some idle fisherman might not find a little piece of Ed on the end of his hook? There's only so many lies one person can tell, after all.

Thirteen

I push the door when it starts to open. He stands back, hands up in a gesture of submission. I don't care. I walk through to the living room, pace between the sofa and the new widescreen TV. He's been playing games. The screen is paused on a map of somewhere called 'Liberty City'.

'Jesus, Dave!' I say.

He ambles into the room and flops on the sofa. Raises his hands. 'What?'

'What?' I could laugh. It's pushing at my chest.

'Yeah, what?'

'You sent the police to my house!'

'His mother sent them here first.'

'What, this is pass the parcel now? I could have . . .'

He shrugs. 'Aye, but you didn't. What else was I going to do? You have to keep acting like everything's normal.' He scratches at his chin. 'You did act like everything was normal, aye?' He's calm. Not just stoned calm, but completely unbothered calm. 'You spent anything yet?'

'No.'

'You should.'

I laugh, then. Turn and look at the TV.

'For crying out . . . Did you have this on when the detectives came round?' It's a new set. Brand new. The packaging is still beside it, like Dave couldn't be bothered tidying up before having a play with his new toy.

Impulse control. Something men seem to have trouble with.

'Yes.'

I can't even think of the words. Instead, I make a sputtering sound.

He just sits there, shaking his head.

'Dave,' I say, 'I'm serious. You're the one who said we had to be careful. With the money. And the . . .well . . .the . . .you know . . .'

'Aye, the product, I know. I am being careful. Couple of people Ed used to know came looking for him. They said he used to sell some stuff. I said I thought I knew where he had some spare. They gave me cash.'

'And you bought that?' I point at the TV.

'Great for gaming. And check out the new surround system too.'

I look at the corners of the room. The speakers on the stands. The trailing cables. I think I want to slap him. But instead I just take a deep breath.

He says, 'Live a little. I mean, who notices a new telly, right?'

'Everyone,' I say. 'When you keep the packaging right there beside it.'

I flop down on the sofa beside him. He grins. 'Beer in the fridge, if you want.' He takes the controller from where he dropped it off the floor and resumes the game.

I watch for a while as the character onscreen runs round a city causing mayhem and destruction. Dave whoops it up.

People die on screen. Pixelated blood flies. The character Dave controls takes an incredible beating, runs over health packs and just goes back to normal, like nothing happened.

I wonder if when Dave saw Ed's body that night, whether he was able to distinguish between the fact that what he had to do was dismember a real corpse or whether he saw the world around him as some kind of computer-animated fantasia. Unreal. Two dimensional. Inevitably unimportant.

* * *

Three hours later. A bottle of prosecco from Oddbins. Flicking through movies on demand. I would be reading, but my brain can't really focus. I was halfway through a book about a childhood friend of Mary Shelley's when Ed died. Good stuff, but the fact she killed her husband and was sentenced to an asylum just seems like too heavy-going, in the circumstance.

Perhaps Dave's right. Maybe I should just enjoy the money. Let it go. Accept that all of this is over. Even if the police find Ed – or part of him at least – what does that really prove?

My flat is peaceful. There are no ghosts. Even the earlier interrogation seems like a tiny blip, something unimportant. Now that it's been and gone, the worst is over.

I killed a man. And got away with it.

Why am I not more bothered by the idea?

Because of what Ed did? Or because, in the end, it wasn't really my fault? The entire incident coming to accident and circumstance. Why should I pay for something that I never intended to do?

I settle on the Sherlock Holmes film with Robert Downey Jr. Some fluff. I need to relax. Turn off my brain. Stop trying to think about why I'm not feeling the way I expect to feel.

I click yes, I accept the charge. In HD, too. Sod the expense. I want to see those hazel eyes in all their detail, lose myself in them.

I sit back, try and forget that niggling concern that somehow, without ever intending to, I've got away with murder.

PART TWO

SMILEY'S PEOPLE

Fourteen

Three weeks.

A whole new wardrobe.

A replacement cooker.

Fresh coat of paint in the front room.

A little too much?

Maybe.

But I don't feel the prick of conscience anymore. What happened to Ed was an accident. And they can't connect it to me. I wasn't the one chopped him up.

So what about the money?

Who'll connect that to me?

There are doubts. Lots of little moments that threaten to drive me crazy. But they're getting less and less. I'm not going too crazy. Doing my shifts at work, same as ever. People are jealous of the holiday to New York City I have coming up in the next month, keep asking if maybe I have some rich boyfriend I've not been talking about.

The best response?

Smile and say nothing. Let them make up their own minds.

Not like they're going to wonder if I happened to get the cash by murdering Ed and keeping the drug money he'd been hiding in my flat.

Even I don't believe that. And I was there.

* * *

I come home from another shift. I haven't been so tired lately. Maybe because I don't feel I need to worry about much for a while. The money's a cushion, and all those things I used to want before I got it, they suddenly don't seem so important.

So it's great. The only other person in the world who knows what happened is Dave, and it's in his interest not to talk to anyone about it.

If I have any nagging doubts in my mind, most of it's to do with the phone.

I found it the morning after I was late for work, lying in the mess of the cupboard, abandoned among the overturned boxes and the chaos that came about when me and Dave dug through just in case Ed had left me any other little surprises.

But we didn't see the phone.

I recognised it straight away. Ed was proud of the Samsung 6. He always liked to have the latest model, whatever it was. Complete opposite of me. When it comes to a mobile, then as long as it gets a signal, I'm happy.

The battery was nearly dead, but there were several missed calls and messages. How could I resist? How could I not wonder if it was the little barista from the coffee house or some other girl I never even noticed him clocking?

I dialled the voicemail and listened.

'You little shitebasket. We warned you. This was your last fucking chance.'

I dropped the phone before the voice said anything more. The battery died. Later, I went down to the Clyde, threw the phone into the water from the shoogly Bridge.

Three weeks later, and that voice on the phone is nearly forgotten. Like trying to recall a nightmare that seemed so vivid at the time.

I'm a little late back, having stopped off at Sainsburys for the basics. My plan is simple: an evening in with a pizza and maybe finally getting back to reading. Before . . .the incident . . .I read something like three books a week. I don't think I've read half a page in nearly a month.

I'm unpacking the shopping when I see the green light blinking on my phone. I stop for a moment and walk over, thinking it'll be some kind of marketing call. Double glazing. Conservatories. PPI, maybe.

I click Play.

'You have one new message.'

'Jen . . .' It's Dave. Maybe he has a cold. His voice sounds rough, like he's swallowed a cheese grater. 'Jen . . .you need to call me back. You need to–' There's a noise on the other end of the line. A banging sound, like someone kicking the walls.

'That was your last message.'

There's a sick feeling in my stomach.

I check my mobile. It's been on silent. As usual, I haven't really been bothered about checking it. Who calls me about anything important?

Five missed calls.

All from Dave.

Leaving the fridge door hanging open, not bothering to change out of my work clothes, I run out onto the street, head up to Dumbarton Road and hail a cab. When I tell him where I want to go, the driver says, 'Two minutes' walk, love.'

'This is quicker.'

He sighs, but decides a small fare is better than no fare and takes me where I need to go. When I'm getting out he says, 'Emergency, then?'

'I hope not.'

'Want me to wait?'

I consider it. 'Naw,' I say.

'Suit yourself.' He clearly thinks I'm a flake. He should be grateful. The tip I leave is more than the fare.

Dave and Ed share their oversized flat on the third floor of a converted Victorian townhouse, the kind of building where the neighbours are barely aware of who's in the next flat.

I ring the bell.

No response.

Think, Jen. *Think.*

I ring the ground-floor flat. The girl who comes to the door looks a little harassed, and then I see why: a few cats have escaped into the main hall with her. She clearly doesn't want them running out the front door. She's got blonde hair and even though it's only just past eight, she's wearing a thick, dark blue dressing gown. She looks at me and says, 'You know Ed and Dave, right?' Clearly remembers me from when we've passed in the hallways during some of my previous visits. 'Well,' she corrects herself, 'just Dave now, I guess.'

'He's not answering.' I must look crazy to her. Wide eyed and panicked over nothing.

'Maybe he's out.'

'Look, just let me in!'

She looks at me like maybe she wonders if I'm on some of the product she knows Dave likes to use. But maybe she sees something sympathetic in my face, or maybe she's just too concerned about the cats escaping out onto the road, because she relents and lets me in.

While she herds cats back into her place, I go up the stairs.

I hear her talking: 'Mycroft! Come here! No! Naughty puss!'

I get to the second floor. A lot of stairs, this building being the size it is. Clearly I'm not in as good shape as I thought.

The door to Dave's flat is closed. I knock.

Someone's coming up the stairs.

I try the handle.

The door swings. Usually it's locked from the inside. But today it just opens inward. Like the flat was expecting me.

I walk in. 'Dave?'

No answer.

Through to the living room. The big telly. The sofa. And again, that same screen, the map of the city from the computer game.

But Dave's not playing.

He's on one of the chairs that used to be around the dining table near the back of the room. It's been moved into the middle of the floor and he's been tied up so that he has no choice but to stay upright. He's naked, too. Flabby, pale flesh on display for all the world to see. His penis is shrivelled up, looks faintly ridiculous flopping about beneath his oversized and pale belly.

Something acidic assaults my nostrils.

I see the water at his feet.

And more.

The blood on his chest, forming a small trail that runs between his man-boobs. Not that he's embarrassed to have them any more.

Not that he's embarrassed about much of anything.

'I just had to check that everything was allr–' The girl from downstairs. She stops in the door and stares, jaw doing that whole hit-the-floor thing.

'Jesus! Is he–?'

I just nod.

She just stares.

Dave stares back. Glassy eyed.

Fifteen

'Ms Carter,' Crawford says, as he walks into the room.

I'm in the downstairs flat, in a small room that serves as an office, to the rear of the property. There's a computer and several bookcases, as well as a cheap sofa-bed, where I sit, waiting to be interviewed. When the police arrived, they'd isolated myself and the woman from downstairs. She was in her front room. I was back here in the office. Guess the idea is that we don't have a chance to sync up our stories. Allows the police to check for any inconsistencies. In case one or both of us turns out to be the guilty party.

I spend most of my enforced alone time scanning the bookshelves, figuring whoever she is – the downstairs neighbour – she's probably in academia, judging by most of the heavy books with titles like *The Encyclopaedia of Philosophy of Mind*. The framed PhD on the wall is a giveaway too.

Crawford stays standing this time, when he comes into the room. I'm the one sitting down. 'Can I get you anything? A glass of water?'

I shake my head.

His attitude is subtly different to last time. Weirdly, now I'm an actual suspect – oh, I know he says I'm a witness, but you'd have to be soft in the head not to think that this was looking less like bad luck and more like something sinister – he seems to be treating me with some degree of compassion.

But, still: he has the notebook out. And the pen.

He's a detective, after all. Still looking for the guilty party. And right now, he knows that the one thing connecting these deaths is me.

Doesn't take Sherlock Holmes to put two and two together.

'Can you tell me how you discovered the body?'

I hesitate. What do I say?

'I know this is tough . . .'

I shake my head. Make like I'm clearing my throat. 'No, no,' I say. 'It's fine. It's . . . Look, he called me.'

'You and Mr Miller are friends?'

'Yeah.'

'This friendship, it started before or after your boyfriend's disappearance?'

I try not to infer anything from the question. 'Before, but . . . I mean, not good friends. After Ed went walkabout, though, we'd check in once in a while, in case either of us had learned something. About what happened to Ed.'

He makes notes, only glances at me. But I don't think he really sees me. Crawford seems like one of those people who does a lot of thinking, gets lost in their own head when they're trying to figure something out.

'Walkabout,' he says, and maybe there's a hint of a smile. 'Okay . . . so you were here to, what, have a chat about your ex? Or just for a drink? Or . . .'

I stick with as close to the truth as I can. 'He called me earlier. Sounded . . . upset.'

'Upset?'

'Scared, maybe.'

'Did he say he was scared?'

'No. He just asked me to come over. I mean, he left a message on my answering machine. Something in his voice, though.'

Crawford nods. 'We'll need the message.'

'Of course.' I try to remember what he said on the message. Whether there was some clue that would lead Crawford to suspect what really happened to Ed. The way he mocked me for using the word 'walkabout,' I figure he has to suspect something even if he can't prove it.

'Well?'

'What?'

'We'll need your phone.'

'No,' I say, maybe a little too fast. 'He called the house phone.' I don't want him to listen to the messages Dave left on my mobile. I haven't heard them. I need to hear them before I know that it's safe for Crawford to listen.

Thinking about what happened to Dave, I wonder if 'safe' is a relative term.

'Okay. We'll send someone over to collect it.'

'Uh-huh.'

There's silence for a moment. Crawford looks around. He looks at the books on the shelves. Then he looks at me. 'This has been a rough month for you, hasn't it?'

'I just . . . I'm not going to sleep tonight.'

'We can send an officer home with you, if you like. If you feel unsafe.'

I think about the cash I have in bags in the cupboard, and how anyone who noticed them would probably start asking questions. 'No,' I say. 'No, no. I just . . . I don't know why anyone would . . .' I take a breath. There's a lump in my throat. I'm about to start crying. I'm actually about to start crying, and I don't want Crawford to see that happen. I don't know why. I just imagine he'd believe it to be a show of some kind.

Crocodile tears.

That's how Crawford would see me. I'm sure of it.

I swallow and blink and say, 'He was a nice guy, Dave. Not romantically or anything, but . . .' I stop talking, think about what

I'm saying. My thought process is becoming more and more fractured. I need to focus. 'He was a stoner, sure . . .'

'Aye?'

'Same as a lot of people.'

'Same as you?'

I hesitate. Sensing a trick.

'I'm just looking for the full picture,' Crawford says. 'Not to get you for a wee bit of weed or anything. Not really my department, anyway. Just trying to work out who might have wanted to harm your friend there.'

'He didn't deal,' I say. 'Far as I knew. Just . . .he liked a wee puff now and then.' But I can't stop thinking about when he took Ed's drugs for himself. The powder was too hard for Dave, but chances were that he knew people who'd want to buy. So maybe it wasn't someone looking for Ed's cash, but someone he ripped off – probably by accident – or someone looking to sample the product without paying. If there was one thing I had learned from watching too many late-night movies it was that people killed for powder wrapped in plastic bricks. And they did it violently. Brutally. Usually as a warning to other people.

'But it's possible?'

'Maybe. I mean, did you find anything up there?'

Crawford shakes his head. 'We're still looking. It's just strange that whoever killed him didn't take anything.' He looks directly at me. 'Makes me think it's personal.'

I don't say anything. But I'm thinking you really don't get much more personal than murder.

'I'm sorry for your loss,' he says, habitually. 'These last couple of months, I know you've gone through more than most of us would want to deal with.'

'Can I go?'

'I'll have an officer escort you.'

'That's not–'

'Indulge me, please.'

'You know what you're doing.'

'We'll talk again in the morning,' he says.

'Okay.'

I stand up. He gestures for me to hold on a moment and leaves the room. I look at the books again.

The Ethics of Everyday Life.

Nothing everyday about what's happening to me.

Crawford comes back into the room with a beat officer. She's five-nothing at best, but looks like she knows how to handle herself. The way she walks is confident, and I have this idea of her taking down thugs with little more than harsh language. Her face is somewhere between severe and soft, but it's hard to tell. I suppose it probably depends on who you are and what she wants from you.

'This is Constable Deeren. She'll escort you home.'

I nod my thanks and make for the door. Deeren follows, and outside she walks me to a police car. She opens the back door. I get in the back. Not in the front, where I can cause trouble.

I lean forward as we drive and watch the road from between the front seats. I'm feeling itchy, now. Nervous. I have to say something, have some kind of conversation. Just to stop my mind wandering.

'Been on the force for long?'

She just looks in the rear view.

'Just wondering,' I say.

'I'm sorry you had to find your friend like that.'

'Aye, so am I.'

'Crawford . . . I don't know him, but I know he'll do his best to find who did it.'

'Aye.'

'But anything you think of . . .'

'So he said.'

82

We turn onto my street. I direct her where to pull up. 'I'll come in with you.' It feels ludicrous, her driving me back. I live too close. The drive was nothing.

'No,' I say, a little too fast. 'I mean, its fine. It's okay.'

'If he asks,' she says, 'I can say that I did everything to ensure that you arrived safely.' I see her face in the mirror. She's smiling, but it's a genuine expression. She's got no ulterior motive. Maybe Crawford hasn't clued her into the idea that I might have killed my ex.

What's the point in arguing? I wait for her to open the back door. The cop equivalent of child lock, I guess.

Criminal Lock?

When she lets me out, I walk right up to the front door of the building, which hangs open.

'Always like that?'

'Sometimes,' I say. 'The old dear on the top floor, sometimes she forgets to close it behind her.'

Deeren nods, but her face is concerned. She's thinking worst-case scenario. Maybe that's what the training does to you. I think there's such a thing as being over-cautious. But of course I would. I don't want her in my apartment. I don't want anyone in my apartment.

As I walk in, I check my mobile. Just to avoid talking to Deeren any more than I have to. Three missed messages. From Caroline. *Where RU?*

I could kick myself. At work, I told her I'd join her at some bloody ceilidh in the centre of town. I'd forgotten about it before I even got home.

The door to my flat is open too. Same as the main door. I know I locked it. Ever since Ed, I've become paranoid about checking and double checking.

I can see into my hall, to the cupboard, where someone's in there looking for something. He's a big man, dressed in a dark

83

suit, and he doesn't know we're here. Deeren looks at me, a silent question in her eyes. I shake my head: no, I don't know this man. She urges me back and steps forward, through the door.

'Police,' Deeren says. 'You are trespassing on private property. Turn around, slowly.'

The man holds up his hands. He turns around. He's big. Not just tall, but beneath the loose-fitting suit, he's a mass of solid muscle. He grins when he sees Deeren, and then he looks at me for a moment before focussing his attention on her again. She's clearly more of a threat.

The intruder is bald, but I can't tell whether that's natural or if he shaves his head. He has a big nose that's been broken before and left crooked, and a prominent, puckered scar that runs angrily down his right cheek. It's an old scar, the kind that never really heals. It's a part of him, and it tells you everything you need to know about what sort of man he is.

'What are you doing?'

There's the hint of a chuckle before he says, 'What does it look like I'm doing?'

'Stay where you are,' Deeren says, stepping forward. She's inside the flat now, reaching for the radio on her shoulder.

'I wouldn't,' the bald man says.

She looks at him. He jerks his head towards the kitchen, out of my field of view.

She doesn't touch the radio. Instead, she swallows and raises her hands.

The bald man looks at me now. 'Come in,' he says. 'The more the merrier.'

Deeren shuffles towards the living room. I walk into the flat, and look to the kitchen where I see a younger man dressed in a white suit and dark shirt. He's got light brown hair that he's let grow out. Any other day, I'd say he was off to some '80s party dressed as someone out of the original *Miami Vice*. He thinks

84

he's it, too. Has this cocky look I recognise. Reminds me of Ed before . . .well, before.

'Awright,' he says, speaking out of the corner of his mouth. I realise he's chewing gum. 'Mind closing the door behind you?'

He's holding a gun. I couldn't tell you anything about it, except it looks like every weapon I've seen in the movies: black and dangerous. Maybe it's a toy, but I figure Deeren thought the same and then decided it wasn't worth the chance.

I close the door.

The young guy grins.

I try not to shiver.

Sixteen

They make us sit on the sofa. The guy with the gun is jittery: can't stand still, hopping from foot to foot. Makes me think of a child who needs the toilet but can't go.

A child with a gun.

Don't forget the gun, Jen.

Never forget the gun.

Dereen keeps looking at him oddly, head tilted slightly to one side. Like she knows him from somewhere, but not well enough to call him out on it. Maybe she's seen his face in a book of suspects. Maybe just passed him on the street. But she keeps looking at him like she wants to say something, but can't find the words.

The younger guy's partner, by way of contrast, is stillness and restraint. Clearly in charge. He's maybe in his forties, but he hasn't developed a gut or any sign of middle-age spread. He's built big naturally, but I get the feeling he looks after himself too. Lots of hard men go to seed with middle age. This guy's all too aware that he can't just rely on being large – he needs to be able to back himself up.

He makes me think of Kat, and the continuing mystery over why she disappeared. No, not Kat. Her family. I remember meeting some of them a few times. Her cousin Ray was the scariest. He never seemed quite human.

This guy, well, I can't tell. Yet.

'I'm sorry,' he says. 'If you'd just been a few minutes later, then all this would be academic.' Something in the way he speaks makes me think that he's got brains as well as brawn. He's got the traces of an east-end accent, but there's something else in there too. Like he's learned how to make himself understood to anyone not from Glasgow. He holds himself tall too. Maybe he's military. Maybe I'm just looking for something about him to remember later.

If there is a later.

Maybe this is what they call karma. I never believed in it, but how could I have believed there wouldn't be consequences after what happened with Ed?

Deeren says, 'It's not too late to do something about this.' She's calm. Controlled. Like this kind of thing happens all the time. What gives her away is the deep breaths she takes when she's not speaking. She's struggling to keep it together. Sweat too, on her forehead.

'I rather think it is too late.' He shakes his head, sits down in the armchair across the room and looks at Deeren. 'Ask you something?' She nods. 'My face, you don't know it, do you?'

'No.'

'No reason you should. Never been arrested. Never been caught. Lived my life under the radar.'

'And we want to keep it that way,' the younger guy says. He's dancing even more frantically now. It's not the desperation of a kid needing the toilet, but one who has something to say. Or one who's come down on Christmas morning and been told to wait five minutes before opening those presents.

'But I know you,' Deeren says. 'Don't I?'

'Knew this was a bad idea,' the younger guy says. 'Fuckin' knew it.' He points the gun at Deeren's face. 'Was really hoping it didn't have to come to this, you know? That you and me could go our separate ways, never think about this again. That we—'

'Michael,' the bald man says, not even looking at the younger man. 'Shut the fu—'

The gunshot is deafening. And then I can't hear anything except for this buzzing in my ears. It's like I've blacked out. I don't know what's happening. The world loses all coherence. My vision blurs and everything loses its shape. My stomach churns.

When everything comes back, I slowly turn my head and see Deeren still on the couch. She's slumped back with this ragged, red hole between her eyes. I can see blood and bone and bits of grey matter. And the sweat from earlier too, mingling with the blood, giving it this odd, slick sheen. I don't want to think about. I know what the back of her head will look like. But I try not to think about it.

The bald man's on his feet, and he has the gun now. It's like I've jumped forward in time a few minutes.

The younger guy, Michael, is on the floor. I've just switched channels on the TV, coming into the middle of a scene with no context to ground me.

Thinking of it like that is the easy option. It allows me to sit back from everything, removed like watching a screen where I know nothing is real. All of this is pretend, make believe. It has no effect on me.

' . . .ck're you thinking?' The sound creeps in now too. The bald man kicks at his associate, who just stays where he is. Not acceptable. The bald man holds out the gun, hands on the grip, fingers snaking to the trigger. The business end is pointed at the younger man's head.

'Naw. Please.' This isn't a game any more. No more excitement. Real fear. Sudden and sickening.

'You killed a fucking polis.'

'Naw, naw.'

'Yes, yes, y'wee bollocks!'

'This is fucked.'

'And you're the one who fucked it. We could have dealt with her, easy. Quiet-like. But *oh no*, you fucking coked-up wee bollocks . . .'

Gingerly, I stand up, making as little noise as possible. I can run while they're distracted. This tiff is good news for me. Get out the flat, down the stairs, in someone's front door, on the telephone.

What's your emergency?

There's a bald man, a dead policewoman and an injured psychopath in my flat. If I'd called you the other week, then it would all have been okay. But this is my own fault, so why don't you come here, arrest them and maybe arrest me too?

I'm ready to make a break for it when the bald guy turns and points the gun at me. 'Don't make a fuckin mistake,' he says. Then, looking down at the younger man, Michael. 'Get the fuck on your feet.'

Michael does as he's told. Despite the suit and the thick hair, he doesn't look quite as in control as he was earlier. The suit's too big now. The psychotic glee at the prospect of using his gun is long gone, replaced by a pathetic air of fear that even has me feeling repelled.

Bald guy says, 'We're leaving. This is fucked.' He looks at me. Then he does something odd. He ejects the cartridge from the butt of the weapon and pockets it. Then he pulls back on the gun and ejects a solitary bullet, with which he does the same thing. Then he walks towards me.

I don't think I can breathe. No, I can't. I can't breathe. My lungs won't work. My chest is going to explode. But at least then I'll be dead. All of this, I won't have to worry about if I'm dead.

He then slips his hand inside his sleeves and wipes at the butt of the weapon, careful not to touch it with his skin. I watch him do this, standing like a lemon, unable to figure what he's doing.

Then, still using his hands inside his sleeves, he holds out the gun to me. 'Take it,' he says.

'What?'

'Take the fucking gun.'

I do so.

'Put your finger in the trigger. Hold it like you're going to shoot me.'

I look at him, not quite believing what he's telling me. But he's insistent. He barks at me like a drill sergeant: 'Do it!'

I do as he asks. Gun or no gun I get the feeling he's a dangerous man. More than his friend, anyway, who I think needed the weapon to feel big.

He turns to Michael. 'Get her to the car.'

Michael takes my arm, like he's leading me off on a date. Except he tugs and insists more than I like my men to do. 'Okay,' I say. 'Okay, okay.' My choice is to go with him or have my arm ripped off. Not that he's threatening, but more that he's every bit as scared as I am.

I can't process what happened to Deeren. The idea that he just shot her in the forehead. For no reason that I could figure either.

I guess his bald friend feels the same way, judging by the way he beat the shit out of Michael for what he did. Maybe if I hadn't stood up, Michael would have a bullet in his head too. Maybe not. Maybe I'd have one. A triple homicide. A triple tragedy. Questions would be asked, but I doubt anyone would get to the bottom of it.

Maybe baldy isn't as smart as I thought, after all. Or else he's seeing something I've missed.

As we head out in the hall, I offer up a silent prayer that someone must have heard the noise. Someone has to be calling the police.

But there's no movement anywhere in the building.

So much for the power of prayer.

Michael hustles me down the stairs.

Outside, we cross the street. I twist my neck to look back at the building. Lights are going on. Finally. Someone on the third floor is looking out the window. Do they see me? I want to wave and shout, but instead I keep quiet and let this guy in his ill-fitting suit force me into the back of a black BMW.

The bald guy's in the front almost instantly. Michael's in the back with me.

'Fuck,' Michael says. 'Fuck, fuck!'

The bald guy passes something back to him. 'Don't fuck up,' he says. It's the gun. He's decided to give Michael back the gun.

Is it loaded again?

Do I want to risk it?

Baldy starts up the engine. As he pulls out, like he's off for a Sunday drive, nice and calm and collected, he says to Michael, 'You say another fucking word, though, you useless we prick, you'll be wishing you'd died quick as that polis.' I can see him in the rear view and I know he can see me. Those eyes – grey and clear – lock onto mine. 'As to you, this could have been so fucking simple. Still can be, if you behave yourself. Yeah?'

'Yeah,' I say, and, acting on instinct, I grab at my seatbelt and pull it on. 'So . . .where are we going?'

Neither man says anything.

Definitely not a good sign.

Seventeen

We drive out onto the M8 and pull off at Tradeston, and park near the new developments.

The bald man turns around and says, 'Let's try the introductions again, aye?'

I nod.

He nods to his friend. 'This is Michael,' he says, in case I hadn't already noticed. 'As you can tell, fucking eejit thinks he's Clint Eastwood. Nah, maybe Mel Gibson. More his generation. They call me Smiley.'

I nod again. Maybe there's a question to ask about the name, but I don't ask. In my head, I visualise the shop and the shelves where we keep the Le Carré books.

'And you're Jen, right? That's the name fat boy gave us. Before . . .' He lets that hang in the air. Not cruelly, but more that he doesn't know how I might react. Things are calm now. He doesn't need them kicking off.

'Uh-huh.'

'Know why we were in your flat, Jen?' I remember a customer service course I took once. They told you that once you know the customer's name, you should use it as often as possible to make them feel familiar with you, create a false sense of intimacy.

Smiley doesn't strike me as the customer service course type, though. They were a different breed of sociopath.

'No.'

Michael makes a buzzing noise. 'And our survey says . . .nah!'

Smiley says, 'Oh, give the girl a chance.' Then, his full attention back to me. 'You know Ed, don't you?'

I hesitate.

'Don't deny it. I know exactly what you were to him.'

'Aye?'

'It was the fat fuck,' he says. 'He was the one who gave us your name and address. I think he tried to leave you a message.'

'I heard it.'

'That's what the business with the police was all about?'

'Yes. You didn't have to kill him.'

'He was being uncooperative,' Smiley says. 'Things got out of hand. Not as bad as with the policewoman there . . .' He gives Michael a pointed look, and then drops it again. 'But there you go. Dave wasn't someone who wanted to talk, who wanted to help us retrieve our . . .personal property.' He takes a moment to let that sink in. 'But you, Jen, you look like someone who's eager to please, happy to help.'

'I don't know what–'

'Ed was your boyfriend, right? What we managed to get out of Dave, anyway.'

'Aye.'

'And you knew what he was into?'

'I knew he was into being a fucking idiot.'

Smiley nods. But he still doesn't smile. I'm beginning to wonder if it's one of those ironic nicknames. 'Good, good,' he says. 'Very good. I only met him once or twice, but enough to know he was an arse. Must have had something, though?'

'Big cock?' Michael says.

No one laughs.

'Something that made you care for him?' Smiley says, as though the younger man had never said a word.

'Not any more.'

93

'Trouble in paradise?'

'I kicked him out of my life about six weeks ago.'

'Six weeks?'

'Uh-huh.'

'When he vanished.'

'What?'

'Six weeks ago, me and your wee boyfriend, or whatever you want to call him, we had a little meeting. A chat. See, he's the kind of man has the patter, all the rest of it, but when the shite hits the fan . . .well, let's say he didn't like paying his bills on time.'

'Who does?' I don't know where the mouth is coming from. Adrenaline, maybe. Acting like someone else to cover how scared I am. Something similar to the way I dealt with Ed and what happened there.

I make a vow never to get on the psychiatrist's couch.

'You want to know what he owed us?'

'Probably not.'

Smiley's silent for a moment. Those grey eyes stay fixed on me in the rear view. I think that I haven't seen him blink during our whole conversation.

Basilisk.

'He owed close to a million. Imagine that.'

'How?'

He shakes his head. 'You don't want to know. He was supposed to do a few favours for my boss, and instead he screwed everyone over. Thought he was big time. Truth? He was just another bawbag in a world filled with them. A man who thought he was king shit, but didn't have what it took.' He takes a deep breath and says, 'So now you know and you can tell me where he is.'

I look at Michael, who still has the gun. He's holding it low. I can't help but think he believes he's a film star. Everything he does seems affected, like he's impersonating someone else, behaving the way he thinks he should. There's nothing natural or authentic about him. Making him and Smiley the ultimate murderous odd couple.

'You killed that police officer.'

I don't know if it's my imagination, but I think Michael goes pale when I say that. All the posturing in the world can't disguise that he's in over his head. He's probably thought about killing before, but I'm guessing this is the first time he's done it.

And it was an accident. I'm sure of that.

Because there's something else in his expression. I'm missing a piece of the puzzle. He's not just afraid of his partner's wrath. There's something else. What is it?

Smiley says, 'I need you to focus, Jen.'

He's so different from Michael. I get the impression that Smiley has been stuck with the younger man. I know that Smiley has killed before. He's too calm and collected. Death doesn't shake him.

I say, 'I want to know why he killed her,' nodding at Michael.

Smiley shakes his head. 'I was hoping we'd have that conversation in private. But the girl here, it's a good question she's asking.' In the rear view, his eyes flick onto Michael for a moment. 'So, yeah, why'd you pull the fucking trigger?'

'Fuck. Fuck.' Michael takes his eyes off me to look at Smiley. 'You said it, man, she wasn't supposed to be there and sooner or later she was going to try something.' He talks fast, words running into each other.

'And we'd have dealt with that.' The contrast between them is clear. Smiley enunciates clearly, keeps his voice clear. 'But now she's dead. Know what's worse than hurting a polis?'

Michael says nothing.

Smiley gives him a moment before providing the answer. 'Killing a polis. The kind of storm that comes from that?' He shakes his head. Then looks at me. 'Think they'll have found her by now?'

95

'The whole building will have heard,' I say. 'Someone will have come to check on me by now.' I try to remember if we left the door open.

I think of the age of some of my neighbours. Feel worse about giving an old woman a heart attack than Deeren being shot.

What does that say about me?

What does the fact that I never told anyone about Ed say?

Maybe I'm finally in the right company with these two.

Michael laughs. 'Think they'd know it was a gunshot? In Partick? West End Wendys and all? Think they'd know what a gun is?'

'Then, what? A car backfiring in my living room?'

Smiley, eyes on the road but still listening, nods. 'They'll have called the police by now. Found the body in your flat.'

'Uh-huh,' I say.

'That's not going to look good.'

'No.'

'What will you say when they ask you?'

'I don't know.

'No?'

I think about it. How ludicrous my story would sound. 'Maybe that two psychopaths came into my flat and asked for money owed by my ex. The same ex who went missing six weeks ago, who I already told I didn't know where he was.'

Smiley shakes his head. 'I have a good idea when people lie to me, Jen,' he says. 'I wasn't always a shylock, you know.' It's an odd reference for him to make. But I don't have the time to press him further on the point.

Of course, he's right.

I know where Ed is.

Thing is, what Smiley doesn't know is that even if I'm lying about not knowing where he is, finding out won't do him any good. Hard to collect your debt from a dead man.

Smiley strikes me as the kind of man who wouldn't hesitate to kill someone if they were in his way or no longer of any use. The moment he finds out about Ed, I think he'll cut his losses and toss me aside. I can comfort myself with the idea that it won't be anything personal.

'Hey,' Smiley says. 'Are you going to say anything?'

'I know where he is,' I say. 'Dave would have told you too, I think. Because he knew.'

'Aye,' Smiley says. 'He was a surprisingly stubborn bastard for an overweight pothead. Almost admired him.'

'I can take you to Ed,' I say. 'But, look, where it is . . . I could direct you. But it would be easier if I drove.'

Jesus, Jen, what are you doing?

What are you doing?

Michael shakes his head. He raises the gun. I try not to shrink back from him. 'No way, no fucking way,' he says. 'Nuh-uh.'

Smiley says, 'You can direct us. You're not driving. And there's no room for negotiation, either. You have a dead policewoman in your flat as proof of how serious we are. But tell you what, we're not heartless. You take us to Ed, we get to talk to him, we'll let you live. How's that for an offer you can't refuse?'

'Aye,' I say. Negotiating was never my strong point. Whenever I try – like attempting to bring down my broadband bills at the end of a contract – I always feel like somehow I come out worse off than when I went in.

Here, I don't think there's a better off to be found, anyway.

Smiley looks at Michael, 'Looks like we've got a plan, then.'

I take a deep breath.

Okay, so I've bought myself some time. But what am I going to do with it?

Eighteen

I'm calm.

That's the strangest thing.

As I'm thinking I'm about to get myself out of this, I don't feel panicked or afraid. My heart doesn't race. My breathing doesn't get shallow. My mind doesn't race.

I'm calm.

Cool.

Collected.

Is this what it feels like to go into shock?

There has to be only so much a person can deal with, after all. Seeing Dave dead, witnessing Deeren's murder, being forced to go and show a couple of thugs where you buried your ex-boyfriend, all of these things have consequences.

Maybe this is what happens: after a while, the brain decides the best way to cope is just to behave as though everything that's happening is perfectly normal.

Another day in Paradise.

Okay, I'm definitely in shock if I'm using Phil Collins songs to comfort myself.

Smiley, in the driver's seat, following my directions, looks at me sideways, as though trying to work something out. Maybe he suspects something. I don't see how he couldn't. He's not stupid. He's a violent man – you can see that in the way he moves, hear it in his voice – but he's not cruel or stupid.

I think about telling him the truth, but remain silent. It's not simply his reaction that worries me. Whether he gets angry or simply accepts what happens doesn't make a difference in the current situation. No, what worries me is that talking about what happened to Ed will only make it real.

The last few weeks have been a dream, and if I talk now, I'm going to wake up and realise the truth.

'We could have worked something out,' Smiley says. 'Me and him. Your boyfriend, your ex, whatever he is to you now.' He shakes his head. 'I know you said things ended, but if you know where he's hiding, that means you still care. And I want you to know I offered him every chance to make things right. I'm not a thug.'

In the back seat, Michael is sitting low and quiet. Like a child sulking because his parents won't take him to McDonalds.

I keep my eye on the road. I don't think I want to talk to Smiley. But he's insistent. Like he has to figure me out. Like he knows there's something I'm not telling him but he really doesn't know what it is.

'No one had to die,' he says. 'But he decided to run rather than face the consequences, own up to things like a man. That makes him responsible for Dave, and that policewoman.' He hesitates. The unspoken words are *for you*. After a moment, he continues. 'If he had come to me or to my employer, tried to work out a deal, then no one would have had to die.' Another pause. I know he's trying to make sure that I understand what he's saying. And I do. Maybe I even agree with him, but I don't see the point in saying so. 'He was the one killed them, really.'

I keep my eyes fixed ahead. The white lines blur.

Ed may be ultimately responsible, but Smiley was the one who tortured Dave and killed him, while Michael's finger was on the trigger of the gun that went off in Constable Deeren's face.

I can't say any of that, though.

Or maybe I won't. I'm still two steps behind myself, observing rather than acting. Whatever I say or do, I don't feel like I have any control over my own actions.

'Who is your boss?'

That gets him. 'Come on, lass,' he says. 'You know better than to ask.'

'Just curious,' I say. 'I have a feeling it doesn't matter if you tell me.'

I know he won't let me live. All along, I've been dead. From the moment they saw me. I can give a good physical description of them, to go along with their names. Which could be just enough to help the police track them down. It makes sense to kill me. I accept that with a flat fatalism that is unfamiliar.

I wonder how long it is until I reach hysteria. I'm too calm about everything. I'm too removed. I don't know why. All I know is that sooner or later, it will erupt. Until then, all I can do is keep going.

We take the side road Dave drove me down over a month earlier. I've never come back this way, and yet I know it intimately. The route is stuck in my mind. Landmarks, even in the dark, seem familiar. I know where we stopped. I recognise the line of the trees, the ragged line of the side of the road.

I say, 'Pull over here.'

Michael finally speaks: 'What the fuck is this?'

Smiley remains silent.

He's waiting to see what happens next.

I get out the car. Walking a little too fast. Smiley's out, and after me. 'Whoa, slow down!'

I lead them through the trees and the long grass and to the edge of the drop where we threw out the pieces of Ed's body.

The water is calm. Almost black.

Smiley says, 'What? He's wearing camouflage? Living off the land? Has a campsite out here?'

I point at the water.

Michael says, 'He's not a fucking fish.' He peeks over the edge.

Smiley remains where he is. Everything falls into place. Like I said, he's not stupid.

'Jesus fucking Christ,' he says. 'But he is sleeping with them. Luca-fucking-Brasi.'

'What?' Michael says, looking at the water.

My mind is still calm. What happens next is done without thought or planning – the most natural thing in the world.

I push Michael in the small of his back as he peers at the water. He loses his balance and windmills his arms.

I spin and start to run.

Michael grabs at Smiley to steady himself, the bigger man trying to fend off the clawing fingers. I see this in my peripheral vision. My senses feel heightened. Time slows. I can observe every detail.

Smiley pushes Michael away from him. The last thing I see as I turn my head around to look where I'm going is Michael going over the edge and grabbing at Smiley's sleeve. Smiley is trying to follow me, but again his younger friend is the one stopping him.

I keep my head low as I run for the car.

I don't look back.

Hear a splash.

One or two bodies?

Do I really want to go back and check?

I get in the car. Smiley left the key in the ignition. Too concerned with making sure I didn't run off to double check that little detail.

The engine sputters. That wipes the smile from my face. What am I doing wrong? What am I doing?

I try again. This time press down on the clutch. My foot slips and again the engine doesn't catch.

Smiley is coming through the trees. One body, then. He couldn't have climbed out of the water so fast. Not even him.

The engine fires. My foot's on the clutch. I tug the gearstick into reverse.

Smiley's hands are on the passenger side handle. The door clicks open. He makes to reach inside.

I release the clutch and hit the accelerator, taking the car backwards. I spin the wheel. The car bumps over uneven ground.

Smiley's caught off balance. He hangs onto the door. Tries to use the momentum to fling himself inside the vehicle.

I make the turn wide. The momentum throws him out of the car instead of in. But still he grips that open door.

Clutch down. Stick into first.

Accelerator.

Half his body's in the car now.

'Bitch!'

I press down my foot even harder. The car roars and protests. The back half sinks into the grass and the earth, even as the front wheels bump onto the smooth road.

The vehicle wrenches forward.

Smiley falls onto the passenger seat.

Heavy hands grab at me, and at the gearstick.

I pull into second.

He falls away, out of the open door.

I see him in the rear view as he rolls along the ground and then comes to rest on his back.

Shift into third.

Fourth.

Fifth.

And away.

In the rear view, I see Smiley getting to his feet. He doesn't run after me. Instead, he makes the shape of a gun with his fingers and points them towards me.

Message received.

Loud and clear.

What the hell do I do now?

Nineteen

Back on the A82, I slow right down. A few people overtake me, probably cursing as they do. One guy flashes his lights, and I catch a glimpse of an extended middle finger as he goes past.

I don't care.

I'm shaking.

My limbs are awkward and unresponsive. My chest is tight. Each breath comes shallow and disorienting.

I drive like a granny back into the city. Overly cautious. Probably more of a danger than someone speeding.

Do I have a plan?

Beyond saving my skin?

At the very least the police will now have realised Deeren is missing. They'll know the last place she went to was mine. They'll have called. They'll have gone to ask me questions. They'll have found her body. And the cash that was hidden deeper in the cupboard than Smiley got the chance to look. They'll have gone over the place with those fancy UV lights they use in *CSI*, seen the blood spatter that Dave couldn't clean from the floors.

They'll have put two and two together, come up with something close to the truth, but not quite there.

What do I do? What do I do?

Because even if I tell the truth, they won't believe me.

I wouldn't believe me.

I drive in via Great Western Road. Head for the city centre.

I need to talk to someone, and there's no one left except for the person who might just understand or at least sympathise.

Caroline. I think about calling her, but then I remember that my phone is at the flat. I left it behind after running out to get to Dave. Stupid move. Who does anything without their mobile these days?

I get this pang of anxiety. Starts just behind my ribcage. Makes my lungs breathe shallow.

I hit the centre of town, navigate to St Vincent Street in the town centre. The Royal College of Physicians and Nurses. That's where this ceilidh's being held. That's where Caroline is.

I just need a friend. A familiar face. Someone who can help me think all this through.

She'll tell me to hand myself in. And she'll be right. But I need her to say it. I need her to pull me out of this panicked flight I've been on ever since Ed got stuck with that knife.

I park just down the street. When the engine stops I take a deep breath. My stomach tightens. My throat closes up.

I screw my eyes shut and grip the steering wheel.

'Come on,' I say, quietly. 'Come on, come on, come on.'

I open my eyes again. I breathe slowly.

I used to do yoga. I remember the breathing techniques.

In. Out.

In. Out.

Think only of the sensation of breathing. Don't pay attention to anything else.

In. Out.

My heart rate slows. My stomach loosens. My throat opens up.

I open my eyes, feeling a little misty. I look at myself in the mirror. Not crying yet, just a little bit of dew. Like I've been chopping onions. No worse than that.

I take care not to look too flustered or draw attention to myself as I walk to the college. On the street, I feel exposed.

Are people watching me?

Are the police looking for me?

At the far end of the street, a jam sandwich passes. I tense up, expecting the blue lights to flash and the siren to blare. But the police are on their way elsewhere. Right now, they're not on the lookout for a woman in her late twenties suspected of murdering three people in cold blood.

I take a deep breath and walk up the steps of the Royal College. Two guys in suits on the door. They're big, but compared to a man like Smiley, they're cuddly teddy bears. 'Help you?' one of them says. He's got a goatee that softens his face. Without it, he'd look a little like a young, pumped-up Ian Rankin. The effect is a little disconcerting. We've had a few signings with the man before, and I almost want to ask the bouncer how he's doing and what possessed him to grow the beard.

'There's a ceilidh tonight,' I say.

Bearded Rankin's friend looks me up and down with suspicion. Of course he does. I'm dressed in tatty jeans and a t-shirt. Hardly what you'd call my dancing shoes.

I say, 'My friend's in there. I need to speak to her.' It doesn't sound convincing enough. So I add: 'A family emergency.'

Silent suspicion. These two take their job seriously.

'Really,' I say, 'it's important.'

They share a look and then the one with the goatee nods that I can go on in. 'First level,' he says, 'Up the stairs.'

'Thanks,' I say.

Inside, I'm conscious of how I'm dressed. The building's deceptively large, with a sweeping staircase and ornate decorations on the wall. You can sense centuries of ceremony and learning within these walls. Old white men stare at me from wood-framed oil paintings. Their eyes disapprove and I try to tell myself they look the same way at everyone. All the same, I'm aware of my faded jeans, my Converse, the old stripy top that I wear when I'm doing a shift in the stock room.

It's not hard to find the hall. The jaunty sound of fiddles and accordions accompanied by a subtle bass echoes down the stairs. I just follow the noise.

Inside, there must be around one hundred people. All dressed up in gowns for the girls and full kilt regalia for the boys. A few people close to the door look at me as though I'm a streaker running onto a football pitch.

I scan for Caroline, see her on the floor being burled around by some guy with dark curly hair and the kind of arms you'd imagine would be bulletproof if they were wrapped around you.

I push through people and grab her shoulder. She breaks away from her partner and looks at me as though I'm some lunatic who just came up and accused her of being an alien or something. 'I thought you knew there'd be a dress code.'

'I need to talk.'

She nods. Understands I'm being serious. Just the look in my eyes is enough.

She turns to her partner. 'I'll see you at the bar, aye?' He shrugs, gives me a look that speaks of daggers and leaves the floor.

Caroline and I slip away from the hall and down the stairs to the first-level landing.

'This had better be good . . .'

'I need your help. I need . . . I need to crash at yours for a bit. Just tonight.'

'What's wrong?'

All the calm I felt earlier has dissipated. I feel this surge in my stomach, and it's not nausea, but laughter. It works up into my chest and I fight to hold it in. The worst case of the giggles I've ever experienced.

'Jen, what's –'

'I'm in trouble. Real trouble.'

She looks like she's about to walk away, and then she looks at

106

me and her face drops suddenly from tight anger into a softer expression. Her eyes go wide, and she says, 'Jesus, Jen, what's happened?'

'It's Ed,' I say.

Not exactly the clearest explanation of the century.

'He's back? Oh, Jen . . .'

'Not . . .' I hesitate. 'Not exactly.'

She scratches just above her eye for a moment. Playing for time, giving herself a moment to think. Maybe torn between her clearly distressed friend and the hunk in the kilt. Without context, I'd find it a difficult decision to make too.

'Just give me a moment,' she says. 'Aye? Just hang on here a second.'

She runs back up the stairs.

I take a deep breath, put a steadying hand on the bannister. I don't have a plan. I just need to find a space to breathe, somewhere I can feel safe and gather my thoughts.

I haven't been thinking straight since I killed Ed. Something like that, it's bound to put everything out of whack.

But this isn't something simple. Something that will readjust after a few days. I knew it when I killed Ed, and I ignored it: everything about my life has changed. Everything about who I am has changed. Whatever happens from this point on, all the things I used to believe in are no longer applicable.

The old plans, the old dreams – they don't matter any more.

And the sooner I understand that, the sooner I'll be able to find my way forward.

Twenty

'This is new,' she says as we climb in the car. Like she wouldn't clock it. I don't have a car. Haven't had one since I started work in the shop. No commute, good public transport, why would I need one? I only learned to drive because I was a teenager who lived out in the country. Soon as I came to the city, I stopped.

'Uh-huh.' I start up the engine. The dashboard lights up like the controls panels of some sci-fi TV show.

'Fancy. Must have set you back.'

I don't say anything. What do I know? It's a car. It moves forward and back. I can't tell you the make and manufacturer. All I know is that it's what saved my life.

She indulges my silence until we're heading down the road, towards the West End. 'Okay, have you won the lottery? I mean, lately you've been spending like—'

'Can this wait until we get back?' I say, sharper than I intended. 'I mean, it's a lot to explain.'

'Okay,' she says. 'Okay.'

I keep my focus on the road, but I'm aware of the expression on her face: a mix of concern, apprehension and compassion. Those eyes, always so expressive. Her ex used to call her Bambi because of those eyes. Big, dark, soulful. I was always a little jealous.

'Just tell me,' she says, 'when you're ready.'

* * *

At Caroline's, there's always a bottle of wine on the go. Red, usually. She'll drink prosecco with me, but given the choice, she likes her wine heavy and full of flavour. Tonight, I don't feel like arguing the point. She brings two glasses through while I sit on the sofa. The lights are low, the way we both like them.

Through the window, there's a decent view of the city, looking out across to the Mitchell library and then the centre with all its lights and traffic and people bustling together. This building is new, an adjunct to one of the older properties, designed with modern aesthetics in mind: big windows, clean lines. Caroline bought it after an unexpected inheritance from an uncle she barely knew. She calls it her one extravagance.

Can't say it's to my taste – I like old and solid and cluttered – but the place is impressive in its way, and she clearly loves it.

She sits beside me on the sofa, sips from her glass and says, 'So?'

'It's not easy.'

'So maybe a wee drink'll help. But I'm not about to have cut short a sure thing this evening for nothing.'

I take a deep breath. 'Ed didn't exactly leave when I said he did.'

'What do you mean?'

'He came back that night. After we were out drinking.'

She purses her lips, and their colour drains a little. Those eyes go narrow and tight lines appear around her mouth. 'Okay,' she says.

I know what she's thinking, and horrible as it might have been, I almost wish that was what had happened. At least then I wouldn't be to blame for what happened next.

'He'd been hiding things at my place.'

'As in his stash?'

The surprise is probably clear in my face. 'You knew?'

'Who didn't? He dealt a little puff,' she says. 'Good prices.' I try to hide my disapproval. But I can't. She shakes her head. 'No secret I like a wee bit now and then. And he was a dick, but what he got was good product. I mean, I know how you always felt about it, so I never . . .well . . .'

'What he dealt, it was more than weed.'

'Oh.'

'He'd been storing money too. A lot of money. In bundles and bags. And powder in these little wrapped bricks. I don't know what it was exactly, but it was all there, in my flat. And he came back to get it while he thought I was out.'

'No wonder he always kept you sweet,' Caroline says, shaking her head. 'You were his perfect alibi. I mean, why would the police even think of searching your place, right? Little Miss Innocent? No record, not a hint of wrongdoing.'

'Not even a parking ticket,' I say, still proud of it. Although I'm pretty sure that murder cancels that one out.

'And you didn't want anything to do with that side of his life.' She shakes her head, takes a sip of wine and then looks right at me. She wants the details, the gossip. 'So, what? He came back asking for it?'

'Not quite,' I say. And I tell her. Everything.

* * *

When I get to the part about Smiley, she holds up and hand says, 'As in . . .?'

I shrug. We're booksellers, so of course the first place we'll go is *Smiley's People*. Thing is, I doubt that Michael does much reading, but Smiley? I don't know. He's smarter, more controlled. That much is obvious. But maybe he gets called that because all he does is frown, or maybe it really is his name. An unusual one, right enough, but still perfectly plausible.

I try and picture him settling down in the evening with a good book.

The image doesn't stick.

'It was the name he told me, anyway.'

'He's who Ed owed money to?'

'No. I get the impression he worked them, though. Whoever they are.'

'Right.' Caroline's having a hard time with this. I can't blame her.

'Jesus,' I say, and shake my head. Trying to get everything to fit, to fall into place. The world feels fractured. My mind can't quite figure out how everything fits together.

I try to make sense of it all by telling Caroline. About the policewoman. About Dave. About the trip to the loch. The whole story.

As much for me as her.

When I'm done, she looks at me like I'm insane.

'I wasn't really thinking,' I say. 'I think if I'd stopped to think, I'd be dead.'

'Aye?' She laughs. It's a manic little sound, and she cuts if off fast. Looks at me with a serious expression. 'And what are you going to do now? Now you can think straight?'

'I don't know.'

'I'm an accessory,' she says. 'Now that you've told me, I'm as guilty as you.'

'I don't think that's how it works.'

'You're a legal expert now?'

'You're going to turn me in, then?'

'I should.'

'That's not an answer.'

There's silence for a moment. Neither of us know how to process this. I just wanted a familiar face and some support. Selfish, really. I never considered how Caroline would feel.

'You have to tell the police,' she says. 'I mean, better late than never.'

I say, 'Can we turn on the TV? The news. I just . . . I need to see.'

Caroline nods. She turns the set to STV. The news. Live report. My street. My flat. The subtitle:

POLICEWOMAN FOUND DEAD IN PARTICK FLAT.

Twenty One

'What do I do?'

'You know what I think you should do.'

But I can't turn myself in. The idea of admitting what's happened, of events being twisted, it terrifies me.

So, what? I go on the run? Stay here?

'I think I might be sick,' I say. 'I don't know . . .'

'You should take a shower,' Caroline says. 'Maybe that'll help. Wash away the cobwebs, that kind of thing?'

Maybe it will. I thank her, and then lock myself in the bathroom. I look in the mirror for a long minute, holding my own gaze, expecting to see a girl I don't recognise. Someone who could kill her boyfriend and then keep living her life. Someone who could escape from two hitmen determined to put a bullet in her head.

But I don't see anything. Just the same eyes I always had. My expression is a little more drawn, perhaps. The worst I could say is that I haven't had enough sleep. Which seems strange, considering that I've had no trouble drifting off each evening.

Maybe I still haven't accepted the truth about what happened. Consciously, I mean. That tired look could point to something I'm in denial about.

I shake my head to clear out my thoughts, and turn on the shower. Push the heat as high as possible and stand under the water.

I don't do much other than that. I just close my eyes and let the stream pound off my skin. I need the heat. Thinking that somehow it might strip away the layers of my skin and the layers of my sin too. I think about the monks who used to whip themselves in order to atone for their sins.

When I'm done, maybe ten minutes under the water, I feel a kind of strange loss in my stomach, an emptiness that threatens to overwhelm. The only way I can think to avoid it is to keep moving.

I dry myself off with a heavy towel, scraping as hard as I can at my reddened skin. After, I get dressed. Caroline's loaned me jeans and a top. We're about the same size, thank goodness.

I hear a noise out in the hall. A buzzer. Shake my head. This time of night? Who's going to be ringing the buzzer?

Unless . . . Did Caroline call the police? Did she rat me out?

I head out into the hall. 'Thanks,' I say as I walk into the living room. 'Look, I was think–'

Caroline holds up her hands. 'I didn't call them. Honestly.'

A man steps forward. 'She didn't. But now we're here, we don't want any more trouble, do we?'

He's dressed in a police uniform. The stab vest. The radio. The whole works. But he's not a policeman. He can't be.

Michael. He's here. He found me.

'If you come quietly,' he says, 'no one else has to get hurt.'

Caroline looks at me, pleading. She doesn't know who he is. He's just a policeman to her. How he knew I was here doesn't matter. He has the uniform. Why wouldn't she believe him?

He holds out his hand; a gesture for me to come forward. A challenge, maybe? Like he's daring me to call him out.

No.

Enough people are dead. I don't want to add my best friend to the list.

I look at Caroline, then, reluctantly, I follow Michael out of her flat.

PART THREE

THE WAY WE DIE NOW

THE WAY WE DIE NOW

Twenty Two

In a way, I should be grateful. Events are out of my control now. This way, I don't have to think.

It's over.

Michael takes me to his car. I expect him to put me in the back, but instead he opens the passenger-side door. It's not Smiley's car. It's definitely a cop car.

I remember the way Deeren looked at him. Like she knew him somewhere.

Jesus.

He gets in the driver's side, says, 'You need to help yourself.'

'Uh-huh.'

'No one's looking for you yet. Even if they've found Deeren, they'll still be trying to establish what happened.'

Something grows in my chest. A tight, terrifying sensation.

Michael engages the central locking. He hasn't turned on the engine. We're just sitting on the street. I see people pass by. I should start to shout and scream. But I can't. The relief I felt earlier is gone. All I feel now is a sense of dizzying momentum.

He says, 'I'm trying to control myself here. Alright? My arse is on the line too. I panicked, right, killing the constable?'

'Her name was Deeren.'

'Aye, whatever. I mean, killing there and then, like that. A fuck up. Now I get to make up for it.'

'How'd you find me?'

'I'm no an idiot. I'm a real fuckin' polis. So I went back to your place – they've found the body, by the way – pretending I heard the call on the Airwave. I checked your answer phone. This girl, Caroline, she seemed a good bet. Her or your mother. The only two people you talk to, aye?'

Seems like he has a brain when he's not panicked, then. People really can surprise you.

'So all that nonsense earlier,' I say, 'was about impressing Smiley, was it?'

He doesn't say anything. Instead, he waits for a moment and says, 'Where's the money? Where's the stash?'

How much of the truth do I tell him? 'The money was in my flat. Dave, he held the . . .stash. And he's not talking. For obvious reasons.'

'You had to put some of the cash in the bank, aye? A rainy day fund?'

I decide not to answer. Hold some power over him. For a while. I think to myself that if I could, I might kill him. I've killed before. I think I could do it again.

He seems to read my mind. 'What you did to Ed was an accident,' he says. 'And running from me and the big man . . . You were scared. You had every right to be.'

'Should I be scared now?'

Michael shakes his head. 'Not of me. Look, I'm just the errand boy. And it's not all bad.' He thinks about something for a moment. 'Piece of advice, though? I'd lose the attitude. You can still make it out of this.'

I don't believe him, but I keep quiet.

'Trust me. It's good to talk,' he says, and dials in a number on the mobile. Holds the phone to his ear. 'It's me,' he says, when someone answers on the other end. 'I've got her here. But she's not talking.' He looks at me, as though this is my final chance. For just a moment, I think I see something that might be sadness or regret, but it's gone quickly, tucked away as though he's embarrassed by the emotion.

I give him the stony stare. The silent treatment.

He nods, turns away as he continues to speak into the phone.

'Aye, okay. I can get her out. See if you can get some sense out of the bitch, then.'

He hangs up. His eyes don't return to meet mine.

Twenty Three

'So, you're just a bad cop, or do they have something on you?'

Every crime novel I've ever read, the bad cop turns out to have a divorce he's paying for, a gambling habit or an unfortunate incident where he ran over a child in his car and didn't tell anyone.

Michael doesn't even look at me. Just fires up the engine, reverses out the space. He puts on his seatbelt once we're moving. That kind of driver.

'Come on', I say.

'That's all you can think to ask?' he says, 'When I'm taking you to see our mutual friend Smiley again?'

As we head down to the city centre, he looks at me every few seconds like there's something he can't figure out. Maybe it's that I'm remaining so calm. Once again, I'm an observer on my own life, watching this woman and wondering who she is, why she doesn't just break down under all this stress.

As we hit the M77 heading towards Newton Mearns, I say, 'So where are we going?' It's a useless question. Michael's decided to meet silence with silence. Playing some kind of mind game, I guess.

We take the exit to East Kilbride, get lost among low-built warehouses and retail centres. In the dark, with next to no traffic, the streets feel empty and abandoned. It's the kind of area that only ever bustles in the daylight. At night, there's the feeling there might be something dangerous lurking in the shadows of the buildings.

I think of Smiley.

'Just tell me where we're going.' All pretence at politeness gone. A tightness in my chest. An anger.

Still the silent treatment. There's something almost childish about it, as though he's taking a petulant revenge for my earlier refusal to talk.

I try not to think about where he's taking me.

The car turns into an empty parking bay outside a low-level brick building. There are no signs outside, no sense that anyone even owns this place, never mind conducts business inside.

Michael kills the engine. 'You're not going to run, are you?' He doesn't sound like he looks forward to the prospect or that he really cares if I do.

He actually sounds bored.

'Do I need to?'

'Just tell the truth. We can sort this out. It's still no too late.'

'You believe that?'

He doesn't say anything. Maybe that's my answer.

I don't think he wants to hurt me. In a way, I feel sorry for him.

'Come on,' he says. 'Out.' Going for gruff. Missing the mark.

I climb out. I can hear the whoosh of traffic from the motorway overhead. But down here among old warehouses and storage lots, it feels a million miles away. Another country, even.

We walk round the side of the building, through an innocuous red door with peeling paint. Inside, he takes me to an office on the second level. The interior feels temporary, as though the building is ready to be gutted and rebuilt.

In the office, a man sits in a faded office chair with a high back and arm rests. He looks at me as I enter, with his head to one side. His face looks slightly squashed, and the wrinkles around his eyes and on his forehead can be taken for laughter lines if you don't look too closely.

But there's a cruelty in the way his thin lips slash into a smile, and when he breathes, there's a sick sense of excitement that makes me want to find a place to hide.

'This,' the man says, 'is our . . .femme fatale?' He's got a definite touch of the South Side to his accent. Educated, but no denying it. Govanhill, maybe. I imagine if you asked him, he would claim to be self-made.

There's another man standing to one side of the chair. Completely still, like a robot awaiting instructions from its creator. But he's not impassive. He looks at me with barely restrained hatred.

Smiley.

Bloody great.

There's a cut across his face that looks raw and fresh. His expression tells me that he's looking to take out his frustration on the first person he sees.

Which, of course, happens to be me.

But he keeps his mouth shut. One thing you can say about Smiley is that he's a professional through and through.

'The bitch,' Michael corrects his employer.

The old man waves his hand dismissively. 'No need to be rude,' he says. Then he stands up. He's small. Just over five foot. Or just under if you're feeling cruel. He walks up to me. 'You have something that belongs to me.'

'I don't. I mean . . .not all of it. Not any more.'

'The lads here say otherwise.'

'I can give you some of the money,' I say. 'What I have in my account, although I made sure not to deposit all of it. The rest . . . The rest is in an evidence locker by now.'

'Oh?'

'It was in my flat. The one where these two shot and killed a police officer. They'll have searched the place. They'll have found it.'

The old man turns his head from one side to the other. Looking first at Smiley, and then at Michael. 'Let me guess which one of you was impetuous enough to do that.' He doesn't even bother to hide his smile.

Michael cracks instantly. Can't help himself, it seems. All that calm talk in the car was about the most he could manage. This is the real Michael: quick on the trigger, quick to rise to his own defence. 'I didn't have a choice! I didn't–' He cuts himself off, then, maybe seeing the expression on his employer's face. That smile is anything but amused.

The old man turns back to me. 'Had to be a frightening experience,' he said. 'Seeing that kind of violence up close. You're just a citizen, right? You don't get mixed up in this kind of thing.'

I don't say anything.

He goes back to his chair and sits down. He looks at Michael. 'I'm forgetting my manners. Please get our guest a chair.'

Michael leaves the room.

I stay where I am beside the door. Part of me still thinking I can make a run for it. Somehow.

There is silence. Empty, deep and overwhelming. I want to scream. I don't.

I will not be the one to break the quiet. They want me to be scared: one woman against three men. Three criminals.

They think the very fact of their physicality will somehow cow me, make me feel like I can't stand up against them.

Maybe they're right. I've never been in a fight before. I only escaped from Smiley and Michael thanks to luck and the fact I had them off balance. Here and now, I wouldn't stand a chance.

So what do I do?

They want what they want. I can't give that to them. So what happens next?

What happens?

Twenty Four

Michael returns with an old swivel chair. He throws it down in front of me. But he doesn't say anything.

The old man gestures for me to sit. I do so.

Finally, he speaks. 'Shall we begin again? My name is Solomon Buchan.'

Oh, Ed.

Oh, Ed, Ed, Ed.

Only you could get in debt with Glasgow's biggest gangster. The man who killed Kat's uncle, who runs the biggest and most violent sectors of the city's underworld. The defacto Godfather of the city. All criminal accusations unproven except in the court of public knowledge.

'You run nightclubs,' I say, shaking myself back into the room and talking to Buchan. It's true, as well. Every good gangster insulates themselves from illegal activities. Even someone like me – someone who's never had a speeding ticket – knows that.

I'm also pretty certain that he'd like me to believe the thing about the nightclubs.

He smiles. 'You like to go clubbing?'

'I prefer a quiet drink.'

'Your boyfriend – your ex-boyfriend, I should say – liked a night on the tiles.'

'Oh?' Check me, little Miss Innocent. Surprised Buchan knows anything about my officially-missing ex.

Pass the Oscar.

'We never met. I didn't know his name until one of my employees came to me regarding his . . .transgressions.'

'Did he steal that money from you?'

'Not exactly. He borrowed. And then failed to pay back what he owed.'

'How does your APR compare with Wonga?'

He smiles again. I think this one might be genuine. He's not without a sense of humour. Maybe if I make him laugh enough, he'll allow me to walk out of here alive. 'Oh, I see why he liked you. Soft, but with a hard sense of humour. It's attractive in a woman, you know. Humour, I mean. I like a funny girl.'

I think to myself, *you wouldn't stand a chance* but decide it wouldn't be the wisest move to say that out loud.

He leans forward. Drops the Grandad act. His face hardens, voice dropping to a savage whisper. 'Don't think it'll do you any favours, though. You chose to take on his debt. If what my friends here tells me is true . . .' he pauses for a moment, 'and I think it is – I think you have a secret side you don't want to let anyone see.'

I don't know what he's talking about.

'It doesn't suit you,' he says. 'Maybe it was easy ripping off and killing a man like Ed . . .'

'No,' I say. 'That's not . . .'

'Please!' He sits back again. 'It's there, in your eyes. You've never had the chance to indulge before. But now you have. And I don't think you'll be able to go back.'

'Really,' I say. 'I don't know what you're–'

'Have it your way then, lass. Tell me where the gear is, at least. The money, we can come to an arrangement over that.'

'An arrangement?'

'One way or another, you're going to prison. I mean, if not for killing Ed, then that police they found at your flat, the one who stumbled over your little secret.'

'Hang on—'

He holds up a hand. I shut up without any further prompting. The man may be small, but he has a kind of presence that you wish would leave you alone.

'No,' he says. 'You hang on. And listen. You have your story, but the truth will be different. When you're interviewed again by the police, you won't mention a word about my friends here. Or that we met. You'll tell a story about how you accidentally killed your boyfriend, decided to keep the money. How you got paranoid and bought a gun. How when that policewoman stumbled on your secret, you killed her.'

'And Dave?'

'You killed him too.'

'They won't believe that.'

'No?'

'Physically, I couldn't have—'

'I'll leave the details up to you.'

'Why would I lie? Why not just tell the police everything?' I nod at Michael. 'Why not just turn this eejit in while I'm at it?'

'That would be unwise.'

'Aye?' Trying my best to appear confident, as if I can bluff my way out of this.

But it won't work. Buchan doesn't see me as a threat. I'm just a wee girl who got in over her head. In his mind, he's giving me an easy way out, I guess. I do the time, he doesn't kill me, and maybe he wipes out the monetary side of the debt if I tell him what Dave did with the product he took from Ed's stash.

'You've been through a lot.' Buchan turns on the charm. He could be my grandfather, the way he looks at me. Concerned.

Give the man an award. Put him on the silver screen.

Stay strong, Jen.

Remember who he is.

Buchan says, 'This isn't fair.'

I answer, unable to stop myself. 'No.'

'Just tell me,' he says. 'One thing. Betwee[n]

'Did you really kill him?'

'I killed Ed,' I say. 'Fine. But I did not

'Okay. Okay. So who did?'

'Dave.'

Standing in the door, Smiley laughs. 'That fat sack of shite?'

I look at the big man. 'He was high,' I say, like it explains everything.

'He was a fucking moron.'

'I called him. He came round.'

'He was in love with you, then,' Smiley says. 'I wouldn't cut up a body for anyone who wasn't paying. Failing that, if I wanted to, you know, get in their pants . . .'

'You forget,' Buchan says, 'the cash. The merchandise.'

They still think I can tell them where it is. And if I don't?

I don't want to think about it.

I take a breath. 'Look, I already told you. There's some in the bank, but the rest . . . Well, it's either still in the flat or the police have it.'

'And the product?'

'Dave did something with it,' I say. 'He's the only one who could tell you.'

Michael says, 'I can get some of the money that's in evidence. Maybe.'

Buchan turns to look at him. 'Oh?'

'I can get some of the money.' To his credit, he doesn't sound enthusiastic about the idea. Like he's trying to think of a way to save his own skin. Which tells me he wasn't supposed to kill Deeren,

'And what about the dead policewoman?' That confirms it.

'No one will know. Three people know I was there. Two of them are in this room. The other . . . Well, she's not talking, right?' Aiming for tough, sounding desperate.

k at you, Michael. You're falling apart. What Smiley here
you're a loose cannon. You can't be trusted. I don't have any
ck with that. Not in my organisation.

Buchan, apparently satisfied, turns back to me. 'You will take
the fall,' he says. 'You are the one who killed that woman. Do you
understand?' He doesn't wait for me to respond. 'There are three
choices you have. You can do as I say, and do your time inside.
You'll be taken care of, I assure you, as a token of my apprecia-
tion. Or you can tell the police what happened here tonight and
take your chances. Believe me, doll, they won't be good.'

I get up the nerve to speak. My voice cracks. 'And the third
choice?'

'Best leave that alone for now.' Still with the grandfather tone.

Maybe that's something I can use to my advantage. I'm just
a wee girl to him. To Smiley and Michael too. What happened
at the loch was luck more than anything, right? I'm not going to
make that mistake twice.

Right?

I smile at the wizened old man. He looks back, no expression
on his face.

'Okay,' I say. 'There's more of the money. Me and Dave, we hid
it. You know, rainy day fund and all. I can get it for you.'

Buchan nods. 'This isn't a game,' he says. 'You know that, don't
you, doll?'

I look at Smiley. 'I've seen how serious you are,' I say. 'And I
don't want to die. Not like Dave.'

Buchan finally smiles. 'And not like wee Eddie either?'

I don't say anything. I just swallow back bile and try to stay
upright.

He looks at me in the rear view. In the half-light, it's tough to read his expression. Maybe he figures that even if he doesn't have a plan, maybe I do. That I've worked out how to escape. Maybe how to kill him and get away with it.

Oh, aye. Criminal mastermind, that's me.

Kill a policeman, escape from under the noses of everyone in FHQ.

Simple stuff.

Lisbeth Salander might be able to get away with it. But then she's a computer hacker with combat skills. I'm a bookseller who nearly falls over trying to run to the subway.

I say, 'Killing Ed was an accident. Everything that's happened to me up until this point was an accident.'

'But you know where the money is?'

'I do. Like Mister Buchan said, I show you where we stowed it, then you take me to the police like you just arrested me, I confess and stay alive. How bad can prison be? It's not all *Orange is the New Black* over here, right?'

He shakes his head. 'That show, it's great, but it's still nothing compared to the reality. I've heard stories about Cornton Vale,'

'I'm talking about the book.'

He looks at me like I'm crazy. Maybe he's not much of a reader.

'Don't believe anything,' I say.

He hesitates. But he moves so that the light catches his face. Even if he's hesitant, he believes me. He thinks I don't have a plan.

And I really do.

Half-arsed as it is.

Twenty Six

'You're serious?' Michael peers forward, looking up at the building. The abandoned structures in Kinning Park loom out of the darkness like monsters from a nightmare. Office buildings and warehouses, they've had various uses over the years, but now stand empty and gutted. These days, they're a playground for urbexers and adventurous graffiti artists. You can often see their work while driving along the M77. For a long time, on the top levels of this particular building, anti-war and anti-austerity messages dominated. The council kept removing them, but the sloganeers kept returning, undaunted.

'Yes.' Not *aye*, but *yes*. Doesn't feel natural. Like I'm playing a part. But he doesn't seem to notice. Or care.

'Okay,' he says. 'Where, exactly?'

'Inside.'

'It's a big fucking building.'

'You have a torch?'

He takes a deep breath. 'If this is some bloody–'

'No, it's not.'

If I get out of this alive, I figure I could go into acting. Lie for a living. I'm getting good at it. All it takes is practice. And the threat of what happens if you don't convince men like Smiley and Michael.

'You left it in there?' He shakes his head, not quite able to believe how stupid I've been. 'Someone will have nabbed it.'

'Dave knew where no one else would find it.'

'And the two of you came out of there unharmed? You know the kind of people who hang about in places like that? They see a wee girl like you, a fat pillock like Dave, they'll be thinking *two easy targets*.'

I don't really have an answer for that. All I can hope is that if I keep quiet, then he might convince himself.

He takes a deep breath. 'Come on, then' he says, and steps forward, towards the hollow building.

* * *

I can't believe I'm even thinking about this. Inside the building – entry easily gained by prising a loose board near one of the ground-floor windows – we climb up to the second level, every step echoing in the shadows. There are noises all around us: shuffling and creaking of old joints. Hard to tell if we're alone. At the very least, I figure there might be foxes in here.

Halfway up, on a landing, he swings the torch at me. I cover my face from the light. 'Jesus!' Colours swirl. When I remove my hands, they remain. The world has blanked out completely.

I blink.

Things swim back. My retinas ache.

'You don't seem so certain now we're in here,' he says. 'Thought you said you knew where fat-boy hid the stash.'

'I'm allowed a little uncertainty,' I say. 'The last few weeks . . .' My mind is racing. What was I thinking? I thought I could lose him in the dark. Maybe, when we got up the stairs, get close enough to give him a shove so he drops the light, maybe even breaks his neck, and then make a run for it.

Run to where?

I don't have an end game. I'm just surviving one moment to the next.

I should be dead by now.

But other people keep dying in my place.

'You're trying to fuck me over,' he says. 'You're scared. I was a fucking idiot for believing you in the first place.'

'Aye? I'm not the fucking idiot letting myself get owned by a gangster.'

Left field, but it does the trick. Sets him off balance.

'What?'

'Come on, what did you do?' Push it further. Get him angry. Because that means he's either going to start making mistakes or he'll just get it over with and kill me. I feel oddly relaxed about either outcome. 'Must have been something bad for them to hold this much power over you. Drugs? Drink? Gambling?'

'You don't know what you're talking about.' He talks through a jaw that's gone tight. 'That crap in the car–'

'You ever killed anyone else? Other that Officer Deeren, I mean.'

'Who?'

'The police officer back at my flat.'

He thinks about that for a moment, 'I think I'm about to.'

'Fuck you.' Oh, brave words, Jen. Brave bloody words. Taunt the crooked killer cop. Brilliant.

He's three steps above me. He steps down one. Torch shines in my face again. Every time I blink, colours explode behind my eyes.

He's close now. His breath is sour and tickles my skin like a cooling fan on the back of a computer. I can't really see his face. He's just one blob among many.

The torch lowers. I try to focus.

He could be about to kiss me. I can smell something that might be rotting behind the mint he chewed in the car on the way over. More than just bad breath. Bad tooth, maybe? All that stress rotting away his gums.

'Tell me,' he says. 'Tell me the truth.'

'Okay,' I say. 'I lied. Had some stupid–'

The back of his hand – sharp knuckles, I don't know why that surprises me – connects with my face. I'm not expecting the blow. My head snaps to the side. I feel something across my cheek. Maybe a scratch. Maybe worse.

I look right at him. He's back in focus now. No longer just one dark blob among others. He has features. He is distinct. Real. Not a dream or a nightmare.

He looks right back.

His eyes are empty. I never noticed that before. He will kill me. Nothing to do with sex or gratification.

Pure anger.

I step to the left. Michael tries to counter by swinging harder and wilder, but I step to the side while dropping down a step, so I'm lower than before. He can't quite compensate. I step up again, and in towards him. He's spun so that he's at a sixty-degree angle to me. I push into the small of his back with both hands.

Michael was already off balance before I pushed him. What happens next is inevitable.

He tries to right himself, but he can't and – with oddly balletic grace – his head falls forward first, followed by the rest of his body. His arms go out. A protective gesture. His fingers splay. The torch spins up in the air and strobes for a moment before clunking down onto the steps. The light goes out.

I hear Michael fall. In the sudden darkness, I'm completely blind. He doesn't say anything. Just crashes hard against the steps. I can hear the impact. I think maybe he falls past me.

But he doesn't make any noise. No scream. No sound of pain.

I stay where I am. I know that if I go upstairs all I can do is hide. If I go down, there's a way out. But he might be there. Waiting for me.

Do I risk it?

135

The lights from outside come in softly through a window, providing only the barest of illumination. Enough that when my eyes adjust I can see the stairs, but not the bottom where I presume he has landed and where I guess the torch has clunked down to.

I need the light.

I need to get out.

I step forward, arms out as though I can see through my fingertips. Stupid. Childish. Like when I was a girl wrapping my arms round my head when I got up to go the toilet at night. Working on the principle that if I couldn't see the ghosts then they couldn't see me either.

I don't fall. That's the main thing. I don't stumble. I'm wearing flats. Converse. Sensible shoes for a sensible situation. So there's that.

My eyes adjust with each step. Not much light, but I can see shapes. One of those shapes, at the bottom steps, is what appears to be rags abandoned on the floor. They weren't there when we came in.

Michael.

He's not moving. I'm still not going near him.

Last step, on the ground, finally. My toe touches something. The torch. I pick it up, shake it and the light sputters on. I spin round on Michael.

He moves. Limbs twitching, neck moving spasmodically. Reflex action or is he conscious? He mumbles something. I don't hear it. He repeats: 'Fucking bitch.'

I tense up, ready to run. He tries to roll over, stand up. One fast movement. Smooth. He's not going to let me go.

And then he screams. High and loud and piercing. He flops down again.

I keep the torch on him. I should run, but I'm fascinated.

'My leg,' he says, voice cracking. 'My fucking bastarding

arseholing leg!' He lifts his head to look directly at me. 'So, what? You kill me now? That's it? Then the money . . .the stuff that's not in the evidence locker . . .you, what, you know where it is?'

I feel sorry for him, in a way. He doesn't want this to be an accident. He wants it to be a movie, maybe, where he's the antihero or just the guy caught up in a bad situation.

I say, 'Sure,' like, if he wants it to be like that, it can be.

'So kill me,' he says.

I shake my head. 'Broken leg,' I say. 'If I leave you, maybe someone will come for you. Or maybe you'll die. Shock. Infection. Whatever. All alone in here. I haven't seen anyone else. And I have to figure that if there is anyone lurking in the shadows, their first thought on seeing you is not going to be calling for an ambulance.'

'You're a cold-hearted cow.'

'Uh-huh,' I say. 'Where are the car keys?'

'Fuck you.'

'Give me the car keys.'

'Or?'

Good question. I've been doing a good job with the posturing. But it's not me. Not really. I don't know what I'm doing.

But I know he has to believe that I do.

I step forward. Which of his legs are broken?

Okay, best guess. I get as close as I dare. Stamp down. All my weight into my right foot. All the power I have.

The scream makes birds take off somewhere on the upper levels.

'Cunt!'

I stamp again. I don't mean to, but the word makes me do it. I get the tone behind it. The intent.

He screams hoarsely this time. Maybe if he passes out, I can search his pocket for the keys, but that seems like it could get oddly intimate and really I don't fancy going anywhere near there if I can avoid it.

'Okay,' he says, gasping. 'Okay.'

Trouser pocket. Like I feared. He throws them up at me.

I don't say thanks. 'Phone,' I say.

He hesitates.

I raise my foot.

'Fine, fine,' he says. 'Take the bastard fucking thing.'

I look at him. He's pathetic, lying there on the ground. A man with no control over his life. All that anger and rage, whatever happened to him, he just wants to get back at the world. He's not angry at me.

It would be a mercy to kill him.

Jesus, Jen, when did you start thinking like that, you wee psycho?

I take his phone. Pocket it.

'Whatever happens to me,' he says, 'you're dead. Fucking dead.'

I don't doubt it. But at least I'm in control. For the first time since any of this started. Maybe even before. I'm making my own choices.

I turn and walk away.

He continues to shout threats and retribution, mixed with pleas for me to help him. I ignore them. I have other things on my mind.

Outside, I go to Michael's car. I place his phone behind the rear driver's side wheel. I position it carefully. It's real retro. A brick of a thing. Maybe that works better for people in his line of work. Too easy to trace a smartphone. Old school might ironically be less easy to trace now. Didn't I read that somewhere once, how old-fashioned safes might be more secure than banking online?

Then I get in the car, reverse over the phone, and drive off.

Knowing he's right. Whatever happens to him, I'm still not safe.

Twenty Seven

Back again. Outside Caroline's place.

Why return here?

Michael isn't dead. He knows where she lives. He knows she's important to me. She shouldn't be involved, but whether she likes it or not, she is. I need to warn her. It's the right thing to do.

I should have called, but the problem is I don't remember her number. Not by heart. Mobiles make a lot of things easier, but we rely on them too much. All the numbers are stored in my phone's memory. And when it comes to the crunch, I can't remember any of them. Besides, I ran over Michel's phone, and when I think about it I can't remember the last time I saw a working payphone.

The sun is starting to come up over the city. There's a sense after a few hours of stillness that Glasgow is coming to life again.

The hours between half four and six are strange. My first job was in a fast-food chain that opened around seven in the morning. I worked the opening shifts, where we cleaned the place from top to bottom and got the breakfasts ready for that strange breed of people who come in early enough to have that first plastic egg and compressed-shite patty of the morning. The restaurant was down Argyle Street and back then I lived in the South Side, which meant a strange commute for me across the city during those sleeping hours. There's a stillness in the air which you imagine is what it might be like when the apocalypse finally hits: expectation mixed with uncertainty.

And then it begins. The slow movement. The yawn of the first commuters emerging, blinking, onto the motorways and city-centre streets. The magazine deliveries, the posties making early collections. Not so many milk trucks, but it's comforting to think even they might be out there somewhere.

I lock the car with the clicker. Stand there for a second, feeling sick. Then I cross the road, buzz Caroline's bell. Once. Twice.

Three times is the charm. She answers, groggy.

'It's me.'

'What?'

'Me.'

'They let you go?'

'Let me in.'

'Jen . . .'

'Let me in.'

She buzzes me up. I bound the stairs. She meets me at the front door, holding herself upright against the doorframe. 'They let you go?' Repeating the words like she doesn't know what else to ask.

We go into the living room.

She's wearing a fuzzy purple dressing gown and her hair is a mess. She looks like someone set off a grenade on her scalp. Her hair is everywhere, twisting and turning on itself, sticking out at angles that don't even seem possible.

Her eyes are heavy. She keeps blinking. 'Why'd they let you go?'

'They didn't,' I say, sitting on the sofa. 'That policeman, you didn't think it odd that he just turned up?'

'He said they were contacting anyone who knew you . . .'

'On his own? No partner, no backup.'

She looks at me like I'm speaking another language. Caroline's never been into crime novels. She thinks they're a waste of time.

140

But it explains why Michael's behaviour wouldn't have seemed suspicious to her.

'I told you about Ed,' I say. 'And those two thugs who showed up.' She's still not getting it. 'The policeman . . .he was one of them.'

She nods, slowly.

'Caroline,' I say, 'Please. Say something.'

She looks at me. The space between us seems vast, suddenly.

She'll have been watching the news. I know that I'll be painted as some insane killer: maybe there'll be talk of mental health problems. I used to suffer panic attacks, and I wonder whether they've got that little bit of medical history on their radar yet, using it to demonise me.

Reporters claim to be impartial, but like anyone else, they just want a good story, a narrative they can latch onto. We all know it, too. But we deny it. We like the narratives and the stories. We want to believe them. Until they contradict what we believe.

Maybe the only people who'll believe me are the die-hard Scottish nationalists, the ones who claim that the BBC betrayed them during the referendum.

A name flutters through my mind. Stuart Jeffries. The landlord everyone thought killed his tenant because she was young and good looking and he was middle-aged and odd. The media looked for anything in his past that could fit their narrative. And they found it. Used it against him. Fitted up an innocent man because they wanted him to be guilty.

We all have skeletons. We all have secrets. That doesn't make us bad people.

'I believe you,' Caroline says.

She's just saying it. Look at her, the expression on her face, the blankness in her eyes. Not just because I woke her up. She's trying to pacify me, keep me calm. Maybe she's afraid I'll kill her too, if she says the wrong thing.

But she's the only hope I have left. 'I don't know what to do,' I say.

'He was dressed like a police officer, for fuck's sakes!'

'He was a police officer . . . Is a police officer. Whatever. Does that make him the good guy by default?'

'I . . .' She hesitates. 'I don't . . .' She can't finish the thought. She grips at the arm of the sofa, putting all her stress into the one gesture, forcing herself to remain calm.

'All the same,' she says. 'They can't all be like him. I mean, if you go to the station yourself . . .'

I think about it. Remember Crawford. He was tough, sure, but at least appeared to have his head screwed on the right way, morally speaking, anyway. I didn't really like him, but did that mean I couldn't trust him?

'Crawford,' I say. 'DI Crawford.'

'So phone and ask for him.'

I hesitate.

'How much worse can this get? What, you're going to spend the rest of your life hiding out on my couch? If you even try and go back to work, they'll arrest you there. Try and use your credit cards, they can track you that way. You're a celebrity now and not in a good way. You know that your Twitter feed gained over 15,000 followers overnight?'

I laugh. From a measly 100 to 15,000 in the space of a few hours. Kill a couple of people – intentionally or not – and you have your fast track to celebrity. 'Maybe I should check friend requests on Facebook,' I say.

She shakes her head.

I take a deep breath. 'You're right,' I say. 'I panicked. Everything that happened . . .well . . .I wasn't thinking straight.'

'If you don't call them, I will,' she says. 'Just tell them the truth. Innocent until proven guilty, right?'

I nod. I think I might cry, but I swallow it back.

'Borrow your phone?'

She nods.

The door buzzer sounds.

I look at her. She shrugs. No deception, I'm sure. Besides, she hasn't been out of my sight the whole time. No chance she had another opportunity to call some other police boyfriend I don't know about.

'Delivery?'

'Don't remember ordering anything,' she says. 'Late-night Amazon binge, maybe.' She laughs, gets up to go answer the door.

Just pick up the phone. Let those fingers do the walking. That's it. What's the number? Do I just dial 999?

I don't know.

Maybe look it up. 'Computer on?' I shout through to Caroline. 'I need the actual number for the station.'

'Of course. Just a moment,' she shouts back. 'It is a delivery. Jesus, Amazon really are serious about delivering on time.'

'Up with the larks,' I say, more to myself than her. I head through to the bedroom where her PC is set up in one corner. There's the musty smell of sleep in the room, and with the curtains drawn and the bred crumpled, I feel weirdly like I've invaded a very private space.

I pull the curtains rather than turn on the light. The room gets brighter with that odd early morning illumination that's more grey than white. I boot up the PC, get asked for a password. Of course I do. Everything's password protected these days. And according to the rules, you should never use the same one twice, even if most people do.

I walk back to the living room rather than shout again.

When I get there, I stop. Dead. If the word's not inappropriate.

The man who rang the doorbell is no delivery driver.

Smiley doesn't smile. His face is carved in granite. He makes sure I see the gun he's got pressed against Caroline's head. His eyes are fixed on me.

'You want a job done properly,' he says. 'Well, I guess you know the rest . . .'

Twenty Eight

I stare at Smiley.

He says, 'A man doesn't die from a broken leg. And he doesn't miraculously lose the ability to work a mobile phone.' His lips flicker, but his expression remains neutral.

'I took his phone,' I say. 'I smashed it up.'

'Police officers have two phones,' Smiley says. 'Check the one he gave you.'

I didn't even think when he handed it over. It was chunky. Old-fashioned looking. I take it out of my jacket. Look at it again.

'That's an Airwave handset. Police-to-police communications. No use to you without the code. No use to him if he wants to call a private number. But clearly it was enough to get you off his back.'

Jesus.

Bloody idiot, Jen.

Aye, there's your dangerous criminal mastermind right there. The media are going to love that one. Femme Fatale makes bloody stupid mistake. I should have been more careful. Acted on that instinct about how old-fashioned the bloody thing looked. But I just wanted to get away.

'I can't work out,' Smiley says, 'if you're stupid or the most psychotic individual I've ever met.'

'Can I be both?' Getting hysterical now. I want to laugh. Collapse to my knees and weep with laughter. But I stay standing.

Because he has a gun pointed at my friend's head.

The line between tragedy and comedy is thin, but not that thin.

Caroline is holding it together, but only just. She's shaking, but there's no hysterics. No screaming. No questions. No crying. She doesn't know what's going on. Except that there's an evil bastard threatening to blow her brains out, and I'm probably the only one who can stop him.

No pressure, then.

'Okay,' I say. 'I get it now. I'm in over my head. Like Mister Buchan said, I'll go to the police and say how this was all my fault. How I was the one who murdered two people–'

'Three.'

'What?'

'A broken leg won't kill you. But a knife across the jugular will.'

'Jesus.'

'The old man's getting bored, doll,' he says. 'All this messing around. Maybe it would be easier if you would just die. Maybe then, the losses could be cut. The longer this goes on, the more danger there is that this comes back to him. I mean, you could have got off easy, you know? He's got a thing for women, young women. Not like that. A father thing, I guess. Maybe something in his past, I never asked. But . . .men like my former partner, they never get a second chance. I bugger up, it'll be the same thing. Which is why I never have. But you, he showed you what would happen and he let you live. He let you take the easy way out. Believe me, if he'd found Ed first instead of you, it would have been a different fucking story.' He shakes his head. 'Me? I don't care much for men, women, whatever. I do what I have to do.'

He squeezes the trigger.

I don't even think about why he's doing it.

When the explosion comes, I barely feel it.

Two women shot through the head in almost twenty-four hours now. Both of the connected to me.

146

This time, my best friend.

There's a spray of red and then she's down, and I don't want to look at her because I know what I'll see.

Just a pile of flesh and bones. Not real any more. It's not her now.

Smiley holds his arms wide. 'I remove obstacles.' He steps forward. 'Take the quickest path to what I need. It's nothing personal.' He raises the weapon.

I think I should scream or run.

But I stay still. Keep my eyes on his.

'No need for caution now,' he says. 'The way they're speaking about you on the news, I don't think anyone's going to be shedding any tears over your death. Especially when they think you killed two other women.'

'With a gun I don't have.'

'Don't think we can't plant the evidence.' He shakes his head. 'I've done it before. Murder suicide pacts . . . I don't think I've ever known one that's real. And yet ordinary people – like you – they eat them up.'

I back away. The sofa's behind me. I can't retreat any further.

I don't look at Smiley any more.

I look at the gun.

Twenty Nine

Everything goes slow.

His movements. The way he brings up both hands to steady the shot. His fingers curve around the butt of the weapon, right index snaking to the trigger guard.

I watch all of this. Think, *at least it's going to be quick*, and then wonder how I can be so calm, knowing that I'm about to die.

All that's happened in the last month:

Ed.

The money.

Seeing a dog rip out a man's throat.

A policewoman shot in the forehead.

My best friend executed only a few feet away from me. Her blood is on my shoes, still wet.

And now it all ends.

A few more seconds.

The bullet will enter my skull, plunge into my brain. I figure that at least it won't hurt.

I hope it won't hurt.

It seems a good way to go, all things considered. Your brain won't have time to panic or send pain signals. Just: bang, and the lights are out.

This is how it ends.

Maybe I deserve it.

I'm not a criminal. I've never had even a parking ticket. All I wanted was a quiet life, doing what I wanted to do, no one really noticing me.

Two months ago, I'd have said someone like me deserved to die. Not that I would bring back the death penalty, but something like this, where I wouldn't have had an active say in what happened, well, I would have figured that's how these things go sometimes.

People who do what I've done deserve to die.

The backs of my legs press against the sofa.

Something in that sensation is like a jolt of electricity passing through me. I've been passive for the past few minutes, just waiting for the inevitable to finally happen. The touch of the sofa against the rear of my thighs reconnects me to the real world. Makes me realise: if I don't do something, I'm going to die.

And I don't deserve that.

Move or die.

I move. Flipping round and running towards the bedroom.

'Where are you going?' Smiley says.

I don't answer. Keep low – as though that might make me a small target – and scuttle towards the open door. I slam it shut behind me.

He takes his time. Not worried. Where am I going to go, after all?

I hear him on the other side of the door. 'You're only delaying this. It doesn't have to be drawn out. This can be over in seconds.'

Because I'm not an idiot, I keep to the side of the doorframe and catch my breath. A few seconds. I have that at least to try and think how I get of this.

I look at the window on the other side of the queen size, and realise I'm dead if I try to jump for it. Third floor is still too high. Even if I survive the drop, I'm going nowhere. Not much effort to shoot me as I lie on the pavement. And even then, I have to open the window. I don't know if Caroline keeps them locked or if I'll waste precious seconds trying to force them open. Plenty of time for a man like Smiley to do what he does best.

'I promise you won't feel a thing.'

I wish he'd shut up.

I look around the room. The pebble lamp by the bed. She bought it somewhere in the West End. One of those boutique shops where you pay fifteen times what everything should cost, but you feel good about it because the word 'artist' might be involved somewhere, and they're always starving, so you should pay a little more for their product.

Desperate times.

I grab the lamp and it resists. The plug. I fumble behind the bedside table. Why am I not more scared? What the hell is wrong with me?

I take a deep breath. The plug comes out. I grab the lamp, shake off the bulky shade. The side I need is that massive stone pebble. It's lumpy, like it just came out the sea. And heavy. That's the important thing. It takes heft to wield it. Lugging boxes all day for a living means I'm not too intimidated by the weight. My arms are only deceptively skinny.

I wait beside the door. Keep my breath quiet and steady. Blood flows through my veins faster than usual, a tingling sensation that comes frighteningly close to pins and needles.

'Okay,' Smiley says from the other room. 'We'll do it the hard way, then.'

The handle turns. The door opens.

Gun arm first.

I pivot on my feet, like an awkward kid playing rounders.

Luckily, Smiley's head is bigger than a tennis ball. The base of the lamp connects with a crunching sound against the side of his face. Not a direct hit, but good enough. He falls. Tries to raise the gun. I stay to the side of him, swing the lamp again, bringing the oversized pebble base down on the top of his head. The impact sends him down, face-first into the carpet. He drops the gun. I kick it away.

Looking at his cracked head, maybe I can see white among the red, as though I've broken right through to his skull. Maybe it's my imagination.

I had to hit him as hard as I could, make sure he went down.

But he's not dead. He moves, his arm twitching. He's trying to get up.

'Fucking . . .' he says, between other words that are less clear.

'Four people are dead,' I say. 'And I know they're all going to get blamed on me.' Right enough, I was responsible for one of them, but that seems unimportant in the bigger picture.

'Should've just . . .' His words slur together. I wonder what I managed to do with the pebble lamp. I don't know much about how concussion works, but at the very least, I gave his brain a good shake.

'Should've just nothing,' I say. He's no threat to me any more. He can barely move. I doubt he really knows what's going on.

I pick up the gun.

I've never held one before. It's lighter than I expected, although the weighting feels a little strange. I hold it gingerly, making sure that the business end is pointing away from me. I try and emulate Smiley. Two hands, one on the bottom of the grip. My index finger snakes out to the trigger guard.

Smiley raises his head. The second man I've had at my feet today. Both broken and bleeding. What's that say about the choices I've made lately?

'You won't do it,' he says, clearly fighting through the pain. 'You're not one of us, Jennifer. You're not a killer. You've never fired a gun before. I can see your hands shak–'

What cuts him off is an explosion. My hands jerk back. Maybe I've gone wide, missed him completely. The noise and recoil judder my bones. A high-pitched whine starts up inside my head, drowning out all other noise.

I drop the gun.

Expect Smiley to pick it up again, finish the job he started.

But he doesn't move.

Because in spite of myself, I've shot him through the top of his skull. I can see flesh and bone and blood and spattered bits of grey matter that I guess have to be brains.

I step back.

Stop breathing.

That whining noise is still there.

I collapse on Caroline's bed.

I didn't mean to do it. I just meant to scare him, show him I meant business. But the trigger was too sensitive. Or I couldn't hit the backside of a barn door. And now, another man's dead.

Five bodies to my name.

Chalk up prison time no matter what I tell anyone.

Bloody hell.

The tabloids are going to love this.

PART FOUR

THE SILENCE OF
THE LAMBS

Thirty

THREE WEEKS LATER

The hair dye washes down the drain.

Watching the dark-brown liquid mix with the water, I keep thinking of the shower scene in *Psycho*. They used black syrup instead of red dye. It came up better on screen.

Someone told me that once. I remember reading the original book by Robert Bloch. Enough to give anyone nightmares, more than any movie.

Some nights I dream of someone ripping open the shower curtain and stabbing down at me. But not with a knife: with a pebble lamp like the one I used to bring down Smiley.

It would be a blessing, in a way.

I finish my shower, get dressed, then look at my face in the mirror. The woman who looks back is the same but different. She seems harder than I used to – something about the eyes and the severity of the pixie cut. On some girls it might look cute. On me, I don't know: there's something butch going on. Fine by me. Long as I no longer look like the Most Dangerous Woman in Scotland.

Sorry, Nicola, darling. Didn't mean to topple you off the top spot.

* * *

Downstairs, my mum is cooking breakfast. I smell sausages and bacon frying on one of the rings of the Aga. The crackle and spit of fat brings back odd, nostalgic memories that feel at odds with the childhood I want to recall: the lonely, uncertain one that I felt blessed to escape.

We rewrite our histories all the time. Ask my mum, she'd say I was a happy child. Ask me, I felt like the leper of all the kids, the weird girl no one knew how to talk to.

Perspective.

Learned a lot about that over the last few weeks.

As I walk into the kitchen, Mum looks at me and shakes her head. 'It's like having a stranger live with me.' Meaning the way I look. Her idea, this changing the way I look. Anyone asks, I'm her sister's daughter getting work experience on the farm. Seems a flimsy lie, and yet we both know no one in the village will really remember me: I escaped as soon as I could. The hair dye, the pixie cut and the change in wardrobe should be enough to fool most people if I keep myself to myself.

'What's on the agenda today?' I want to help where I can. Mum believes in me, after all. The least I can do is help out.

After Dad's death, I could never get my head around how she ran the place all by herself. She'd laugh and say that the McAllister women were born tough. She started using her maiden name the day after the funeral. Never quite been sure what that said about the way things were between her and Dad at the end.

'You really want to,' she says, 'you can check on the sheep.'

Sure. Fine by me. I signal my agreement by nodding and then sit down at the oak table in the centre of the room. She dishes up and I get a scent of nostalgia for the good mornings of my teenage years. I always felt safe in here with Mum. I'll give her that. Everything I wanted to escape from, none of it was to do with her or Dad.

I eat breakfast and then get my boots on, trek up to the fields at the foot of the hills. Since Dad's death, Mum has people who work for her on a casual basis, but she likes to do most things herself. Sheep, cows and a nice turnover mean she's going to do okay until she gets too old. She denies it, of course, and she's in fair shape for a woman in her mid-sixties, but more and more I'm starting to realise that she might be frailer than she lets on.

It's the little things. A more haggard look to her face. A slight tiredness in the eyes. The occasional moment of frustrated confusion that doesn't chime with the Mum I remember from when I was growing up. There's a vulnerability that frightens me.

Does it come for all of us?

* * *

I'm in a reflective mood. Standing at the gate, looking at the sheep grazing in the field.

My face still appears on the telly, but less often now. I'm an open investigation. The police have been up to the farm more than once. Mum has friends down in the village who phone up when they see the police on their way. They think they're just giving her a friendly warning before she gets too upset at their sudden appearance.

The truth is it gives me time to get out to Maiden's Bower, spend time in the shadow of old caves and rocks at the base of the Lomond Hills. I have some camping gear at the ready in case I need to spend time there. The hope is that it won't come to that. My agreement with Mum is that after a month, I'll move on. When things quiet down.

I don't know that she believes me when I say I'm innocent. But she's my mum. She does what she has to do.

I'm not sure how I feel about that.

I trudge into the field, check the sheep over when I encounter them. Note the tags, the numbers, give them a good feel for any injuries or obvious physical issues. They're perfectly calm and welcome me like an old friend. Maybe I should have stayed on the farm after all. Maybe I'm not as bad with animals as I used to believe.

I hear the noise of a car, and turn to look back at the road. A Jeep rumbles along, the kind of showy 4x4 that most people keep for the city instead of the country. It looks too clean. It stops by the gate and someone gets out. A man is as much as I can see from this distance. He wears the farmer's outfit of wellies and a fleece, topped off with a silly woolly hat in Dundee United orange. I think the colour's a coincidence more than a show of support for any team. He keeps waving every few steps as he walks towards me.

I brace myself.

He's in his late thirties or early forties, I reckon. Maybe from one of the neighbouring businesses. Could be an owner or a worker. Hard to tell sometimes. When I was young, the farmers all seemed ancient and liable to roll on in their positions forever: a constant on the farms, fields and sheds. Now they were succeeded either by their sons or workers who decided to buy them out. Meaning the new breed of farmers, even those in their forties, just looked too impossibly young to be in charge of their operations.

'Hey,' he says, waving for the last time as he gets close enough for us to speak. 'You'll be Mrs Carter's niece, then?'

I nod.

He looks at me for a moment, and his brow knots a touch. Just a second, however, and then he relaxes and smiles. Up close his face is familiar, with a strong chin that's clear even when hidden underneath the black bristles that fight the grey invasion. There are lines about his features, but the clear, blue eyes are . . .

'I'm James Johnson,' he says, holding out a hand.

I blink. 'James,' I say. 'No, I'm not James. I'm . . .Linda.'

'You don't seem sure of your own name,' he says, with a hint of a smile. He never was one for smiling. I remember that now. One of the reasons I used to have a crush on him. Always just the right side of serious, and there was the impression that you could break the sternness to something more tender underneath.

Rewriting my teenage years through rose-tinted specs? Oh, Jen, don't be that girl. Really. Seriously.

James Johnson. I haven't thought about him in over ten years.

'I'm sure about my own name,' I say. My heart's thumping. But not for the same reasons it once did. He was ten years older than me, and viewed me as little more than a pest. All I can hope is that he doesn't remember me well enough to make the connection.

'I can see the family resemblance.'

'Aye?' *Thumpa-thumpa-thumpa-thumpa*.

'Her daughter, Jen – I guess you just look a little like her.'

'Right.' My heart slows. Just.

'Sorry, I don't . . . I just wanted to say hello was all.'

There's silence for a moment. 'Good,' I say. 'Nice to see a friendly face.'

'The pub,' he says, nodding back towards the main road. 'In the village. They do a good steak pie. I mean, if . . .'

'I'm kept pretty busy.'

'Sure.'

'But, you know, I'll think about it.'

There's silence again between us. It goes on too long. I can't tell if this is flirting or something else. It's too intense for flirtation, I think, and more and more I'm sure he's suddenly going to realise who I am.

'It's a shame,' he says. 'About what happened.'

'What?'

'With your aunt . . . your whatever's . . . daughter.'

'Oh. Aye.'

'She never heard from her? I mean, after she . . .'

'Aye,' I say. 'She vanished. Maybe died. I mean, no one's heard from her, have they? I don't really ask M . . .my aunt. She's got enough to think about. But I read the papers. Watch the telly. After something like that, you know, what do you do? Where do you hide?'

'I'd've thought she'd have come back home.'

'Stupid move, really,' I say. It comes out as a croak. My throat is tight and scratchy. My stomach is churning. 'Who'd do that?'

One of the sheep ambles over to us. I start giving it a quick feel, try and make it clear I have work to do.

James Johnson stands there and watches me. Can't the lad take a hint? I guess he couldn't when I was younger, so maybe it's still the same. Just in reverse.

After a moment where I don't look at him, he finally cottons on and takes a step backwards. 'I'm serious about dinner,' he says. 'On me. Just dinner.'

'Maybe.'

'Mrs Carter will have the number.' Not pushing it, but still hopeful.

'I'm sure.'

He starts to walk away. 'I hope she turns up,' he says. 'Alive. I mean, what she did was horrific, but she grew up around here, you have to wonder . . .'

'Aye,' I say. 'Aye.' Conversation over. Piss off. I have things to do. Like touch up a sheep.

He shuts up and walks down the field.

I wait until I hear the engine start down near the road. Then, still holding onto the sheep for support, I breathe in deeply, and begin to wonder if coming back home wasn't nearly as good a plan as I'd originally believed.

Thirty One

'It was going to happen sooner or later.'

'Maybe. Maybe. But still . . . you're sure he didn't recognise you?'

I shake my head. Mum's white as a sheet and even though she started this conversation sitting at the other side of the table, she gets up and starts pacing the kitchen. The momentum keeps her from descending into pure, unadulterated panic.

Better than panicking and killing someone. Guess I didn't inherit her self-control.

'I'm sure he didn't. I mean, family resemblance and all, but what did you think would happen if someone got that close? That's why we said I was your niece, right? Instant deniability.'

'Or a bloody stupid idea,' she says. 'I believe you when you say you didn't kill those people, but what are we supposed to do?'

I can't look at her. I told Mum as much of the truth as I could, but telling her that I was the one who killed Ed or what really happened with Smiley was too much. Not lies so much as gentle embellishments. The kind of thing I used to do all the time as a teenager.

Mum doesn't notice my reaction. She's caught up in her own train of thought. 'I don't know how you get a fake passport or change your name or whatever it is people do to run away from the police. But is it really that easy?' She thinks about it. 'I saw something on telly, though. Phil was talking about on *This Morning*. This thing, The Dark Net.'

It's all I can do not to laugh in her face. *The Dark Net*. Christ.

'I mean, how do you access it? They weren't really that clear.' She's speaking more to herself than me. Adrift on a sea of possibilities. Clutching at straws. Virtual straws.

'I think you need to be geekier than either of us, Mum,' I say. 'Besides, I don't think it's as easy as just logging on and asking for a whole fake identity.'

'Well? What's your suggestion, Miss Cleverclogs?'

That hangs between us for a moment before we both burst out laughing.

Miss Cleverclogs. She hasn't called me that since . . . I was still living here at any rate.

The laughter clears the air. It hurts, too. Just a little. Like exercising a muscle you haven't used in a long time.

I force myself to take deep breaths. 'Seriously,' I say, 'one way or another, this isn't going to last forever.' I shake my head. 'He asked me out to dinner.'

'Oh?' Mum's caught between the idea that someone thinks enough of her daughter to ask her to dinner and the knowledge that our little lie could be so easily unravelled.

'I'd have killed for that when I was sixteen.' I realise what I've said as soon it's out of my mouth. I feel my cheeks burn. Again, Mum doesn't notice, or at least pretends not to.

'You couldn't have had a drink when you were sixteen.' More silence. She looks at me oddly for a second. 'You weren't drinking when you were sixteen, were you?'

I don't know if she's joking. We've always been an open family, but like any daughter, I needed to have some secrets from her and Dad. We never talked about me drinking, but she must have known.

She must have. Right?

'I should call the police right now,' she says, finally cracking up again.

That does it. Both of us doubling over, unable to control ourselves. It's the first time I remember laughing since that night in Glasgow, and it's a liberating sensation. I feel like I'm floating higher with each breath, and I lose myself in the sound.

When it ends, neither us can breathe.

'Come on, you wee lush,' Mum says. 'I'll open a bottle of the good stuff.'

* * *

I leave the curtains open at night. My room is at the back of the house and looks out onto the fields and the hills. I took to leaving it open as a teenager, and I'd stare at the night sky for hours trying to work out whatever drama was occupying my mind at the time. There's something about the dark blue broken by the near-black clouds and the pale light of the moon that's reassuring. Perhaps the simple fact of it being a childhood memory.

Tonight, I do the same thing I always did. Lie here. Try to lose myself in the sky. Pray for rain. Because the sound of rain against the window always helped me sleep.

But I can't sleep. Not really. Fits and snatches, here and there. Five-minute cat naps I don't even realise I'm taking until my eyes snap open.

Smiley's dead. But I'm not safe. Nowhere near it.

Smiley's gone. But Solomon Buchan still wants my head.

Thirty Two

Six in the morning, the doorbell rings.

This is it. Whoever's on the other side of that door, I'm either dead or going to jail.

The bell is insistent. Only people I can think of who would ring like that are the police. Which means that this is all over.

Accept your fate.

I get up, pull on the jeans beside my bed and shrug on a jumper. No bra. No time. I have to wonder why they're ringing the bell, though, and not just using the battering rams. Kind of how I figured it would all end: a rush of shouting and violence and someone slapping the cuffs on me as I scream about my innocence.

I head downstairs. Maybe it's going to be quiet. After all the blood and the horror, maybe this ends peacefully. A whimper, not a bang.

I wouldn't mind that.

Mum's at the door already. I can't see who she's talking to. Is she buying time? Waiting for me to leg it?

'James,' she says.

I breathe a sigh of relief.

'We need to talk,' he says, walking right through to the kitchen. Clocks me instantly. 'Good,' he says. 'You're up.'

'What's this about?' Mum says. But look at her face: she knows. Everything's about to fall apart.

It was always going to be the case. The lambs were never going to talk, but the minute I got within spitting distance of another person, of course they were going to realise. We were foolish to think this wasn't going to happen.

'I did a wee bit of checking,' James says. 'After our encounter up at the fields the other day. You know, it doesn't take too much. The internet, anyone can be their own private eye these days, if they have the patience. And the Google access, of course.'

I try to keep calm. Could be anything.

'Your sister, the one you mentioned, she doesn't have a daughter.' He grinned, showing his teeth. Maybe thinking he looked like a wolf.

He was acting, though. I knew what real killers looked like. This one, he was a chancer. I felt a little pit of dismay form in my stomach; disappointment at my younger self for her pathetic crush on this arsehole.

'Okay,' Mum says, trying to keep calm. 'Okay, so you're cleverer than you look.'

'Jennifer,' James says, ignoring my mum now. Looking right at me. 'I bloody knew it was you.'

'Aye,' I say. I lean against the warm top of the Aga, try to look relaxed. Like this isn't something to worry about. So he knows, and what's he going to do about it?

A tingling sensation starts in my arms. I recognise it from the night I killed Smiley. Adrenaline spiking. That sense of self-preservation. That sense of retreating into myself.

I'm calm and collected. I don't want to kill him. But I know I'll do whatever I need to in the name of self-preservation

James walks over to me. 'I couldn't believe it when I saw the news. What they said you'd done. You were always a quiet wee thing.'

'I didn't do it.'

'No?'

'Not all of it, anyway.'

'Killed a policewoman, your ex-boyfriend, his flatmate, your best friend and some random guy. That's what they're saying.'

No mention of Officer Mason. Maybe the news haven't reported it, maybe no one's made the connection.

'There's an explanation,' I say.

'Most dangerous woman in Scotland. I'm sure there is.'

'What do you want?' Mum says, loud and sharp, as though to remind us that she's in the room too.

'What do I want?' He turns to look at her again. 'That's a good question. I'm trying to decide whether it's worth turning her in.'

'If you were going to do that,' Mum says, 'you'd have done it by now.'

'Aye, aye,' James says. Then he turns to me. 'The news said you ripped off some bad people for a lot of money.'

'Did they now?'

'Your ex was a dealer. You killed him for his stash. Which means you have some moola on you. I mean, you clearly weren't dumb enough to put it all in a bank, right?'

I don't say anything.

There's silence for a moment.

Mum says, 'So you want money?' She sounds faintly disappointed.

'How much?' I say.

He looks at me. Finally, he smiles. All these years of waiting, I see his smile and I realise that I don't like it after all. 'You had several thousand, they said. I think you have more.'

'It's not here,' I say.

'Then where?'

I edge along the Aga a little. Natural as I can. He doesn't notice. 'It's about a half-hour drive,' I say. 'I can go get it . . .'

'. . .Or you can take me there.'

'Right,' I say. 'Whatever works. Long as you just take it and leave.'

166

'I knew your father, James Johnson,' Mum says, full-on parental authority in her tone. 'I know what he'd say if he knew that–'

'Don't give me that crap!' He turns to face her, suddenly angry. I get it then, that he's nervous about what he's doing. He's not so cool and collected as he's trying to make out. Probably his first time blackmailing someone. He doesn't really know what he's doing.

My fingers sneak out behind me, along the rim of the Aga. Mum likes to have the kitchen ready for breakfast the night before. Part of her ritual. Always has been, even when she's had more than a few glasses of wine. Meaning that everything is there. Including the steel-bottomed frying pan I used to struggle to lift when I was a girl, trying to show I could help out Mummy in the mornings.

Now, I'm not so little.

I swing hard. One-handed, but it's enough. Catch him in the back of the skull. He goes to his knees. The reverb shoots up my arm and into my shoulder. But I don't let go of the handle.

He's not down and out. He reaches to the back of his head, tenderly. As if not quite sure what's happened. I swing again, catch him with the base of the pan at his crown, and he falls forward on his face. He makes a soft little noise like someone waking up from sleep.

I look down at him.

I think about what happens if he leaves here. What he's going to tell people. He's not going to stay quiet. Not forever.

He's vulnerable here. Look at his feet and his hands twitching. Pathetic. Piteous.

I can stop him from telling anyone what happened. This is my chance right here.

Don't think.

Just act.

I swing the pan one more time with all my strength. Something cracks as I connect. He jerks once and then lies completely still.

'Jennifer!' My mum, unable to believe what she's watching. She's panicked, as though the reality of who her daughter has become is only just hitting home. 'Oh my God! What have you done? What have you done?'

I look at the pan. It's covered in blood. So are my hands. And my clothes.

Then I look at James. His skull has completely caved in.

Thirty Three

'I had to. You know what would have happened if I hadn't.'

We're in the front room. James's body is still in the kitchen. Since he stopped moving, neither of us have touched him. Anyone who walks in will see him, but it seems like a minor concern compared to getting Mum to accept what just happened.

I have to wonder if I'm losing my humanity, somehow. If all this death has inured me to the reality of what's happening.

Desensitised.

Too many horror movies. Too many computer games. People are desensitised to violence.

What about books? I read more books than I watch movies. And I don't play computer games. You don't hear the tabloids talk about how reading too many books makes a person into a killer, do you?

Milky tea has helped Mum a little. But she shakes as she brings the cup to her lips, and she's sitting forward in her chair, like she's getting ready to make a bolt for it.

She keeps looking at me and then looking away. Takes her a few attempts before she can hold my gaze properly. And then, finally, she asks: 'Is this like what happened with Ed?'

'No,' I say. 'Not exactly. That was an accident.'

She considers this. 'So what was this? What happened in my kitchen? Exactly.'

'He was threatening us, Mum.' She has to see that. She has

to understand that I did what I did in self-defence. Same as I attacked Mjchael. Same as I shot Smiley.

'You told me you hadn't killed anyone. That what happened. . .it was all other people.' She knows the truth. Maybe suspected it all the time. And now she can't escape it.

I rub at my forehead as though I might massage my brain into saying the right thing. But it doesn't work.

I still have to say something. She expects me to. It's in her eyes. Same look she gave me when I was a stroppy teenager. So I stumble out an explanation. 'It wasn't . . . I didn't . . . I killed a man, Mum. To defend myself. Because he killed my best friend. Because he set a dog loose on another man. Because I knew what he'd do to me.'

'James wasn't that man. He wasn't threatening you like that. What do the police call it? Appropriate force?'

'I didn't know he had a skull like an eggshell!'

'He thought he knew you,' Mum says. 'Like me. I thought I knew you too. He thought, whatever happened, she can't be that dangerous. She's still that wee teenage girl used to make doe eyes at me. He thought that the threat of him going to the police was enough.' She shakes her head. 'He was always an odd one.'

What can I say?

She lifts her head to look at me. 'You're not my wee girl any more,' she says. 'I can see that in your eyes.'

'Mum,' I say, but can't finish the sentence.

'I love you,' she says. 'That's why I'm not phoning the police. Why I'm going to let you deal with this the way you want. But the truth? I'm scared, Jennifer. If you can do something like this without even thinking about it, then maybe I have to be careful myself.'

* * *

Where is the line drawn between 'like' and 'love'?

My mother loves me.

My mother is scared of me.

How far will love take her? She's sheltered me for the past several weeks. But now she's seen me kill a man. She can no longer hide away from the truth of what I've become. Does she love me enough to continue protecting me? Or is this beyond the pale?

What do I think?

I think maybe I'm too far gone now. I've killed at least two people deliberately. I am indirectly responsible for several others. Mostly through inaction.

I'm a fugitive and I no longer have any excuse as to why.

The most dangerous woman in Scotland? I'm really starting to believe it.

Upstairs, I rip the shower curtain from the railing and drag it down to the kitchen to wrap the body. I grab the tractor from the shed, and bring it round to the front of the house. Mum tells me she has to go to bed. She can't watch.

I tuck her into bed, and think that this a strange reversal. She looks older and frailer than I've ever know her.

Have I done this to her?

'Your dad,' she says, as I leave the room. 'Your dad would have known what to do.'

I pause in the doorway, but don't turn around. 'I know.'

'Do you miss him?'

'Every day.'

She makes a sound. It might be approving. Then she starts breathing loudly. Probably she thought she'd never sleep again, but then I remember how I was after Ed, the way that exhaustion enveloped me before I was aware of what was happening.

It's for the best, I reckon, that she sleeps through what I have to do next.

An old Kipling poem runs through my head.

Them that asks no questions, never hears no lies.

* * *

I drive across to the silo. The body bounces in the shovel on the front of the tractor. It's early enough that no one's on the farm yet. None of Mum's part-time help. The only witnesses are the cows peeking out from their sheds as the rumble of the tractor's engine disturbs them.

They won't talk.

I hope.

The solution is simple. Hide the body.

Maybe it will be found one day, but by then I doubt it will matter. The point is to solve the problem instantly. If I leave the body intact, then they might even think it was an accident. God knows what kind of accident, but a tragic one nonetheless.

As I roll him into the tower and shut the door, I wonder when I started thinking like this.

A few months ago, it was equal parts heartache and lust with Ed. I would go to work, panic about being late, sometimes fantasise about some cute barman I met with Caroline after work when I went drinking. But always back to Ed, like I knew all I was doing was fantasising. I'd settled myself to life with a dick. God knows why. Everything else seems petty, too. I'd worry about whether I set up the Sky box to record *Nashville*. Normal, everyday concerns. Tiny things. The possible implications surrounding the discovery of a corpse were not a part of my thought process.

And now?

Is Mum right? Have I changed? Or, worse, was this always a part of me?

It would be easier to turn myself in. That's what I should do. Everyone tells me. Caroline told me. Mum keeps hinting at it.

Maybe if I did that, the bodies would stop piling up.

So why don't I?

As I turn on the grain silo, I think about whether I should just call Crawford like Caroline told me to all those weeks back. Tell him the truth, and to hell with him if he doesn't believe me. I'll go to jail, I'll do time, but I won't be constantly looking over my shoulder like this or second guessing myself. The idea of being able to live with what I've done in a small way is appealing.

Maybe. Maybe.

The grain drops through: a roaring, consuming sound. I stand there for a while, feeling like I'm lost beneath it. Then I turn and walk away.

I drive the tractor back to the house. The rumbling of the machine distracts me.

And then I see the car in the courtyard. New model. An Audi, I think. Silver, recently cleaned. It looks like the kind of car a middle manager would drive, and what I immediately think is plain clothes police.

Crawford.

Has to be.

He's found me at last.

The relief is overwhelming. I can finally unburden myself. I can tell the truth and do my time and who cares what happens to gangsters like Solomon Buchan, or whether everyone believes I'm a killer. It'll be enough for all of this to be over.

I almost bound into the house. Floating on the idea of giving up my freedom to choose to run. I can't escape any more. I can't run away.

It's finally over.

And then I walk into the living room.

And stop.

Dead.

Thirty Four

The old man looks up as I enter. He stands in front of the fireplace, arms folded, head cocked to one side, eyes on me.

Mum is in her chair. She looks at me too. Her body language is stiff and guarded.

Two men mill about near the window. One I don't recognise. He has a thick neck and small head. A distinctive tattoo snakes out from beneath his collar and ends just below his ear. Black ink. I don't recognise the pattern. He wears gold chains round his neck and a signet ring that could do serious damage. Finishes off his look with the kind of shellsuit I thought went out of fashion in 1996.

The other guy is familiar. He's in crutches. Guess he's lucky that's the worst of it.

Michael.

'Jennifer,' Buchan says. 'How lovely to see you. I was just telling your mother here the story of how we met.'

I look at Mum. She looks back at me. Her eyes are cold. Hard to know what she's thinking. Her face is set in a neutral expression. Her jawline vibrates with tension.

I keep the eye contact with Mum and say to Buchan, 'How did you find me?'

He gestures for me to walk further into the room. I do so.

He looks me up and down. Nothing perverse about it. As an appraisal, it's cold and clinical. 'I don't like the new look.'

'Didn't have you down as a fashion expert.'

'I'm old but full of surprises.' He shakes his head. 'The feminine look suited you. This . . .this androgynous thing, I don't get it.'

'Generational.'

'Maybe.'

We stare at each other, me and the old man.

'How did it feel?' he asks, changing tack. 'To kill someone with intent? Was it easy? I believe this is the first time you killed someone who wasn't directly threatening you. The way your mother tells the story, anyway.'

I don't say anything. Look back at Mum. She turns her head so she doesn't have to look at me directly.

Love and like.

I realise where I stand.

'It's a hard thing for most people,' Buchan says. I look back at him again. He wants my attention. It's best that I give it to him for now. 'They can't handle it. Smiley was impressed with how you coped with what happened with your boyfriend. He thought maybe we could use you in some way. If things had gone differently, maybe you and I would be having a very different kind of conversation now.'

'We'd be talking from the other side of prison bars,' I say.

'Which side?' He allows himself a smile. 'I think we all know you were doomed from the moment you decided not to tell the police what you had done. That was it for you, end of the line.' He smiles. 'Who was in the curtain, by the way?'

'No one important.' I don't have to look at Mum to know she can't believe the callously casual nature of my reply.

But I need to be this person. Play this part. If I'm going to survive.

'Everyone is important if you kill them,' Buchan says. 'I know every man who died at my hands. I know their names. I remember the look in their eyes.'

'Quite the hard bastard,' I say. 'But you're old now.'

'Still dangerous.'

'Gangster number one.'

'More than that.'

'Why don't you just kill me, then?'

'We discussed a compromise before.'

'Bit late now.'

He nods. Slowly. 'No compromise, then?'

'No.'

'You have a simple choice.'

'I turn myself in, take the blame for everything and tell you where the money is?'

He nods again.

'Or you kill me?'

He doesn't nod this time. Just looks at me. I realise I don't remember the last time he blinked.

'If you turn yourself in,' he says, 'you'll be taken care of. Inside, I mean.'

'Aye?'

'Our friend Michael here isn't the only compromised person I know in the justice system. The sad truth is, many of them are worse than men like myself. So the question you have to ask yourself is: who do you trust?'

I'm not buying it. He's acting like a cheap Scottish imitation of the gangster Casper Gutman in *The Maltese Falcon*. Playing on my expectations. He says he knows me. He doesn't know a thing.

'All I need to do, then, is hand myself over to the police and you'll guarantee that my sentence will be as cushy as you can make it? Unlimited access to the prison library, preferred dinner arrangements, that kind of thing?'

He shrugs.

'And what about the drugs? You know I have no idea what Dave did with them.'

'Some things you just have to let go.' He looks at my mother. 'Old age and parenthood brings its own kind of zen.'

He's in his mid-seventies by now, and in a straight fight even I could take him. But just looking at his eyes, it's clear that Solomon Buchan is more dangerous than ever. I doubt he'd give his own daughter a birthday gift without a price attached, opaque or otherwise.

'What else do I have to do, other than take the rap?'

He looks at Mum. 'You brought up a good girl here. Smart.'

'I'm beginning to wonder,' Mum says. It earns her a smile, at least. A genuine one.

'Circumstances,' Buchan says, 'can make killers of us all.'

My mum shuts up again. She's not engaging him.

I say, 'So what do you want?'

He keeps looking at my mum as he says, 'You'll turn yourself over to the custody of DI Crawford. I believe you were considering this the night you killed Smiley.'

I have a sick feeling in my stomach.

He continues, 'You'll state when you hand yourself in that you're willing to give a full and frank confession, but only to him. You will refuse to speak to anyone else.'

Why Crawford? Why him specifically? I can't believe he's in Buchan's pocket. It doesn't gel with the man I met. Unless he's a hell of a good actor.

I don't like where this is going.

Mum says, 'She could just tell him the truth.'

'She could,' Buchan says. 'But your daughter knows that when I say if she dares to even think about messing me around again, I will kill you. She knows I mean it, too. She's seen what happens when people . . .disappoint me.' He steps towards her. 'You seem like a good woman. But know that I will do whatever I have to. And it will be your daughter's choice.'

I look at Mum. She looks back at me, and I see that she knows

177

he's telling the truth. Just one look at my face, I can't hide it from her any more.

I say, 'Please, don't threaten her.'

He nods. His whole demeanour designed to tell me that he's not an unreasonable man. The way he talks – so calm, and the way he moves, with relaxed shoulders and an almost humble tilt to his head – belies the vicious bastard I met several weeks earlier.

Which version of him is the act?

Are they all?

'What happens, then,' I say, 'when I get in the room with him? He tells me what to say and what to do? He's one of yours, right?'

'You do what you seem to do best,' Buchan says. 'You kill the bastard.'

'You're giving me a second chance?'

He shrugs. Gestures for me to follow him outside. I do so. Mum follows behind, Goldie Lookin Chain pushing her so that she gets the point.

Knowing Buchan, whatever it is he wants me to see, it's not going to be pleasant.

Thirty Five

Buchan and Michael walk ahead of us. The old man gestures for me to stop somewhere in the middle of the yard.

Then I hear it: the barking. The growling.

'I don't think you've met Brutus,' Buchan says.

Of course Brutus is a dog. A big one, too, unless his bark's worse than his bite. I doubt it.

I've always been a cat person. All dogs sound big to me. Even the little yappy ones have that edge to their bark that says they'd try and rip your throat out if they could. Cats kill too. But they're smart enough to only attack things that are smaller than they are.

Brutus's growls have a bass-bite that makes the bones in my body shake. I tense up. I don't want to think about what's happening. Buchan and his pals are sadistic bastards, but surely this is going over the score?

Right?

I've told them the truth. But clearly they don't believe me. This is their way of showing me they aren't kidding.

There's a panic starting somewhere at the back of my mind, but this cool, calm, collected thing that seems to control my body won't let it take over. All I can do is scream inside my own skull, while outwardly I remain stoic.

Is this bravery?

I don't think so.

There's a van parked outside one of the sheds. Its maybe ten metres away. That's where the barking comes from.

I turn to look at Mum.

She just shakes her head.

Buchan gestures to Goldie Lookin Chain. The thug walks to the van. He takes his time.

Buchan looks at Mum. 'I suggest, Mrs Carter,' he says, 'that you stay very still. No matter what happens.'

Goldie Lookin Chain opens the rear doors of the van, and quickly steps back.

Brutus comes rushing out. Some kind of pit bull, I think. White and black spotted fur that's so short it could be skin. A pink patch around one eye. Heavy shoulders, built for power. Short legs. Big head with the kind of jaws that would make a crocodile jealous.

Cujo.

Stephen King.

I used to laugh about that book, think it was ridiculous the way he tried to make a family dog so terrifying. I just couldn't believe it.

Now I think the book might be in for major re-evaluation. If I ever get the chance to read anything again.

Goldie Lookin Chain kneels and, unafraid, reaches out to ruffle the fur on top of the dog's head. The dog doesn't seem to mind that, but he's still barking and straining at the leash.

The old man turns his back on the dog to look at me. 'Brutus is a little bastard,' he says. 'Bred for fighting. Won his master more than a few fights.'

'He's a teddy bear,' Goldie Lookin Chain says, looking up now, still ruffling the dog's fur. 'When he wants to be.'

'When he knows someone,' Buchan says. 'And that's the thing – when it comes to strangers, he's a pain in the neck. Or the leg. Or the stomach. Whatever he can get his teeth into. These particular dogs, they have this thing, see. The "hold and shake" attack. Vicious, vicious, vicious. There was this case I read about in America, where the courts said they had difficulty telling the difference between a bite from a pit bull and a bite from a Great White shark.'

Okay, now I'm scared. Out here with no help coming and a man telling how the dog that's maybe only ten yards away from me has the same capacity to hurt someone as bloody Jaws.

The panic in the back of my mind kicks into overdrive. But still can't break through.

I stand perfectly still. Breathing easy.

Behind me, Mum is quiet.

I look above Buchan's head – not too hard given his height – and see that Goldie Lookin Chain's rubbing something over the dog's face. I think of old films where they give sniffer dogs the possessions of an escaped prisoner so the dogs know what they're looking for.

Whatever he has, it can't be something of mine. Can it? They never took my bag or any of my clothing.

My stomach churns.

I can't let them see I'm afraid.

Can't.

For Mum as much as me.

Buchan says, 'Lessons need to be learned. In my line of business, giving people a second chance is a bad idea. They take advantage, you see. Every time.'

I drop to my knees. Finally, I feel something like fear. The last few months, I've been numb. But finally, at long last, there's a rush of sensation and terror.

My breath comes out in short bursts. I should get up off my knees, but I can't.

The dog looks at me.

Buchan says, still standing between us, 'Don't make eye contact.'

181

I don't know where else to look.

Buchan grins. He turns around and winks at me.

Smiley undoes the clasp around the dog's neck. It shakes free and runs forward.

Finally, I find the strength to get up.

But I don't think I can run.

I'm sorry, Mum.

Do I say that out loud?

The old man spins, steps into my body, as though about to start a waltz. He moves me around.

Realisation: Brutus isn't coming for me.

Buchan wants me to see the dog's real target.

Brutus's back legs may be short, but they're powerful, as the dog leaps into the air and goes for Michael. He hasn't even real-ised what's happening, can't do anything but stare wide-eyed at the beast as it slobbers at the anticipation of sinking its teeth into his flesh.

At the last moment, Michael raises his arms to protect his face. His crutches drop. So does he. He screams as he realises his mistake. His voice breaks as he does so. Brutus sinks his teeth into the young man's forearm, the weight and momentum forcing Michael onto his back, screaming and jerking his limbs around furiously.

Buchan makes sure that I'm watching. He says, quietly, 'Hold and shake.'

I watch as man and dog roll about the ground.

Michael squeals at a high pitch, more like a petulant toddler than grown man. Brutus growls through his grip as he tears at Michael's flesh. Finally, he pulls his head up in a harsh, tugging motion. True to form, Brutus hasn't let go. Instead, he's torn away part of Michael's suit and also a chunk of flesh from his arm.

Michael's screams come from the throat now, and maybe that's a bad idea. The dog has his paws on the man's chest and violently nuzzles his jaws past Michael's arm, closing those teeth around his throat.

I try to turn my head away.

'This is important,' Buchan says. 'You have to watch.'

I don't want to. But the old gangster grips my elbow. I get the message. If I don't do as he says, I could be in for some pain of my own.

The jaws grip around the flesh of Michael's throat – suddenly he looks like a boy more than a man – and lock. Brutus's head rips from side to side.

Buchan mentioned shark attacks, but I'm still thinking of crocodiles and the way that they grip onto their prey and roll over until the flesh tears and the beast stops struggling.

The screams stop.

The dog lifts its head.

Blood and flesh arc into the air.

Michael's arms and legs flail around for a moment longer and then go still.

Finally, I look back. Mum is perfectly still. She stares straight ahead. No emotion. She's being strong. For her daughter.

I want to run to her. I want her to hold me.

But Buchan's got a hold of me. He doesn't want me to move. He wants me to know what just happened. He wants me to understand.

The dog looks down at the man's face. He is no longer growling. Apparently satisfied with his handiwork, he hops off Michael's chest, and trots calmly back to his master.

Buchan kneels down and scratches the back of the dog's head.

'Like I said – in this business, second chances are a bad idea. Now, shall we talk about the good Inspector Crawford?'

Thirty Six

I get the train back to Glasgow from Perth. One of Buchan's boys drops me off at the station. I have about fifty quid on me. Train ticket and a cheap meal, if I'm lucky. Nothing fancy. No steak and chips. Maybe an Aberdeen Angus from Burger King.

Not my preferred choice of last meal.

The carriage is quiet. A few people stare at me, but then they shake their heads as though dismissing the idea they might know who I am. One of those faces, maybe.

I'm still a fugitive, but the news cycle has moved on to fresher blood. I'm just a background story: worth updating every few days, but the fact is there's nothing new to report. I still worry that, despite the change of style, people might take a closer look, maybe realise why the think they know me.

And then?

Well, they'll probably run screaming.

BLOODY WOMAN! One of the tabloids had proclaimed in the days following my escape from Glasgow. Mum had shown me the paper. I wasn't sure whether she was proud or disappointed, and I think she wasn't too certain either. Personally, I preferred one of the others that said, **THE FEMALE OF THE SPECIES IS MORE DEADLY THAN THE MALE.** Maybe because the song brought back memories of being a teenager. Odd that I can't really remember who sung it. I imagine at the time I believed they would live on forever in the music hall of fame, but now they've faded like so many teenage memories and dreams.

My seventeen- or eighteen-year-old self would be appalled to know that all I wound up doing was working in a bookstore. A few years, maybe, but I'm coming up on ten now. Although I don't suppose that after the events of the last few months I'll be going back anytime soon.

At Queen Street, I switch to a train that takes me to Charing Cross. From there I walk to FHQ in the city centre. The closer I get, the more lightheaded I feel.

When I see the sign that says POLICE, I fight the urge to turn and run.

I'm committed now. One way or another, this has to happen.

I think of Mum. Her eyes silently asking me to defy Buchan. But with her life on the line, I couldn't do it. Is it cold to think like this? Can saving one life really be worth taking another?

I smile to myself. If I'm not careful, I could end up like Hamlet, endlessly soliloquising and never really taking any action.

Check me: Crown Princess of Hyndland.

Queen of all procrastinators.

Well, not any more.

At the doors, I take a deep breath. Walk inside. I push to the front desk. A few people sitting around, waiting like this is a doctor's surgery, look at me. They sense something's about to kick off. They're not far wrong.

'Excuse me.'

The officer on duty looks up. Bored eyes. Then, a sudden change of expression. They know who I am. Probably burned in her brain. Probably burned in the brain of every police officer after what happened.

'My name's Jennifer Carter. I'm wanted in connection with multiple counts of murder. I'd like to turn myself in.'

* * *

185

They take me to a room on the fourth floor. Taking no chances. Two detectives come in to see me. I haven't said anything beyond my opening statement. The detectives sit down across from me.

One of them – smaller and squatter than his companion – says, 'My name's DI Stringer. This is Detective Constable White. We understand you came in of your own free will, and we'd like to thank you for that.'

I keep quiet. Does he expect a response? I don't know. Is all of this unnecessary theatre? I don't know that either.

The taller detective – White – says, 'Everything in this room is being recorded. Do you understand that?'

I take a deep breath. 'I understand,' I say.

Stringer says, 'Before we can proceed, we need to read you your rights.'

I hold up my hands. 'Before we can proceed,' I say, 'I don't want to talk to you.'

They look at each other. Lost for words.

I help them out. 'I want to talk to Detective Inspector Crawford. Can you arrange that?'

Stringer recovers first. He's definitely in charge. 'Detective Inspector Crawford has a lot of cases to–'

'It's not a request,' I say. 'I talk to him. Him and only him.'

Stringer shakes his head. 'That's not going to happen. You don't get a choice. You're not controlling this situation. Maybe you think you are. Maybe all that coverage in the papers has gone to your head. We get it. They cover killers like they're celebrities. But in this building, you don't have any power. We're the detectives on duty. We say what happens.'

'He knows the case.' I keep my voice deliberately neutral. I have to show them that this is the best decision they can make. I'm in no position to make demands.

'We all know the case,' White says. 'The man on the street knows the case.'

'Crawford,' I say. Laying it out. I'm not budging.

'No,' Stringer says.

'I'm not saying anything else until I see Crawford.'

There's silence for a moment.

Stringer looks at White. The taller detective arches his eyebrows. I get the impression they've worked together for a long time. They use shorthand similar to a married couple. Maybe that's what it like for them. But instead of sex, they interrogate people.

'We'll see what we can do,' Stringer says. 'But believe me when I say it's not going to make any difference to what happens to you.'

'In that case,' I say. 'I'll wait.' I fold my arms.

The detectives stand. They leave without another word. Maybe they're going to get Crawford. Maybe they're just going to let me stew. I'm prepared for the psychological games. Makes a nice change of pace from knowing my life is in danger.

When they're gone, a uniform comes into the room. He doesn't want to engage with me. He stands by the door, stares into space. Maybe thinking about the end of his shift. I don't look back. I just sit where I am. And wait.

Thirty Seven

I'm sitting as still as I can, looking at myself in the mirror opposite the table, when there's a knock at the door. The constable assigned to guard me, who hasn't said a word, answers, and looks surprised to see another uniformed officer standing there. This one is slightly older, beefier. He looks like he wouldn't pass the mandatory fitness tests for new recruits. His nose is red. The kind of red you get from a few too many bevvies.

'Phone call for you,' he says to my guard. Then he glances towards me. 'I'll keep an eye on this one.'

My guard looks at me for a moment. He's not sure this is a good idea. I try and make like I'm not paying attention. I stare right ahead.

'Who is it?'

'Didn't say. Just said they had to speak to you. Look, I can–'

'Nah, nah. Look, just don't even talk to her, alright? Crawford's coming in, he's the one cleaning up this mess. Besides, we don't want her claiming mistreatment or anything, right? She kills one of us, we treat her the same as any other murderer.'

'Right,' says the fatter man. He looks at me and shakes his head. 'Not going to give me any trouble, doll, are you?'

I look up and stare at him with blank eyes. The whole, 'Like I care?' routine.

The younger uniform leaves. The door closes, and the older one folds his arms. I return to what I was doing before: waiting.

'Jesus,' the fat man says.

He reaches into his pocket, pulls out something wrapped in what looks like an old duster. He walks forward and drops it on the table. It thunks down with some weight. Whatever it is, he acts like its radioactive. 'Take it,' he says. 'Do whatever. Just don't you ever dare fucking say I gave it to you.'

I look at him, then at the package.

'Quick,' he says, 'before that bollocks gets back.'

I unwrap the package a little. See the blade. They search you when you're processed, confiscate anything that could be used as a weapon. Sharp objects, even ones that seem innocuous, like hairpins or car keys, get sent to the lockers. They obviously didn't consider me a suicide risk as I've been allowed to keep my shoe-laces and my belt. Or maybe that was wishful thinking. I'm not exactly Miss Popularity among the police.

I tuck the package into my pocket. Questions will be asked later. But I won't say anything. Part of the deal that's keeping Mum alive.

The fat man doesn't say anything else. Just returns to where he was standing before, and sweats.

I don't look directly at him. Just remain aware of his presence out of the corner of my eye.

My guard returns and says, 'No one on the line.'

'Hey,' the fat man says, 'not my problem, pal. I'm not your fucking secretary!' And he heads out of there fast as he can.

'Prick,' my guard says. Not for anyone's benefit but his own.

I might as well be invisible.

I sit there thinking about the last few weeks. Try to remember who I used to be before I became Public Enemy Number One.

* * *

189

When Crawford walks in the room, my stomach heaves with stress. It's all I can do not to vomit all over his shoes.

I'm not sure he notices. Or cares.

He doesn't say anything. He dismisses the uniform with a wave of his hand. Not even eye contact. He walks over to the other side of the table and sits.

Lets the silence hang.

He's got to be the one to break it. Right?

* * *

How do I do it? How do I kill him?

Cut his throat.

When?

Whenever you can. But I want him to know it was me who set this in motion. I want him to know. I need the bastard to know that I have a long fucking memory.

* * *

'Last time we talked, you told me you didn't know anything.'

'Yes.'

'There are four bodies we can connect to you.'

'Yes.'

'Are you here to say you killed them?'

'I killed Ed.'

'Yes?'

'That was an accident.'

'Okay.' He takes a breath. He's looking at me oddly. 'You've been informed of your rights?'

'The two officers who brought me in.'

'Why didn't you want to talk to them?'

I shrug. My eyes keep going to the corner of the room, where the camera looks down at us. I can feel it moving, I can sense the focus shifting. Is there anyone watching us? Do the tapes get reviewed at a later date? I honestly don't know. Was the camera working when that red-nosed officer gave me the knife?

I look at the mirror on the far wall. Remember watching *NYPD Blue* when Channel 4 screened it at stupid o'clock at night. The cops used to line up inside a small room with one-way glass and watch Jimmy Smits and Dennis Franz interrogate suspects.

Mostly, I watched Jimmy Smits. Didn't bother watching his interrogation techniques as closely as other assets.

Crawford says, 'Jen?'

'Sorry,' I say, snapping myself back into the room. It's easy to wander. It might be easier than anything else. Maybe if my mind wandered far enough, I could escape all of this. I've been doing something like it for the past several weeks anyway, taking a mental backseat whenever I've had to do anything unpleasant.

All that blood. All that violence. Why doesn't it touch me?

'Come on,' Crawford says. 'I'm here now. If you don't want to talk, then why ask for me?'

'You have kind eyes,' I say.

'I'm sympathetic?'

I nod.

He shakes his head. 'First and last time anyone's described me that way.' He sits back. 'You want to know something?'

'Aye?'

'Until last year I was a DCI. I worked with the SCDEA up until a few years ago too. You know who they were?'

I shake my head.

'Scottish Crime and Drug Enforcement Agency. We were the ones who took down the dealers and the gangsters.'

'So you were demoted? Why does that matter to me?'

'The SCDEA was disbanded for Police Scotland. The

demotion . . . well . . . You told me when we met that you were friends with Katherine Scobie?'

'Aye.'

'She happened.'

'You were the undercover–?' I remember the stories. Kat's boyfriend had turned out to be a police officer working with a rogue unit who had the ultimate in deniability. Which sounds like fiction until you realise just how often this happened. Look at the girls in England, the environmental protestors who had children with men who turned out to be undercover operatives. Kat never let it get that far. But it was still a fuck up. Enough that she disappeared completely.

He shakes his head. 'No, no,' he says. 'Not me. I was in charge of the operation.'

A man of influence, then. And now he's just a detective like any other. I figure he has to have a lot of dirt on the right people not to have been drummed out of the force entirely.

'And?'

'Everything about that operation went wrong. Kat was never supposed to get caught up in any of it. She was certainly never meant to be in any danger. The idea was to use her to get our operative close to the family. But . . .'

'But . . .?'

He shrugs. 'But things go wrong. That's the nature of life.' He leans forward. 'You know about that, right? How things can just spiral out of control?' I wonder why he's being so open with me. Maybe I just have a sympathetic face. But now I see it. He's using his own story to get me to trust him.

I can't trust anyone any more.

I'm on my own.

No one can help me but myself.

I say, 'You wanted her family?'

'They were criminals.'

And now they're dead. After Crawford's undercover man set in motion a series of events that led to a bloody massacre. I remember the headline in the Herald the morning after:

THE NIGHT GLASGOW'S STREETS RAN RED WITH BLOOD

That was the least melodramatic one too.

'No one else?' I say. 'You weren't looking to take down anyone except the Scobies?'

'They were the focus at the time.' He looks at me for a moment, as though wondering whether I'm trying to say something.

Maybe I am. 'Buchan,' I say. Just throwing it out. And why not?

He sits back again. 'What do you know about Buchan?'

'Enough.'

'Your boyfriend, he owed dealers. Men connected to Solomon Buchan.'

I nod.

'You knew about it?'

'Not until he died.'

'And then?'

'I found the stash in my cupboards.'

'And the flatmate?'

'He was the one who disposed of the body. He came up with the idea. I called him because I didn't know who else to call. He told me that no one would believe what happened.'

Buchan allows himself a grim little smile that doesn't reach his eyes.

'So you're blaming him?'

'Not entirely.'

'Did he threaten to go the police, maybe? That's why he had to go too.'

I bite my lower lip.

'The only person you killed was Ed?'

I hesitate. It's only a moment, but it's enough. I've lost him.

Any sympathy he might have evaporates. I've told a lie. Anything else that comes out of my mouth is now suspect.

'Where did you dispose of Ed's body? Give me that, at least.'

I lean across the table. Can anyone hear us? Is that camera still recording everything that happens in this room? 'I'm supposed to kill you,' I whisper. 'Don't say anything.'

Does he believe me? Does he think I'm insane?

'You killed Ed.' He acts as though I haven't said anything. Is that good or bad?

'Yes.'

'The flatmate?'

'I . . .yes.'

'My colleague?'

'Yes.' The lies come easily. Buchan told me that all of this was down to me.

'You shot her?' His voice rises with scepticism.

It's a good question. What would I be doing with a gun? Where did I get it?

Crawford says, 'With a gun that I presume belonged to your boyfriend?' Practically giving me the story. And he still hasn't reacted to what I said earlier. About killing him. Either I imagined I said anything, or Crawford should quit the police and take up professional poker playing.

'Aye. Yes. I found it with the stash.'

Crawford says, 'The girl too? Your friend.'

'Yes.'

'Four people,' he says.

'Four people,' I say.

'No one else?'

I hesitate.

I try to catch his eyes, try to look for some sign of this being an act. He has to know that I was serious earlier, that I was trying to tell him something.

I'm supposed to kill you.

Did he hear me?

He stands. 'Excuse me just a moment.'

No. No. Don't leave.

Did I just lose my chance?

Instead of killing Crawford, did I kill my mother?

I want to leap from the chair and stab him then and there. But I can't move. Paralysed.

He leaves the room.

Just me and my guard.

I look up at the camera in the corner of the room. Who's watching me? What are they thinking?

What do I do now?

* * *

I stew for maybe forty-five minutes. My guard stares off into space for most of it. Sometimes he gives me the side eye.

Then the door opens. Crawford back in. He dismisses the officer guarding me, grabs his chair and pulls it so that he's sitting right next to me. He looks at me.

I get this tight feeling in my chest. My eyes water just a little.

What do I say?

I look at Crawford. My hand moves down to my pocket. I don't even think about what I'm doing. It just happens.

He still doesn't say anything. Why not? Some kind of mind game? Or . . .?

I need to commit to this.

For Mum.

Even if I don't succeed, at least I can say I tried.

I'm sorry, DI Crawford. It's you or my mother. There's no choice.

Thirty Eight

Crawford shakes his head. 'Killing someone,' he says, 'isn't easy. Most people, even when they've done it before, they're prone to hesitation. To kill someone without thought or doubt is a special psychopathy.' He looks right at me. 'I don't think that's you.'

'No?'

Is he responding to what I said earlier? My fingers, under the table, slip around the blade's handle. It's plastic. Maybe as simple as a large kitchen knife.

Enough to do the job it's supposed to?

I don't know. For all that's happened in the last few months, I haven't actually stabbed anyone. Do you go for the heart? Slice the throat? How do you make sure that the job is done?

'No. I don't think you're really a killer. In fact, the way I understand it, you allowed yourself to be brought into custody. If you were a stone-cold killer, you wouldn't do that. Not without good reason.'

'I still thought I could talk my way out of what I'd done.'

'Good,' he says. 'Hesitation. That's what I'm talking about. Acting on impulse is a bad thing. You know that as well as I do. In some ways, we're kindred spirits.'

Is this a message? Is he trying to tell me something?

I don't know. If he is, I really don't understand what he's saying.

'You have to wait,' he says. 'Until you know the time is right.'

He stands up and walks round the table, leans in close. 'Do it,' he says. 'Abdomen. Left hand side.'

He's telling me how to kill him?

'Do it!'

He stands straight.

I should hesitate.

But I don't. That part of me that keeps reacting in ways I don't expect stands, knife in hand. I think that maybe I meet his eyes, try and apologise silently. He doesn't notice. Doesn't try and defend himself.

This whole thing is like a dream. I still don't know if he really just told me to kill him. I can't be certain I haven't finally cracked up.

I make a feint for his abdomen. He twists further to the side. The chib goes in, and I swear he twists his body. Is he trying to make the blade go deeper? The blood spills over my hand. There's not the resistance I expected. Not at first. Then I seem to hit something hard.

This is different to killing Ed or shooting Smiley in the head. I scream. I back away. The blade remains in him. He drops. Holding the handle.

Does he want to die?

Does he know that we're being watched?

I drop the knife. But I stay on my feet.

The door opens. I feel the bodies rather than see them, as I'm bundled to the floor. Pressure from above. I can't breathe. I think of when I was seven or eight getting into play fights with bigger kids who would always use their mass to try and suffocate me. The same sensation of claustrophobia, of panic.

The side of my face cracks on the ground. My arms are held, my body pinned, a knee in the small of my back.

The pressure lessens a little. I pull in a loud, painful breath. I open my eyes. They've made sure I can see what I've done.

197

Crawford is on the ground, against the wall. The blood slicks around him.

So much blood.

I close my eyes.

They don't open again. Not in that room.

* * *

Ed lies on the gurney next to mine. He's naked. His chest has been opened up with a Y incision. The blood is long dried. The flesh around the cuts has turned almost black. His head is twisted so that he faces me.

I can't move. My head is also turned to the side so that I have no choice but to look at him. His eyes are glassy, and the pupils dilated.

'Eight balls,' he says. 'That's what cops call them. Eight Ball Haemorrhages.'

'You took that from a movie,' I say.

Ed says, 'Hey, babe, you got me. All my best lines, I stole them. Homaged them, if you like. But they worked on you just the same.' Even as a corpse, he's an arrogant prick.

Someone comes into the room. 'I can't move,' I say. The man, dressed in a white lab coat, ignores me. He moves out of my field of vision.

'I can't move my head,' I say Ed.

'He can't hear you,' Ed says.

'Why not?'

'No one can hear the dead.'

He's right. I'm being stupid. So I relax a little. 'Okay,' I say. 'This isn't so bad.'

Ed makes a noise that sounds a little like a snort.

'What?'

I'm aware of the man in the white coat standing over me. He's fiddling with something heavy. I don't know what it is.

'Ed?'

'Look up,' he says.

I can finally move my head. Nothing else. Just my head. I look up, see the man standing over me. His features are indistinct. But I can focus clearly on the mechanical saw he's holding. The teeth are rusted and dripping with fluid from other corpses.

'Oh, God,' I say. 'Oh, God, no!'

'He can't hear you,' Ed says. 'That's the problem with being dead.'

I can't even close my eyes. Can't blink.

The saw starts up.

The whine echoes around my skull.

* * *

I can't move.

I'm in a bed. Sheets tucked tight around me. My arms are by my sides. I try to move them. I feel leather on my wrists. The sheets aren't too tight. I'm restrained by straps. My ankles, too.

I open my eyes. I can move my head. There's no sign of any other corpses. I don't hear Ed laughing or the whine of a buzz saw. Everything is quiet and still.

I'm in a small room. It's a hospital ward. The blinds are closed. The only light leaks through from the small window in the door. There's monitoring equipment, but I'm not hooked up to anything. Nothing beeping. There's water in a glass beside my bed. But I can't reach it because of the restraints.

The door to the room is ajar. I can see someone in the hall. Black trousers, stab vest. A uniformed policeman. Of course there is. I stabbed a detective. I tried to kill – maybe even succeeded in killing – a DI. They're going to have me under guard. I'm a danger. To myself and to others round me.

All I can think about is what Buchan promised me: a cushy time behind bars, and the safety of my mother.

'Hello?'

The policeman doesn't turn. Have I spoken? The dream is still fresh in mind. *He can't hear you. That's the problem with being dead.*

My voice is cracked. My throat hurts.

All the same: 'Hello?'

This time he turns. He opens the door further to look in on me. Barely disguised contempt on his face.

'Where–?'

He turns away again. Closes the door so that I can't see him any more. Guess that tells me everything.

I close my eyes.

Drift.

Thirty Nine

When I wake up again, the straps feel loose. Maybe I'm just getting used to them. I flex my fingers, get the circulation flowing. I move my legs.

The straps aren't loose.

They're unfastened.

I sit up.

The window is open. A cool breeze filters through. I shiver in my hospital gown.

I stabbed a policeman.

And now someone's set me free?

Something is on the pillow, next to where my head had been. A piece of paper. An A4 sheet, folded neatly. I unfold it. Walk over to the window, read the words by the light of the moon.

Run.

There's an address, too. Somewhere in Tradeston.

I take a deep breath. What's the point in heading over there in my gown? I'll be stopped before I even get to the front door. I look around the room. There's a rack with the clothes I was wearing earlier. I get dressed as fast as I can, worrying that at any moment the door will open.

The idea of staying where I am doesn't even cross my mind. Why would it? Running has become my default. It's all I know how to do any more.

I sneak a look through the glass of the door. There's a chair, where I imagine the officer on duty should be sitting. But he's nowhere to be seen.

Luckiest woman alive? Or being set up?

Whoever left the note, they're taking a big chance that I'll go to that address. I could easily decide to simply run off, slip into the night and never be seen again. A little like Kat did last year. Except she was never suspected of murder. She never attacked a serving policeman.

Crawford.

Is he alive?

And do I really believe he's the one who left the note?

He asked me to stab him. I didn't hallucinate that. I'm sure I didn't. The one thing I can be sure of is that I still have all my faculties. I'm not crazy. Despite the straps. Despite what I'm sure they've been saying in the papers.

If Crawford's alive, maybe this is somehow part of his plan.

Don't know if I understand it, though.

I need to focus. Need to find that distant feeling that came with killing Smiley, with watching Ed's dismembered corpse sink beneath the water. It doesn't matter who left the note. They're giving me a way out. Whatever happens now, I can't afford to show weakness. I may not be in control, but I can pretend I'm going to take it back.

And what if whoever left that note works for Buchan?

What if I'm walking out of here to my own death?

Except that doesn't make sense either.

I slip out of the door and down the hall. No idea when or if the officer will be coming back. I make it to the elevator at the far end. Hit the call button.

The wait lasts forever.

The harsh buzz of strip lights illuminates the emptiness of the corridor. The effect is one of disconcerting loneliness. I'm the only person here.

The elevator doors open. Finally. I step inside.

Hospital elevators are disconcertingly spacious. When the doors close, I feel lost. I wonder why I'm not moving and then realise I haven't pressed a floor. I select the ground level, then stand against the rear wall.

When the doors open again, I expect to see a phalanx of uniformed officers waiting for me, armed with batons and scowls.

But there's no one there. It's not just my floor. The entire building is empty. Stephen King strikes again. Where's the clown ready to pop up with balloons?

We all float here, Jen.

Try not to think about it.

When I walk out of the lift and then head out towards reception, I see one. Mopping up the floors and listening to her iPod. White buds in her ears, eyes half closed as she mops in time to whatever rocks her world. I slip past, walking calmly. She doesn't notice. Maybe thinks I'm a doctor or nurse clocking out after a long shift.

Outside, the night air tries to freeze me. I stop and get my bearings.

The building is instantly recognisable.

Southern General. Or the Royal Victoria. Whatever they're calling it now.

I know I can't afford to hang around too long. I don't have a bag with me. Nothing but my clothes. I don't have it in me to try a carjacking.

So I do the next best thing.

The Battlefield Rest is nearby, I know that. Old Glaswegian Restaurant: an odd building in the middle of several oncoming roads. It's closed, of course. Meaning it's late, maybe after midnight. But the Rest resides near a populated area, and I figure enough students live in this part of the South Side that I can hail a taxi without too much difficulty.

Sure enough, with the Rest in sight I hail down a black cab. Climb in the back.

The driver gives me a glance in the rear view. I can see his eyes. They're a little suspicious, but then when he clocks me, he must think I look okay because they relax. He's in his fifties and I think maybe I've got one of Glasgow's famous talkers. Some nights, that's grand. Tonight, I really don't need it. I imagine he reads the *Sun*. Which means any minute now, he might make the connection.

Those are the risks. No one said deciding to escape police custody would be easy.

Although, so far . . .

I smile and settle back in the seat. Try and look a little blootered. Give him the address from the note.

As we drive, he starts in on a monologue about how the clubs are all getting later and later with their chucking out times, how in his day, he'd be home in bed by this time. 'And a weekday too,' he says, shaking his head. 'You students, love.'

I don't say anything, feel pretty good that he thinks I'm a student. Unless he's too polite to add the word 'mature'. But the way he keeps glancing back, I don't think so. I catch sight of a wedding ring as he turns the wheel, so I know I have a comeback if he tries anything.

But I don't think he will. He's Mr Traditional after all, telling me how things were better in the old days, despite all the advances in technology and the fact that telly's way better than it used to be.

'Nights off,' he says, 'me and the Mrs, we watch box sets. On Sky, like. Been watching that *True Detective* thing.'

'Yeah?' I say, turning my face so I'm looking out the window at the streets as they trundle by.

'Oh, it's great,' he says, not caring if I'm actually listening to him. 'I mean, I don't understand a bloody word that McConaughey guys says, but, right enough . . . You watched it?'

'Not my thing.'

'What she said,' he says. 'The wife, I mean. Not her thing either, too violent and all. Too male. Her exact words. I mean, I know men are more . . . We're more likely to be violent. Just a fact and all, but good telly's good telly. You probably watch that *Sex and the City*, aye?'

What I'm thinking about is the fact that I could show him who's more violent. If only I kept Ed's body somewhere it could be found. I could take it out, show people what us weak and feeble women are capable of, even if it's only by accident.

'I really don't watch much telly.'

'Ah,' he says. 'You're a reader. Don't have much time for books . . . Some of the other lads do, on quiet shifts. Me, I read the papers.'

I tense again, but he clearly doesn't read them close enough that he realises who I am.

I drift in and out the rest of the journey. Don't have to listen for the words. Just the pauses. The moments where he expects me to say something, even if he doesn't care what it is.

Finally, we get to Tradeston. Head down roads that are more industrial than residential. 'You sure this is where you are?' he says.

I tell him to stop.

'Look,' he says, 'this isn't the kind of pl–'

'You said you read the papers?' Dropping the drunk girl act, letting him see I mean business.

'Aye,' he says, drawing the word, sounding more than a little wary.

'My name is Jennifer Carter.'

His jaw drops. The gears in his brain start turning. 'Naw,' he says. 'No way.'

'Yes way,' I say. 'I just escaped police custody. You gave me a lift. You're going to let me out. You're going to drive away. And you're going to pretend this never happened.'

'The metre–'

'Your problem,' I say. 'And if you don't want any other problems that could be more terminal, I suggest you do what I say.'

He nods. 'You really killed all those people?'

I get out the cab.

Forty

The taxi disappears round the corner. Part of me feels guilty for what I just did. Being a bore isn't the worst thing in the world. But I had a feeling he wasn't going to let me off with not paying the fare just because I asked him to. It's not the worst crime I've committed. But now that I think about it, what's going to stop him calling the police and telling them where I am? I need to be more careful. Think forward. Stop living for the moment and consider what's coming down the line.

Too late now, of course

Guess I'd better hope it was Crawford left me that message.

The rain falls in a gentle mist. The night is cold but not freezing. There's a stillness in the air. Expectation. The city is waiting for something to happen. Holding its breath.

I allow myself a smile. There's no time for reflection. Much as I want to slow down, I know that I have to keep moving.

The streets here are poorly lit, and there could be anyone hanging in the spaces between the low-roofed buildings or behind the walls in empty car parks.

The building in front of me is a garage. The kind of place where you bring your car after everywhere else has failed that MOT. There's a sign above the display window that says, 'Cheapest Repairs in Glasgow!'

Aye, right.

I wonder where the subsidies for the work comes from, how a

place like this stays in business. It's the kind of question I might have asked idly before. Now I feel like it's the kind of question that needs to be earnest. The kind of question that demands an answer.

I walk into the forecourt and stand there.

What am I supposed to do? I look around, thinking maybe someone's watching. No sign. No movement. Not even the whirr of a camera watching me. The building might as well be dead inside.

Did I make a mistake? Did I get the wrong place?

The sound of a car approaching makes me turn. A black Lexus pulls into the forecourt. Stops right in front me. I lift my hand to shield my eyes, the headlights are turned up so bright.

Two men get out from the front doors. Two shell-suited thugs. One of them stands at the side of the car in what I think is meant to be a military pose. He thinks of himself as a soldier.

Brilliant. Men are always at their smartest when they think they're being macho.

The second shell suit heads to the rear passenger door and opens it. There's a reverence in the way he moves that's almost laughable.

The old man himself climbs out: Solomon Buchan. I can't help but think he crawled his way out of a retelling of Rumplestiltskin. The wizened face, the tiny body, the feeling that he's not entirely human.

Maybe Buchan isn't his real name. Maybe he'll ask me to guess what it is. Three times. What happens when I get it right and he stamps his foot?

Buchan nods his thanks to the thug, and then he walks towards me. Maybe he thinks this is making an entrance. Trying to intimidate me, perhaps.

It isn't working. I'm long past intimidation. I'm tired and I'm cranky and, one way or another, I just want this to be over.

I make the opening move this time. 'I did what you asked.'

'Did you?'

'Yes.'

'So why are you here?' He seems genuinely curious. He looks at me with a slight squint, as though that might help bring me into focus.

'What do you mean, "why am I here"?'

'They wouldn't let you go. They wouldn't. You should be under tight security by now. I was told they took you to the hospital. That you hurt your head while they attempted to restrain you.'

An accident, I'm sure.

There's silence for a second. Is he trying to play me? Is this all some kind of sick game to him? A continual, terrible kind of psychological torture? Showing that the young lad had it easy? That the real mercy was in having a dog rip out your throat?

Then he seems to make up his mind. His spine straightens. His eyes go clear. I see the decisiveness he showed when we first met. 'Get in the car,' he says. 'Now.'

'Are you going to kill me?'

He stays where he is. Impassive. Still.

* * *

Leather seats. From the back seat, I can see a pine freshener hanging over the rear view.

I'm on the driver's side. The leg room is impressive. I can stretch out and still not kick the rear of the seat in front. Not that I'm a giant, of course.

Buchan tries to press me on my story. 'There was a note?'

I nod. I have it on me. I wasn't stupid enough to leave it behind.

Buchan looks at it for a moment. 'I didn't send the note. I don't recognise the writing.'

'Then how did you know I was going to be at the garage?'

'You sent me a message.'

'I did?'

'By text.'

'I don't have your number.'

He doesn't say anything. But his shoulders go tense and his lips press together. I've caught him out, exposed a mistake. I imagine people have been fed to that bloody dog of his for less.

'I see.' Terse. No speeches. No proclamations. He might just be scared. Finally.

'I didn't text you,' I say again. 'And you didn't send me a note.'

'But you killed Crawford?'

'I stabbed him.'

'That doesn't mean you killed him.'

'You didn't see the blood.'

'You told him why?'

'Yes.'

'And you're sure he was dead?'

I hesitate. 'I . . .. There was a lot of blood. But honestly? There wasn't time for me to check his pulse.'

He nods. 'I'm a foolish old bastard,' he says. 'A fucking imbecile.' He's not talking to me any more.

The silence is good, though. Gives me space to think. To figure out what's going on. Why would someone go to all the trouble of making sure I escaped just to send me back to Buchan? And what was Crawford thinking when he asked me to stab him?

It's like being caught up in a wave and just pulled along. Try and struggle against it, you realise you're in even more trouble than if you just gave in.

Buchan snaps back to reality. 'Take off your clothes.'

'What?' I'm part offended, part confused.

He takes a breath and then, like he's talking to someone he considers hard of thinking: 'Take off your clothes.'

'Not without dinner and flowers,' I say.

He shakes his head. 'I need to know you're not bugged. I've been played for an eejit once this evening. It's not going to happen again. This isn't about sex or an old man wanting to see a young woman naked. This is about the fact that if you don't take off your clothes, I'm going to have to assume you have something to hide. And I'm going to have you killed.'

I shrug off my top, feeling self-conscious at not having had time to find a bra during my escape from the hospital

'Trousers,' Buchan says.

'Oh, bloody hell!'

He waits.

I struggle out of them. It takes some doing, squirming around, getting off my shoes as well. There's a lot of room in the back, but it's still awkward trying not to accidentally elbow Buchan or kick him in the face. By accident, of course.

Finally, sitting in my pants I say, 'Happy?'

Nodding, seemingly satisfied, Buchan says, 'Get dressed.' He leans forward and taps the driver on the shoulder. 'We might have company.'

'No one I can see.'

'All the same,' he says. 'Better safe than sorry.'

The car lurches down a side street. I almost fall into Buchan as I'm trying desperately to pull my trousers back on. His skin is battered leather.

He looks at me as I pull back. Maybe he's smiling. It's hard to be sure.

'What's wrong? I did what you asked me to.'

'It's a fucking set up,' he says. 'Some cunt wanted us in the same place at the same time.'

'I don't know anything about that.'

'You keep telling people you're innocent,' he says. 'And yet you tried to kill a policeman because I asked you to.'

'Because you threatened my mother.'

'And you somehow got the better of Smiley, a man who has killed at least sixteen people. This man was not an amateur. Not like the little prick we fed to Brutus. And if killing Smiley was indeed an accident, that makes you either the luckiest or the unluckiest woman in the world.' He pauses for a moment. 'Which is it, do you think?'

'Honestly? I don't know.'

Forty One

The car takes a number of sudden turns. Indicates left when it's turning right. The driver checks the rear view every time, but not to look at his passengers. He breaks speed limits for short bursts, overtakes other drivers with little or no warning.

Finally, when we leave the city, he evens out.

Buchan says, 'Loch Lomond. You know where.'

I settle back in the leather seat and close my eyes. Loch Lomond? Oh, he knows what he's doing, the wily old bugger. Maybe this is finally it. Luck only lasts so long. Except I don't feel like I've been lucky at all.

'Did he offer you anything?' Buchan asks, talking to me now. 'A deal, maybe? A reduction on sentence or–'

I don't even open my eyes. 'Like you did?'

'I was serious.'

'And he wouldn't have been?'

Buchan says nothing.

I keep my eyes closed. I'm so tired. I just want to sleep. When was the last time I really got some shut eye? Even while I was at Mum's, sleep seemed to come in fits and bursts.

'What happened to the rest of the money?' Buchan asks. His voice is the only thing that keeps me from falling completely into the darkness. 'The merchandise?'

'I don't know,' I say. My words are slurred, running together. I

213

think that I sound drunk. Maybe high. 'About the product. That was Dave. He . . .he had his own plans. Didn't want to ask.'

'And he's dead.'

'That was your man, Smiley.'

'He could be heavy handed on occasion.'

'Putting it mildly.'

'I was going to offer you his job.'

I open my eyes. Maybe I have fallen asleep. Maybe I am dreaming.

Buchan's smiling now. 'I'm serious. The thought crossed my mind, momentarily. No one should have been as lucky as you.'

I don't challenge him. What would be the point?

'To kill so many people and come away unscathed? A man might think you had a talent.'

'How many women assassins are there?' I say. 'Outside of stupid Hollywood movies?'

He nods. 'More than you'd think. More than people would suspect. And "assassin" is such an ugly term. Smiley wasn't an assassin. He was a collector. He had the fine art of persuasion about him. He killed more people during his time on the armed forces than he did working with me.'

I figured Smiley for ex-army. Something about the way he walked. Had a date with a soldier once. It ended poorly. The guy had been too intense for me. Maybe just the way he was, maybe the things he'd seen, but I remembered the look in his eyes and now I think about it, Smiley had the same look. But worse.

'He was part of a special unit working to gather information. Which sounds like a dull job for a man like Smiley. Except what he did was extract information from people. People who didn't want to talk. I think you know what I mean.'

I get the picture. Enhanced interrogation techniques is the phrase that comes into my head.

'When he returned home – he was drummed out on a

dishonourable discharge – he found that he no longer fitted into the world. A man with his talents was little use as a civilian.'

'So you offered him a job?'

'I'm not the bad guy here. What I do isn't about being evil or cruel. It's about taking advantage of other people's stupidity or weaknesses.'

'You need to work on the sales pitch,' I say.

Buchan doesn't rise to the bait. 'It's rare for women to work in the profession, but not unheard of. Especially now. I didn't get to where I am by not adapting to the times. I thought, for a moment, you had the potential.'

'And now?'

He shrugs.

So I answer for him. 'Now you see what I really am? Just someone who got in over their head.'

'Yes.'

'What happens?'

'I feel responsible, you know,' he says.

I don't care. 'What happens?'

'It won't hurt. It'll be quick. I'm not a man to hold a grudge.'

'Uh-huh.'

'I know you don't have the money. I know you don't have the drugs. I know you didn't mean to kill Smiley. I didn't want to kill anyone. Even Ed. Even Crawford. That's on you.'

'You still did it, though.'

'Or tried to.'

'But now you're in too deep. You're a real problem for me. I don't know if you've betrayed me to Crawford . . .'

'What is it between you two, anyway?'

'Personal.'

Not the answer I was hoping for, but probably as much as I'll get.

'What about my mum?'

'She'll be looked after.'

'Aye?'

'Aye.'

I close my eyes again. Okay, okay, that's fine. That's absolutely fine.

The car rolls to a stop. We're near the loch. I look out and see a hotel. Buchan says, 'This is where I get out.'

'Right.'

'Deniability.'

'Right.'

'These two lads,' he says, gesturing to the two men in the front seats, 'whatever they do next, it's up to them.'

'Okay.'

'But it'll be quick. I promise.' He actually reaches out and touches my shoulder. I try not to recoil.

He doesn't care whether I die hurting or not. Just as long as I'm gone and no longer a pain in his side.

He puts a hand on my knee. 'I'm just sorry, doll,' he says.

Not as sorry as I am.

He waits as the thug in the passenger seat gets out of the car. Buchan believes in protocol. That much is becoming clear. His power doesn't just come from who he is, but the way he acts. Maybe that's half the battle for men like him. It's not about the blood on their hands or the terrible things they do. No, it's whether they can make other people believe in those things.

Is being a hard man just like everything else in life? A confidence game?

The door opens. Buchan gets out. He makes sure I can hear him when he speaks to the thug. 'Make it quick. All right? And make sure they can identify her body. Any word of rough stuff, I'll take it out your fucking hide.'

Oh, yes. He's all heart.

Forty Two

When the car starts up again, I lean forward, between the front seats. The shell-suit twins don't make eye contact with me or each other. Eyes on the road. I might as well not even exist.

Typical bloody men.

'You could just let me go,' I say. 'Who's going to know?'

They still don't say anything.

The one on the left has softer features. I think he might be younger. He's chubbier than his friend. If you met him on the street and he wasn't getting in your face, you'd think he looked friendly. He's got this bald teddy bear thing going on. If it wasn't for his eyes and the hardness in there, I'd think he was cute.

'Come on,' I say, determined to get a response. 'Believe me, I don't want anyone to know I'm alive. I'm not going to the police. I'd be an idiot to try and get revenge on your boss.'

Still nothing.

One more try. 'He wants me gone, that's all.'

'Nut,' the Teddy Bear says.

One word. A tsunami of force behind it.

I sit back. 'So how are you going to do it? Kill me, I mean.' Doing my best to sound bored and accepting.

My heart is beating though. Maybe I'll get lucky and have a coronary. Or a blood vessel in my brain will burst. All that's happened lately, it's not impossible.

'Don't fucking worry,' the driver says. 'Just shut up and it'll be done with.'

'Aye,' Teddy Bear agrees. An erudite man, then. Jesus.

'So what happens now that Smiley's dead, anyway? Which one of you two lucky men gets his old job?'

'That prick?' Teddy Bear says, and it's suddenly clear that he can talk. 'He was a fuckin piss artist. Had the boss all hooked on his bloody war stories.' In words of more than one syllable, too. Three might be pushing it, but there's hope.

'How he interrogated these fucking Iraqi insurgents and shit,' the driver adds. 'All this bollocks like he was Jack Bauer. Wasn't even fit to lick the Jack's shoes, like.'

'Aye,' Teddy Bear says. 'Prick.' Back to one.

But they've told me a lot about how they viewed Smiley. So maybe there's another way I can get them to rethink the whole killing me and dumping the body thing.

'You know I killed him?' I say.

The two of them laugh at that. 'By fuckin luck!' the driver says.

Teddy Bear turns round though. His forehead creases a little. I think he might actually be falling for it 'How'd it happen? Like, exactly how did the arsewipe die?'

'Maybe,' I say, 'I'll tell you, if you let me call my mum.'

Baby steps. Get them to do one favour, then maybe another. And another. Sooner or later, they'll let me live.

Right?

The atmosphere drops. Teddy Bear turns back round. I get this sick feeling in my stomach and my throat. Something's wrong. All the calm and acceptance I've built up drops away. I think about when Ed once casually suggested, in the middle of sex, that we call Caroline and ask her to join us. It's the same kind of sudden freeze, only I'm seeing it from the other side, this time.

'Hey,' I say, 'I just want to say goodbye to her. She's my mum.'

Teddy Bear looks uncomfortable. I can see his reflection in

218

the front window. Boys and their mums. It can be a touchy subject.

'Nah,' he says.

'Just one–'

'I said fucking no!' He turns and bares his teeth. A predator ready to rip the throat out of its prey.

I think of Brutus, ripping out Michael's throat.

Something's wrong. It's a feeling more than anything, but I know it's more than simple paranoia. 'She's dead,' I say, quietly. Don't even think it before I speak. Only after the words are out there do I realise what I said. 'Oh, Jesus. She's dead.'

'Look,' Teddy Bear starts to say. He knows. He knows. The bastard.

Did I expect Buchan to be a man of his word? He murdered his way to the top of the criminal chain even though everyone knew who and what he was. Did I think he did that by keeping his word? Honour among thieves? Maybe. But not gangsters.

I reach forward and claw my fingers against the side of Teddy Bear's face, reaching round from behind his seat. I've never been one for long nails. Was never that kind of girly girl. But even short nails are enough to do damage. Especially if you get the eyes.

I get the eyes. Pull him back against the headrest and press against his screwed-tight lids with my middle fingers.

He squeals, high pitched and pathetic. Kicks out into the footwell as though he can push himself away from the attack, and flails his arms.

His friend hits the brakes.

I let go of Teddy Bear and he flies forward.

And then I do something I don't expect. I relax. My heartrate slows. I let go of Teddy bear and just flop back as though we're heading off for a nice Sunday drive.

Air bags deploy in the front seat.

I let my body move with the momentum.

I think that this is what Zen must feel like.

The car crunches against something on my side, and the weight tips. The feeling of floating disappears and gravity does its work fast. I crack against the side door, shoulder first. A dull kind of pain. Nothing's broken. I'll be bruised, is all.

I blink a few times in the quiet aftermath.

Did that really just happen?

I gather my thoughts, take a look in the front of the car. The two of them are still in their seats. The driver is slumped forward against the airbag, his face turned to the side. Eyes closed. There's blood on his face. Maybe his nose is broken. He's breathing though.

Same with Teddy Bear. He's bounced back off the bag, and you might believe he was sleeping if it wasn't for the blood. His mouth hangs open and I can see he's missing his front teeth.

They're alive, at least.

I shove the door open and scramble into the night. No street-lights. The only illumination comes from the headlights that illuminate the ditch where we swerved, and the road ahead.

My legs struggle for a few moments, and my vision keeps blur-ring, but I force myself to keep going.

I might be able to follow the road. But I know that's the worst idea I could have. Maybe the light will be better, but the same goes for anyone who might be trying to follow me.

The trees provide cover and darkness. I might be blind as a bat, but if the ugly twins recover in time to follow me, they will be too.

Great plan.

There's a noise, but it's irrelevant. I think it sounds like the clicking of a lock. It doesn't matter.

When did I start to think like this? When did I become this woman?

I feel a pressure on my ankles. A pair of hands grasping at me, tugging my feet back.

My centre of gravity fails.

I crash into wet grass and mud. Face first. My cheek strikes something hard and smooth. A rock half buried in the earth. My teeth bite down sharply into my tongue. I taste blood. My head swims. I roll over.

There are hands on my body. They grip my shoulders. A heavy weight presses on me.

Teddy Bear's clambering on top of me. He's heavy. Suffocatingly so. 'Bitch,' he says.

In the half light, I can make out the cut on the side of his head, the blood streaming down his face. His nose is bleeding too. His eyes are wide with anger and maybe even a little concussion. Not that it matters to him. He's angry. It's all he can think about.

'Bitch.'

His hands move from my shoulders, grab at my neck. His fingers are thick. I think of sausages in the butcher's window. The one down on Byres Road.

Focus, Jen. Focus.

He's too big. Too heavy.

And I'm tired. Finally, I think I've reached my limits.

He's enjoying this too much as he presses his weight down on me and increases the tightness of those fingers around my neck.

I grab at his arms, but it's a half-hearted effort. A reflex. I can't seem to get a grip, my fingers sliding against the disgusting shell suit. My fingers have no strength. I can't stop this.

I'm sorry, Mum.

I'm sorry.

My hand flops useless. Fingertips brush the smooth wet stone.

Mum.

I think about her face, the last time I saw her. The disappointment. She loved me because I was her daughter and yet she loathed who I had become.

Mum.

221

Was it like this? His hands around her neck? The world blacking out at the sides, narrowing to this blood red pinhole of vision, her strength sapping to the point where it seemed harder to resist than to simply die?

Mum.

Was it Teddy Bear who killed her? Or just someone like him? I can't see Buchan getting actual blood on his hands. All the deaths he's responsible for, he's made sure that someone else did the deed on his behalf.

Mum.

The stone. I can feel it. Smooth, loose in the mud.

My fingers flex. I can fit it in my hand.

One last movement.

I grip. I tug. The stone schlups from the wet ground. I follow through, smacking the side of his face that's already bleeding. Something cracks in the night. Not a gunshot, but a sharp, snapping sound that could be mistaken for a rifle firing somewhere.

Teddy bear falls off me.

Not dead or unconscious. Stunned. He groans. Rolls in the mud, like a bear that's been caught by a hunter's bullet.

I scrabble away from him, still holding the stone.

His friend is still in the car.

Good.

I don't care if he's dead or alive. He's not my problem.

I stand over Teddy Bear, holding the rock.

He looks up at me. I say, 'Is she dead?'

He groans. His eyes start to roll back into his skull.

'Is she dead?'

'Yes.' The word comes out thick and heavy.

I don't think about what I'm doing. That empty feeling settles in my chest again. The one I had before I killed Smiley. After I saw the life leave Ed's eyes. Maybe it's a survival instinct. Maybe it's something everyone shares. Maybe it's always been inside me,

222

just waiting for an excuse to come out: my inner psychopath.

Teddy Bear smiles. Shows off those missing teeth. God alone knows why. And maybe not even Him.

Good.

I don't think this needs to be real. The more unreal it is the better. I can finish this if I don't believe in it.

I'm aware – dimly – of the sound of an engine cutting out. Another car?

There's a light from somewhere too, behind me. It serves to illuminate Teddy Bear. I think maybe I'm going crazy. Maybe this is the light of God or something, a way of justifying myself.

'Jennifer . . .'

I hold the rock high.

Teddy Bear's eyes go wide and he looks past me, as though seeing his own salvation.

'Jennifer . . .' The voice is familiar, but distant. It's not Teddy Bear. For a start my name has three syllables, and he's never gone above two.

'Jennifer . . .'

I smash the rock down hard.

Mum.

His cheek bones give way beneath the force of my attack. Something splats onto my shoe. I lift the rock again. Once is not enough.

Fingers wrap round my wrist.

I don't resist.

223

Forty Three

I let go of the rock and get to my feet. Turn round. Nice and slow. The fingers gripping my wrist let go. Cautiously.

I blink to bring the man behind me into focus.

Crawford.

Of course it's him.

'You look well,' I say. 'For a dead man.'

'HR wanted me to take time off.' He's walking funny, as though trying to keep pressure off his left side. Makes sense, given what happened. All the same, something doesn't feel right.

'I stabbed you,' I say. 'I saw the blood. Now, less than a day later . . .'

He grins. 'It wasn't so bad.'

'And you're so dedicated to the job?'

'Had to see this through.' He might be smiling. Hard to tell in the half light. 'No, there was a reason I wanted you to stab me there. Kind of a risk, but . . . You didn't really hurt me. I was wearing a stab-proof vest. The blood was in a bag. I wanted it to look real. For the cameras. I knew Buchan had people inside.'

'Doesn't seem like official procedure to me.'

'You're right. But I never was too good at being that kind of policeman. Why do you think I was demoted? This thing with Buchan, it's not going to be won by people who do things the right way. I'm just sorry you got caught up in it. But this kind of thing, it's getting to be a habit. You know I'm the reason your friend Katherine did her disappearing act?'

'You sent someone in undercover. Her boyfriend, he was working for you all along. But the operation imploded.'

'How much did Buchan tell you?'

'Oh,' I say. 'Enough to know that you seem to be the kind of man who makes big decisions that spiral out of control.'

He nods. 'Aye, well,' he says.

Looking past him, back to the road, I can see police officers pulling the driver from the overturned car.

How the hell did I walk away from that?

What's happened to me? What have I become?

'We were supposed to catch the old man in your company,' Crawford says. 'Make a case from the fact that he offered you protection after you stabbed me on his orders.'

'Right.'

'It was a desperate move,' he says. 'And I know it doesn't seem like it would end well for you. But given that you didn't actually kill me and that you were acting under duress–'

I wave my hand. I don't really care for explanations.

I've been pushed around too easily in recent months. By other people. By fate or destiny or whatever. All my decisions have been taken out of my hands. And now, I just want my life back.

'You sent me the note, then?'

'It wasn't supposed to go like this . . .' He looks at Teddy Bear, now lying completely still in the mud. I think he's still breathing. But honestly, I don't know that I care too much either way.

'I was protecting myself.'

'You could have run.'

'He would have followed.'

'You were about to beat his brains out with a rock.' He pauses, looks at me, biting down gently on his lower lip. 'And if I hadn't stopped you, I think you might have been okay with doing it, too.'

225

I glance down at the Teddy Bear's body. He's not moving. I don't know if he's breathing. I don't really care, either.

'Do you ever think,' I say, 'that we're all just one bad decision away from being public enemy number one?'

He doesn't say anything.

'Seriously,' I say. 'All my life, I've been a good girl. Held down a steady job. Eaten all the shite that life has thrown at me and kept smiling. Then I make one mistake. And that led to another. And another.'

'One mistake,' he says, 'could have been forgiven.'

'Not one like that.'

I think about Ed's corpse. I can barely remember what he was like when I was alive. Whenever I think about him now, all I see are glassy eyes, maybe that last gasp as his lungs filled with blood. I think about the knife in his sternum. I think about him pulling it out.

'It's everything that happened after,' Crawford says. 'Getting rid of the body. Keeping the cash. Selling the drugs.'

I shake my head. 'That was Dave.'

'You were complicit,' he says. 'Criminal conspiracy, I'd call it. You were the one who agreed to the plan. I'm still not sure you weren't the one made the decision to dump the body. Even if you got Dave to do the hacksaw job.'

'I wasn't in my right mind.'

'You covered up the evidence. You didn't come forward. Even after you escaped from Buchan's boys, you could have come in and told us the truth. Things would have been bad, sure. But now they're a whole lot worse.'

I laugh. Can't help it. It's not hysteria. Something more calm than that: a mocking, nearly cruel sound.

Is that really what I sound like? I was always a good girl. Never even swore when I didn't have to. To use those words, to throw them at a man like Crawford who's so convinced of his own righteousness makes me feel oddly free. It's maybe the only real freedom I have left.

'So what happens now? I turn myself in? Get arrested? Go to jail? Do I get protection inside because of what I've done to Buchan and his people? Huh? Tell me, Detective Crawford . . . What happens now?'

'Now,' he says, 'we try and fix this. Together.' He knows the right way to emphasise his words. Has this tone that makes me think of a friend who just has your best interests at heart. Even looking at his face, I might convince myself that he really does want what's best for me. That there could still be a way to make everything work out for the best.

But he just watched me kill a man. Or at least attempt to. There's no coming back. And for all his sweet talking, Crawford knows it too.

For the first time since I killed Ed, I have no excuse for what I've done.

So . . .

Do I give in?

Do I run?

Make a decision, Jen. Before someone else makes it for you.

I look again at the man on the ground. I think about Mum. What he did to her. I've had my revenge, right? That's the end of this, surely? Except it's not. I don't know that Teddy Bear was the one who killed Mum. I don't know if he ever met her. All I know is that I was thinking of her when I killed him, and that he might as well have been the killer.

That's no way to go about things.

No way to think.

I haven't taken my revenge at all.

My mum used to repeat old phrases she heard from her mum. One of those, whenever she opened a bottle of wine and took just a wee glass, was *in for a penny, in for a pound*, as she always uttered right before the second swally that filled her glass near to the brim.

A Mum glass.

In for a penny.

I've come this far.

In for a pound.

What's there to stop me from going further? I'll never live with myself if I don't try. No matter what happens, I'm going to be treated as a killer, a murderer. The papers have already condemned me. The public too. And for all that he's trying to sound like he's my friend, I know that Crawford considers me to be on the wrong side of the law.

We look at each other across this tiny slip of wild grass.

My back is to the shadows. His to the light.

He starts to say something. I see his lips move. Whatever it is, I don't want to listen. If I do, I might not be able to keep going. I might just give in completely.

'Je–'

I turn and run. Into the dark.

PART FIVE

YOU ONLY LIVE TWICE

Forty Four

I stick to the thickest trees and the darkest shadows.

I hear police officers following me. Sometimes their torch beams slice through the dark, and I make out snatches of words and conversation.

I think of the mushers in the opening of Jack London's *White Fang*. Hunted. Pursued. The predators relentless and seemingly never-ending. Sooner or later, you're going to be eaten. But especially if you turn and fight.

I follow what I think is the line of the road, doubling back the way we came. But it's hard to tell precisely where I am. I need to stay deep in the woods as I can, taking cover behind trees and under bushes, moving fast and low.

I think of school. My final year, an outward bound course at Ardeonaig. They split us into groups, sent us off on an orienteering challenge. The idea was to meet at a bothy where we would then spend the night. My group got lost, wandered four miles off the edge of the map.

Guess who was in charge of the compass?

The men's voices echo. I can't tell where they are. Their words bounce and distort off the trunks of trees.

Looking back will get me killed.

Even if I feel fingers – or worse, claws – grasp at my ankles, I need to keep going. My instinct is what will save me. It has kept me alive so far. No reason to think that's about to change.

Don't think, Jen. Just do.

The voices get quieter. Further away. They're losing me.

Losing me.

I think they've lost me.

My heart rate slows. I have no idea how far I've come. My lungs are the kind of cold that burns, and I keep gripping at the trunks of trees to stay upright. The adrenaline burst from earlier is wearing off.

The comedown has begun.

I spy the road through the trees to my left. The sound of an engine approaching. Lights heading my way. More police? Following the tree line where they think I've gone?

Maybe. Maybe not.

I take the chance. *Trust your instincts, Jen.* Head where the trees and the grass thin, in full view of the road. The headlights get closer.

I step out.

Hitchhiking isn't a thing in Scotland. Maybe because the country's small enough that no one needs to arse themselves hiking out a thumb, or maybe because we're a bunch of dour cynics who worry about letting strangers into our vehicles.

But still, the car slows. Stops beside me. A people carrier. Silver. Man at the wheel in his late fifties or early sixties, with a white beard and hair that's thinning but still dark. I think of a well-groomed Santa Claus. He peers at me over the top of his glasses.

'Are you okay?'

'My car broke down. I was trying to talk back to—'

'Do you need a lift?'

I nod, gratefully. 'I'm heading to the West End,' he says.

'The centre's fine.'

'You're sure?'

I hop in the passenger's side. 'Thanks,' I say.

'You don't have a phone?' He starts driving again. Keeps looking at me every few seconds like he half-expects me to turn psycho. I've done that once already tonight, though. Twice would be too much.

'No,' I say. 'Well, yes, but . . .the battery's dead.'

He shakes his head. 'Bad to worse.'

'Oh, aye.'

'We've all had days like that.'

Silence settles. I don't mind. I don't want him to talk. Just drive. He seems quite content. Reaches down and turns up the volume on the CD. 'You don't mind?'

I shake my head. The music's fine. Serves as a distraction. Old-time blues. The kind you hear late at night in jazz clubs. Ed took me to a jazz club once. Bloody terrible. I faked a headache to get out. This stuff's not so bad, though. There's words at least. And a painful melancholy to the singer's voice that threatens to move me to tears.

Soon enough, we hit the edge of the city. The streetlights flash yellow above us. I feel a weight in my body that dully hints at tiredness. I try to think of the last time I slept. I can't remember. I've been awake over twenty-four hours now. Running on adrenaline and fear.

Here in the car with the music humming, the heating gently warming my body, it would be easy to close my eyes and just drift away.

So easy.

* * *

'Where do you need dropped off?'

I sit bolt upright. As though time has skipped forward and suddenly I have no frame of reference. I struggle to think of an answer. 'Um . . .'

'It's okay. You were asleep. Like you say, long day. Where do you need dropped off?'

I almost say, 'Queen Street,' but there's more chance of me being recognised in a high-traffic area. I need to be smart. Without being suspicious.

'Just . . .just near Charing Cross.'

'You're sure?'

I nod, blink a few times to try and get the sleep out of my eyes. 'Yes, yes. Aye, its fine.'

He drops me by the Mitchell Library, but even when I get out the car, he seems concerned. 'Honestly,' I say. 'It's fine. It's fine.'

As he drives off, I make to cross the road towards Charing Cross station. When he's out of sight, I double back and head to a wee pub round the back of the library. It's the kind of pub where the craft beer comes with a big red T on the pump and where gourmet cooking is beans on toast. It's the kind of place where nobody knows your name. Fine by me.

There's a woman on the bar, maybe five-five both lengthways and round her stomach. She's got a cloth over her shoulder. She regards me with half-closed eyes when I take a seat at the bar. I don't think it's because she recognises me. More, it's because she wonders what a girl like me is doing coming through the doors of her establishment without an escort. Judging by her expression, the word *escort* is at the front of her mind when she sees me.

Okay, that's the edited version of the word she's thinking.

'White wine,' I say.

She gets the drink, keeps her eye on me the whole time.

'Do I know you?'

I freeze. My back stiffens. My fingers flex. 'I don't . . .'

'Naw, naw, you just have one of those faces, right?' Is she toying with me? Hard to tell. Just act casual.

I nod and shrug, like this kind of thing happens all the time.

Keep it nice and light. Friendly. *Stay on her good side, Jen. You need all the friends you can get.*

I pay for the wine and let it sit in front of me for a moment. I look at it, think about how a few months ago I wouldn't be have even crossed the threshold of this place.

It's about taking control. I've been running this whole time. Afraid to turn around. Afraid because I know the chances are good that the wolves will eat me alive.

But what's the alternative? Keep running and hope that I'll be saved? That, once again, my life will be taken out of my hands?

No.

It's time to take charge.

I down the wine in one. The woman behind the bar looks at me with those pencilled eyebrows raised high. I don't care.

The wine tastes sharp and vinegary, like it's at the end of its life. I hope that's not a sign.

I walk out of the pub. Knowing where I need to go. What I need to do.

Hoping I can see it through.

Forty Five

I no longer have the card he gave me. But I remember where he lives, what Ed told me about his business, and what he said to me as I left. *No judgement here. Just service.* Well, let's see what the service is really like. Because if I'm going to take control, I need some very specialised assistance.

When he answers, his eyes go wide and his jaw drops. Maybe he's smarter than I gave him credit for. Maybe my new look isn't as convincing as I'd believed.

'You know who I am?'

'Ed's girl.'

'You know what happened?'

'Aye, aye.'

'Then let me in.'

Once I'm inside, he triple locks the door. No chances taken. He looks me up and down and says, 'Did you really do it?'

'Do what?'

'Kill all those people? Kill Ed?'

'I killed Ed.'

'Aye, aye. And the rest?'

I don't say anything. Responsibility seems a slippery concept now. I'm not sure whose deaths are on my hands and whose aren't.

We're in the kitchen. It's a big room, coated with dust, grease and age. Chris lives on take-outs. Boxes and papers everywhere.

No sign the room is used for its intended purpose. I doubt the oven works anyway. Doubt much in this place works.

'What do you want?' He comes out, direct. He's trying not to look scared. Failing. I remember the first time I met him, I couldn't figure out how he did the things he did, dealt with the people he had to deal with.

'Ed said you can find things for people.'

'Aye, aye.'

'Like when I came here, you had what he was looking for.'

'I know people. Someone gave me a bag,' he said. 'Could have been flour, for all I know. I gave you the bag because they gave me the bag . . .'

'And I gave the bag to Ed because Ed asked you for the bag.' Maybe the reason he's been at this work so long is his paranoia. 'Look, Chris, I'm not here to mess you about or to get you in trouble or to kill you.'

'Aye, aye. Good. Good.'

'But I need something from you. For old time's sakes.'

'Old times? I barely know you. We met a grand total of once. Two days later, you killed your boyfriend. A month after, you're the most wanted woman in Scotland.'

I look around the kitchen. Okay, he doesn't cook here, but he has a few things lying around like maybe he intends to. A few knives and forks. And a blender that looks like it could explode if anyone dared plug it in. A microwave so covered in gunk it's a miracle if anyone ever manages to open the door, never mind turn the damned thing on.

My eyes fall on the set of kitchen knives in a wooden block. Heavy black handles. Hints of sharp blades beneath. Never used, never given the opportunity to dull their edges. I sidle over to them, hope that Chris doesn't realise what's going on.

He watches me, but doesn't put two and two together.

I pull on the biggest handle. The blade slides out.

Now the pieces fall into place.

'Whoa, whoa!' Chris says, backing away from me. Arms outstretched, face turned away.

I don't overtly threaten him. Just walk forward casually. Match the speed at which he backs away from me. Make sure he sees the knife.

The female of the species . . . Oh, aye, he bloody well believes it too.

'Chris,' I say. 'One way or another, you know I'll pay whatever you need. But right now I need you to trust me. And do me a wee favour.'

'Look, whatever it is, I don't think drugs are–'

'Not drugs. Or lawyers. Or money.'

'Then?'

'Guns.'

'Guns?'

'Aye. I don't care what kind of gun, as long as I can point and shoot the bastard.'

'Okay,' he says. 'Okay. But . . .look, surely this has all gone a bit–'

'Chris!' He jumps at the sound of his own name. 'Chris, you need to just shut up and talk to whoever it is you need to talk to. I need all of this tonight.'

'Right.'

'And if you try and mess me about . . .' I hold up the knife. 'Well, you know what happened to Ed.'

'Uh-huh.'

'And the policewoman.'

'Uh-huh.'

'And the other guys.'

'I watch the news, all right? I'm no fucking stupid!'

'Except for letting me through the door after knowing what I've done.'

'Aye, aye.' He sounds resigned.

'Long as we understand each other.'

'Aye, aye, we do! 'Sakes!' He straightens up, tries to put this expression on his face, this slant to his walk like he knew all along I wasn't going to hurt him, like he was just playing along. 'And you're good for the–?'

I raise the knife and step forward.

He backs away. 'Course you are,' he says. 'Stupid fuckin question! It's been a long night, okay? Look, I'll do what I can, yeah?'

He starts to leave the room.

'Chris!'

He stops. Turns round. His eyes wide with fear.

'Have you got anything to drink in this place?'

* * *

The kid who comes round looks like he's barely out of primary school, never mind old enough to handle the kind of cash he's asking for. His name is Runt. Guess I see why.

He sits on the ratty sofa in Chris's front room, and keeps looking up at me with this odd leer that belongs to a man six times his age. He wears an Adidas top that's seen better days, loose tracksuit bottoms and trainers that gleam so white they could light his way at night.

'Like that you see?' he says. I try and ignore the double entendre he makes explicit in his tone.

I look at the spread on the coffee table. Have to say that I do. Handguns, mostly. But there's one that attracts my attention. 'What's that?'

'Aw, doll,' he says, displaying those yellow teeth. 'Now you're talking.' He picks up the gun. It's compact but deadly looking: all sharp angles and squares. 'Ruger MP-9, born in the good ol' US-of-A.' He holds it up with one hand. 'Don't worry, it's not loaded.'

I'm not worried. He looks young, but to have these kind of connections, I figure he has to know what he's doing.

'See this,' he says, letting me see the tiny switch on the side of the weapon. 'That's yer safety. Three positions.'

'Three?'

'Back like this,' he says, showing me, 'is yer safety. Then click it once for single shot.'

'Single shot?'

'These babies pack a punch,' he says. 'If you don't know what you're doing.' He looks up at me as though reaching a decision. 'And I'd say, well, you don't know what you're doing. Don't get many birds asking for guns, know what I mean?'

This 'bird' decides she's not going to put her hands round his scrawny neck.

'And finally,' he clicks the switch to the final position, 'ye're at full auto. Bam-bam-bam-bam.' He holds out the gun for me to take. 'Have a feel.'

I take it gingerly. He's trying not to laugh. I probably look pretty scared to him. My heart is thumping and my hands are slick with sweat. My cheeks burn up like they're ready to burst into flames.

Maybe this is a bad idea.

'Hold it,' the lad says.

'What?'

'Hold it, get a feel for it.' He raises his hands in mock surrender. 'Just don't point it at me is all.'

I twist my body to the side and slip one hand around the forward handle while supporting it at the rear with the other.

'Right, right,' the lad says. 'You want to support it . . .like this.' He slips behind me, reaches round to help me balance the extended butt against my shoulder. I can see along the body of the weapon. 'You can see now?'

'Okay,' I say. I try not to think about how much he's enjoying this close contact.

240

'See,' he says, still too close so I can feel his too-hot breath against the lobe of my right ear. 'You let the butt press against your shoulder. Aye? That way you can absorb the ricochet a wee bit, steady yourself when you come to fire the bastard.'

I lower the weapon, shrug him off. He only comes back to sit in front of me with reluctance. I try my best not to shiver, the creepy wee toerag.

'There's ammo, I guess?'

'Aye, aye, all in the package. You interested?'

'This thing, it will kill someone?'

'When you absolutely, positively gottae kill every motherf–'

I hold up a hand. 'I get it,' I say. Last thing I have any time for is some wee nyaf doing an impression of Samuel L Jackson.

'Aye, aye. So it's all paid for, anyway. Whatever it is you're doing for our wee pal, it's got to be worth something, aye?' That leer again.

'You're too young,' I say.

'Twenty-six, sweetheart.'

'Sod off.'

He puts his hand on his chest and closes his eyes. 'Swear to the Almighty His-self, may He strike me down if I lie.' He drops the hand and looks right at me. 'Growth hormone deficiency. But believe me, darling, I'm a man where it counts.'

I ignore the innuendo. 'Do you gift wrap?'

He hesitates. 'Huh?'

Okay, so not that smart. 'Never mind. That, plus some ammo. As much as you can spare.' I look at the table. 'And the Glock.'

'You planning on going to war?'

I don't say anything.

'Hey,' he says. 'Cannae blame a man for being intrigued by a beautiful woman who likes her weaponry.'

'Aye,' I say. 'A beautiful woman not afraid to shoot the balls off men she thinks are creeping her.'

241

He backs off. 'No chance of a coffee, then?'

'No chance.'

He stands up. 'Goodbye hug?'

He has to settle for my middle finger aimed right at him.

Forty Six

I raise the rifle and press the extended butt against my shoulder. Squint down the sightlines. Breathe in. Out.

This is more than dangerous now. I know that. But once you're in, you're in all the way. This is about taking revenge against the people who destroyed my life, who made me do things I would never otherwise have dreamed of doing.

Sure, I conspired with Dave to hide Ed's corpse. But everything else was out of my control.

The girl who looks back at me from the other side of the mirror has been through the wars. She's not wearing any make up. Her blouse is blackened with dirt and sweat. Her jeans are tired. You can see the wrinkles around her eyes that were never there before. Not even forty, the lines shouldn't be so deep. She has this way of standing I don't recognise, a kind of who-gives-a-shite cock to the hips. Hard to tell if it's a new-found confidence or covering for a lack.

'You talkin to me?'

I laugh, and lower the weapon.

There's a knock at the bedroom door. Timid. Hesitant. 'Jen?'

I put the gun down on the bed and let Chris in. He scuttles everywhere. In another life, he could have been Renfield from *Dracula*.

There I go, still the bookseller. Thinking in books.

Maybe that's how I'm keeping my sanity: thinking of everything that happens to me in terms of some kind of narrative.

I am the heroine of my own story.

Except there's no guarantee I'm always going to make the right choice or come out smelling of roses. There's no way back to my old life. In the real world, the status quo never returns.

'What do you want?'

'This is a bad idea,' Chris says.

'You don't know what I'm planning to do.'

'Naw, naw,' he says. 'I have an idea.'

'You really don't.'

'You're going to kill someone,' he says. 'Even money says it's Buchan.' He's a twitchy bastard, but I get the feeling there might be some human feelings in him. Living out here in this place, having that twitch, that way of speaking that I'm sure is trying to hide a bad stutter, I think is just a way to survive. People trust him with things like drugs or guns or deals because he's harmless, because they know he won't make grab for power. He's reliable, and easily scared. Maybe he even likes what he does. He's the middle man. The one taking all the risks but gaining none of the glory. Still, there's got to be a satisfaction there. He's like a retail assistant, I guess. But this isn't the corporate world, and the risks involved in upsetting a customer are far more permanent than a docking of pay or a cessation of employment.

I sit down on the bed. He keeps standing. Nervous to be in the same room. He has that hurried look on his face, like he shouldn't be in a room alone with a girl. Makes him seem younger than he is.

I say, 'If I did plan on killing Buchan, would you think I was stupid?'

'Suicidal.'

'Okay,' I say. 'But, you know . . .sometimes . . .a girl's gotta do what a girl's gotta do.'

That gets a smile.

'It's not going to come back to you, if that's what you're worried about.'

'Naw, naw.' He starts to pick at his fingernails. They're ragged from years of this habit. I get the impression that once he starts, he'll pick and chew until they bleed.

'Then you're okay with me being here for a few days? Until the documents come through.'

'He's good for them.'

'Your wee friend?'

'Aye, aye.' He starts biting down on a chewed-off nail between his front teeth. Then he spits it out, absent-mindedly.

'Chris?'

He stops gnawing at the tips of his fingers and looks at me with wide eyes. I think of the dog we used to have on the farm when I was wee. The way it stopped when you called its name, looked at you like it wasn't sure whether you were going to praise it or give it a ticking off.

It.

Listen to me, the way I'm thinking now.

He.

Wishbone, he was called. Don't know why. Had that name long before I came on the scene. I should have asked Mum and Dad, but I never thought to. There were a lot of things I should have asked them. When Dad died, I had the same regrets, but at least Mum was there if I ever needed to know anything.

But now she's gone too. There are so many things I should have asked her and talked to her about. So many of them are trivial too. That's the kicker. Not the big questions. All the little ones. Those are what you regret not having asked.

'What?'

245

I realise I haven't said anything for a few moments, suddenly lost in my own thoughts. Bad sign. Bad move. 'I just . . . Thanks.'

'Aye, aye,' he says. 'No problem.'

* * *

When I wake up, loose springs dig into my side. I'm still fully dressed, thin covers wrapped tight around me like a cocoon. For a few moments, as I try to remember where I am, the world feels oddly normal. Like the last month or so has been a bad dream I might shake off when I manage to wake up completely.

But the sinking feeling in my stomach reminds me of the truth.

I ignore the dread, sit up and swing my legs over the edge of the bed. The bare floorboards are rough, and I remember to slip on a pair of socks before risking splinters.

With the sun coming in through the windows, the spare bedroom doesn't look so bad. Put in some half-decent furnishing and give the place a good clean, it could be a halfway comfortable space.

It helps to tell myself that, anyway.

I get up and stretch. I sit cross-legged on the manky old rug I made Chris pull out of a cupboard for me. Before all this kicked off, I'd been doing yoga as a way of relaxing my body. With the house in silence, I close my eyes and recall the routine, stretching my way through and focusing on nothing except the movement of my body and the rhythm of my breathing.

Breathing is important. I know it will keep me calm when I finally confront Buchan. What that plan is, I'm still not sure, but the gun on the bed will help.

And after that?

There's a good chance I'll be killed. The old bastard has lived this long going up against the meanest, baddest psychopaths that gangland Glasgow can throw at him. I'm just a wee girl in over her head with some weird idea that I can get close enough to pull the trigger. He'd laugh if he knew what I was planning.

I'd laugh if I stop to think about it.

But I have to try.

When I'm done with the yoga, I look at myself in the mirror. The glass is greasy, and my features are obscured by dust and greasy marks. All the same, I look okay. I need a shower, maybe. But I'm putting that off as long as I can. Hot water is a minor miracle in Chris's place. Nothing to do with him paying the bills, but more that this place is rotting from the inside out. The guy he rents from takes the money but nothing more. He doesn't ask what Chris does here and he doesn't care. Absentee landlordism at its finest. I have my doubts as to whether Chris's name is anywhere on the deeds.

A knock at the door. 'Jen?'

'What?'

'Come downstairs.'

'Why?'

'TV. Um, aye, Breakfast News. You'll want to see.'

I take a deep breath and go downstairs. He moves ahead of me, almost skipping with the speed in case we miss it.

When I get to the living room, I see Crawford's face on the flatscreen.

' . . . cannot confirm or deny that the body belongs to Jennifer Carter . . .'

Body?

' . . .the investigation is ongoing, and we are asking any members of the public who may have been sheltering Miss Carter or who may be aware of where she disappeared to following a month-long spree of violence . . .'

I read the ticker tape at the bottom of the screen. *Breaking news.* A body has been found floating in the Clyde and they believe it to be mine.

'You're dead,' Chris says. Is he laughing?

'Jesus,' I say.

'How's it feel, aye, aye?'

It feels good. Liberating. One more step to disappearing completely. I know the documents are due today. If I want, I can vanish completely, become someone else, leave all of this behind.

But I can't.

Unfinished business and all.

I say, 'Thanks.'

'Aye, aye,' he says.

I smile.

Forty Seven

Dorothy Rose Harrow.

I'm not sure about the name.

'Howsabout if they call you Dot?'

That's not so bad, I figure. Yeah, *Dot*. It works. It's fine. It's good.

I look at the passport and driver's licence. 'This still work like it used to?' I ask. 'Like in the books, where they get a name from dead babies?'

Runt smiles. He doesn't answer. Probably best not to ask. 'They're biometric and all that,' he says. 'Passport control in the EU, you tap and go.'

'Nice.'

'Oh, aye,' he says. 'Beaut, right? I mean, not that we'll have it for much longer or anything, given what happened last year. But long enough for you. How'd the other items work out for you?' He won't say what they are. Being careful, perhaps. Walls have ears. Or at least microphones.

'Fine,' I say.

'Good,' he says. He stands.

'You've been sweet,' I say.

He stops just before leaving. Turns back. Glint in his eyes. Thinks his luck is in. Especially now I'm on my feet and walking towards him.

'Aw, no,' he says, doing the false modesty thing, giving it jazz hands. 'Not at all. It's business.'

'I know,' I say. 'But doing all this on such short notice.'

'Y'know how it is,' he says. 'Any friend of Chris, and all.'

My arms are out. Oh, he really can't resist. I embrace him. He wraps his arms around me, takes a wee sniff at my neck, maybe thinking I won't notice, maybe not caring if I do.

And then his body tenses.

'Oh, fuck.'

I step back. I don't keep the handgun pressed into his side any longer than I have to. Don't want him thinking he can take it off me.

'What're you doing?' he says.

'What's it look like?'

'I don't carry cash,' he says.

'Not what I'm after.'

'Then what?'

'You have other clients besides Chris,' I say.

'Aye.'

'He knows. He told me. Gave me names.'

Runt looks at me for a second as though seeing me for the first time. And realisation sets in. 'Aw, fuck's sakes,' he says.

I say, 'Man like you, you think you can play both sides against the middle, right? Bet you've been doing it all your life. Telling yourself it's just what you do to stay alive in this world.'

'On the telly this morning, they said you were dead. Had this picture. You looked different, but I kent it was you. And the man tends to pay well, know what I'm saying?'

'These passports, they're the real deal?'

'Got 'em ordered before I saw the news. That and the contacts, everything I set up, it's all real.' he says. 'That was all before I realised you were . . .well, you.' He shakes his head. Grins. 'Jesus, the fucking Angel of Death.'

'What?'

'That's what he called you.'

'Buchan?'

'Aye.'

So maybe he thinks I really am a psycho.

'He hoped you were dead. Said if anyone heard anything, we were to go straight to him. But I never thought . . .'

'No.'

'Chris vouched for you.'

'He did.'

'Fuck.'

'He's not dead.'

Runt looks at me with his head cocked to one side.

'Chris, I mean.'

'Oh.'

'In case you were wondering. I'm the Angel of Death, after all. He popped out for a while because he knew what I was planning. He thought you were going to be pretty upset. Not really sure he'll ever come back.'

Runt laughs. Cuts it off fast, though. 'He's no that daft, then.'

'No.'

'Unlike me.'

'Unlike you.'

'Fool for a pretty face.' He gives me a wink, but this time it's half-hearted.

'Flattery could get you killed.'

'Always a danger.' He claps his hands together. 'Right, so what happens now?'

'You call the old man,' I say. 'And tell him you've seen me.'

'At least I'm no lying.'

I gesture with the Glock that he should take a seat. He does so, sitting on the ratty old couch. 'Got any cigs?'

'No.'

'I tried the vapours. No use for me.'

'I never smoked.'

'You should live dangerously.'

Maybe he's right. 'This is dangerous enough for me.'

'Aye, good point.'

'You should call him now.'

'Now?'

'Arrange to meet him tonight.'

'Where?'

'Kinning Park,' I say. 'You tell him the truth, as far as seeing me goes, but you tell him that's where the handover's happening.'

'He'll not come alone.'

'That's fine,' I say.

'Are you mental? You have a gun. He has a fucking army. Army of morons, like, but all the same . . .'

'Maybe,' I say. Then I wave the gun to remind him I'm holding it. 'I've used one of these before.'

'I know,' he says. 'You really killed Smiley?'

'Yes.'

'Then I'm dialling the fucking number,' he says, reaching into his pocket to pull out a phone. 'Fast as I fucking can.'

∗ ∗ ∗

The girl in the mirror isn't tired. She's angry.

I move closer. Try to see something else about her. Anything else. A person isn't a simple reduction of one emotion. There has to be more to them.

But right now, anger is all she has.

And a name.

Dorothy Rose Harrow.

Dot.

The name feels younger, softer than the girl I see. Maybe she

252

will be. Not soft like a pushover, but soft like people want to be around her. Fun. Reliable and dependable. But fun.

Like I think I used to be.

I won't be Jen Carter again, but maybe Dorothy Harrow – Dot – will know better than to make the same mistakes.

I smile at myself in the mirror.

Nothing to say she's not a lesbian. Maybe the best way to avoid this situation happening again. All of this, it was the fault of men, after all.

Ed.

Smiley.

Buchan.

Even Crawford.

Nah, it wouldn't work for me. I know that. You feel how you feel and women never did it for me. Maybe if I met the right one, but I doubt it. What I'm sure of is that no matter who I appear to be to the outside world, I'm not really going to be able to trust anyone again. Not intimately. Not like that. When you have a secret to hide that could unravel everything, trust doesn't come easy.

Maybe I'll just get a cat.

Wherever I end up.

Forty Eight

Runt asked for his reward to be brought in cash: 200,000 in a duffel bag.

I worried this would be too much or that paying in cash would seem unusual, but it all seemed above board. 'Cash is the way to go,' Runt said. 'Everything I do, I deal in cash. Easier to hide from the tax man these days, aye?'

The *Daily Mail* crowd would love Runt. Pulling in thousands and still claiming benefits. Don't know why he dresses like he does, though. Maybe feels he has to. Homage to his roots or something. Or just that he doesn't want to stand out, the kind of places where he walks. The kind of attention he might draw.

He has a car. A banged-up old Fiat Ibiza with dark green body work and rusted trim. The wheels look ready to wobble off and roll into the night, but he assures me that it's passed its MOT with flying colours. I don't ask how much he paid for that to happen. I don't want to know. Or even think about it.

As we drive out, he asks if I think I can really do this.

When I don't say anything, he presses the point, 'Why would you, anyway? Why not just run away?'

'I might have,' I say. 'Or turned myself into the police, even.'

'Aye?'

'That's what I planned to do. What I would have done. But he was the one who made it personal. He made a promise to me and then he broke it.'

'What promise?'

'To let my mum live.'

Everything else – all the violence, all the death, all the pain – I could have let it go. I could have admitted defeat and just tried to live out my life quietly in some other country, maybe, just making my way, day by day.

We're silent for the rest of the journey. The radio in the car is broken. He claims that he lost the code, can't be arsed paying to have the radio reset or hunting down the manufacturer's codes online. 'Music in my head,' he says, 'is all I need.

I have no doubt he hears all kinds of strange sounds rattling around that tiny skull of his.

I have a bag on my lap. Inside the bag is the Ruger. Runt has now told me that the automatic is something of a collector's item, that they stopped making these after 1996. He brought it along because Chris told him money was no object. He assures me that just because it was discontinued, that doesn't mean there were issues. 'Bloody reliable,' he chunters. 'American made, with all the quality that implies, aye?'

Aye. He already gave me the sales pitch. Maybe he just needs to talk. Whatever. Long as what he sold me does the job I need it to.

* * *

The empty building looms. We're here early. That's fine.

The idea is for Buchan to catch us in the act. I've thought this through. I know what I'm doing.

Or at least, I tell myself that I do.

Runt looks up at the building with wide eyes as we stand outside. 'Aw, Christ,' he says. 'I'm not going in there. No fucking way!'

When I urge him with the Glock, he relents. I carry the bag with the Ruger over my shoulder. The Glock is what I want to use in the final instance. Something about a handgun seems personal. The Ruger's what you use to clear the room.

When did I start thinking like this?

I can't stop thinking about Smiley's face when he died. When he knew that I was going to kill him. He'd been smiling – no, *smirking* was more like it – right before I pulled the trigger. Like there was some joke being told that he'd already guessed the punchline to.

Maybe because, in a roundabout way, he knew he'd won. Not in the way he expected, maybe. But instead of killing me, he'd turned me into a killer. Everything that went before was an accident.

Everything after?

Deadlier than the Male, the tabloids said. They didn't know the half of it.

'You're sure no one's dossing here?' Runt says.

'If they are,' I say, 'they'll know better than to interfere.'

'Aye,' he says. 'Fuckin right. A girl and a wee lad. That's what they'll see in the dark. Deadly, right enough.'

I ignore him, put the Glock in the bag and heft out the Ruger. The bag stays on my shoulder. I check the clip's in the barrel and relax my grip. For now, all we can do is wait.

'Then they'll soon learn their mistake,' I say.

'You're a cold-hearted bitch.'

I don't say anything. I try to think about what I have to do. Instead, I think about Mum. I can't help it. The thoughts have been there, waiting. I can't hold them back any more.

When we last spoke, I remember thinking that she loved me, but she was afraid of who I'd become. If she was here now, she'd hate what I was thinking of doing.

But maybe if she'd had everything taken away from her, she might feel differently. Maybe even understand. If she'd lost not just the people she loved, but everything she believed to be true.

I haven't just lost my mum, my friend, even my ex-boyfriend. My entire life.

I've lost myself.

Runt gets fed up standing around in silence. 'What happens now?'

I don't answer his question.

'Should I be doing something?'

'You should be telling me what the fuck is going on is what you should be doing.' Buchan's voice cuts through the dark with the force of a hurricane. Hurricane Bawbag, if you want to get specific.

I turn to face him. He's flanked by two men I haven't seen before. Big and burly. Both carrying shotguns.

'Oh,' he says. 'Don't think I didn't come prepared, doll. This prick,' meaning Runt, 'he doesn't just call up out of the blue.'

I look at Runt. He shrugs. 'I did what you asked. And what he asked.'

Both sides against the middle. Prick. 'You're dead,' I tell him.

'Death,' Buchan says, 'is like a bit of slap and tickle compared to what I'd put him through. And he knows it.'

I raise the gun.

'So you're going to kill me?' Buchan says. 'You're one woman with a gun. My friends here are armed too. Even if you kill me, they kill you. If you kill one of them, the other gets you. So, what? Is it really worth it?'

'You tell me.'

He looks at Runt. 'And you? Y'wee fucking shitesack. We had an agreement.'

Runt starts letting out sharp little breaths, like he can't quite get the words to follow. He's been caught out and he knows it.

Buchan turns back to me. 'I've always thought someone should put him out of his misery, the wee shite. You know he has to pay girls, right? And even then it's because those he does sleep with, I tell them it's in their best interests to do so.'

Runt is shaking with rage. But there's nothing he can do. He's the only one at this party without protection. From what Buchan just said, I guess that's the story of his life.

'Just fucking kill her,' Runt says. 'Tell you what, I'll only take half the cash. I mean, she's here, isn't she? Like I said.'

'You'll take your life and be grateful for that.'

I look at Buchan and his bodyguard. They're standing maybe five feet away now. Buchan cool as anything. He probably believes bullets will bounce off him. He's Glasgow's only surviving original hard man. Whole armies have failed to bring him down. What's a wee lass like me doing to do?

'I know you're desperate,' Buchan says to me. 'For the record, I didn't ask those twats to kill your mother. They took it upon themselves to do a wee bit of improvising. It's the trouble with the younger generation, you see. We've bred a nation of bloody psychos. The boys, anyway. Boys like that.'

'And what about me?'

'If you were the killer the tabloids made you out to be, the kind of madwoman that Smiley thought he was dealing with, then you'd have had the sense to lay low. Not come out in the open like this.'

'The girl they found,' I say. 'The body in the Clyde. They said she was me.'

'Mistaken identity,' said Buchan. 'I don't know who she was or who she pissed off. But she looked enough like you that they misidentified the body. Well, the fact that I greased a few palms may have helped with that too.'

'Why?'

'I thought it might bring you back out into the world, love. If you were what I thought you were – and you are – then you couldn't stand by and watch someone else be mistaken for you. The way you killed that boy by the side of the road . . .the one who killed your darling departed mother . . . That was impressive.'

'He's definitely dead?'

'You beat his brains out with a rock. Don't pretend you didn't know.'

I just have to pull the trigger. The gun was on automatic. Runt had told me about how many rounds it expelled per minute and per second. Even if the recoil caught me off guard, I'd still be able to take someone down. Maybe both those bastards, before they had a chance to blow my face off with their own weapons.

'Look,' Buchan said. 'You're itching to either kill me or go down in a blaze of glory. Fine. But listen to me, lass. I like what I see. And there's one thing you have to consider before you pull that trigger.'

'What?'

'I want to offer you a job.'

Forty Nine

'Jeez-o, man!' Runt says. 'Are you high?'

Buchan ignores him. Keeps his eyes on me. 'Specifically,' he says, 'Smiley's job. I want you to come and work for me. I want you to keep stupid pricks like your ex-boyfriend in line. I want you to deal with traitorous bawbags like your wee friend here.'

'I'm sorry?' I say.

Maybe I'm hallucinating. Finally gone mad.

'Your answer probably determines if we all walk out of here alive. Well, except wee Runt. He's your first assignment. Just kill him and I can make everything better.'

'This is a joke,' Runt says, voice rising high into a near-squeak. 'Big fucking joke. Ha-ha. Okay, just fucking kill her.'

'New name,' Buchan says. 'New face, even. Come on, it's been done before. A wee bit of plastic surgery's nothing to be frightened of.'

I snort. Can't help it. He's having me on. Buying time.

Nah.

It's not going to work.

Runt's voice breaks the silence: 'Joke's over! I did what you asked and brought the cow here. Our deal's done. You don't even need to pay me. I'm fucking loyal, man, I fucking swear it. Swear it! Jesus, I'll kill her myself, show you how serious I am.'

Seems like he's no longer so sweet on me.

The guy on Buchan's right raises his shotgun. A small

movement. I'd been looking somewhere else, I might not have noticed.

I react fast. Raise the Ruger. No time to aim, or press the butt against my shoulder. All I can do squeeze the trigger.

The kickback is intense. I'm holding the weapon and it jerks my arm back so I elbow myself in the side. Stupid idea setting it to full auto. The gun jumps in my hand and the short spray fires high. The sound echoes. As much physical force as the bullets. Shakes my bones, destroys the inside of my head.

The guy with the shotgun jerks his head back. I see three clouds of red mist that I realise are blood. The shotgun jerks up as well and a low boom echoes as he fires harmlessly upward before dropping the weapon.

The other guy moves as well, while Buchan retreats behind him.

I spin on my heels and dodge to the side as I let off another short burst. Finger on the trigger for maybe even less than second. The bone-rattling power of the weapon – belying its small size – is terrifying.

For a moment, embarrassingly, I feel like I want to cry.

This time I keep my shot low and the thug doubles up with bad stomach ache. Doesn't even get a chance to let loose. He drops his gun and face-plants.

Buchan turns to run. I raise the weapon.

A weight pulls me to the side. I fall off-balance as I squeeze. I let loose maybe four or five shots and then I'm on my knees, realising that it's Runt who's jumped up and grabbed at my forearm to stop me from killing Buchan. He's not up for this any more. Thinks he can save his own life by saving Buchan's. Trying to prove where his loyalties lie. Thinking that's how he saves his own skin.

Even I know that's little more than wishful thinking.

The lies we tell ourselves.

I land awkwardly on top of Runt, my head to the side, looking at Buchan instead of my attacker. The old man falters and falls. Whatever happened, I know I got him. How bad, though, is another question.

I'm still holding the gun, but Runt's holding my arm down. Both hands wrapped around my forearm, all his weight keeping me pinned. For such a wee guy, he's got more muscles than you expect.

He twists underneath me and pulls my arm down towards his face. He bites. Hard.

I scream and finally let go of the Ruger. Pull myself up and away from Runt, but his front teeth have a grip of my upper arm and won't let go. I push my weight back down again. He's not expecting that, and moves with me, single-mindedly concentrating on keeping his teeth in my arm. The back of his skull cracks against concrete and his jaws finally slacken.

Jesus!

I roll off him and onto my back. I breathe, staccato. I want to just lie there and recover, but there's no time for sitting about.

Adrenaline does its job. I get to my feet. Glance at my arm. Bite marks. Blood. Fine, I'll get tested later. If there is a later.

I look at Runt. He's on the ground. Groaning. There's blood on the concrete. Maybe I've done him some real damage. Not that it matters. Bastard deserves what he gets.

I kick away the Ruger. Just in case he gets an idea.

Runt tries to sit up, but doesn't seem to have the strength or the co-ordination. He gives up, falls back down. Settles for looking up at me. His eyes don't quite focus. He moves his lips, but he doesn't manage to say anything.

I see the bag on the ground nearby. I take out the Glock.

But there's no need. He's not moving any more. There's a stillness that I've seen too many times recently not to recognise it. There is a difference between playing dead and being dead, and now that I know it intimately, I understand what it is. Maybe even welcome it a little. Like an old friend.

I walk over to Buchan.

Calm.

The heels of my boots click on the concrete floor.

He didn't get far. He's been trying to drag himself with his fingers, but even that's too much of a task for him now. He rolls over to his back when he realises I'm standing over him.

I stand back and aim the Glock.

Right at his face.

I want the wizened old gnome to see it coming.

This is it. What I was looking for. Right here.

'He was right about you.'

I should pull the trigger.

Instead, I hesitate.

'Who?'

'Smiley. He said you were a killer. Same as him. He was right.'

'No. Not the same.'

'You killed two of my men tonight. And unless I'm very much mistaken, you just spilled Runt's brains all over the floor.'

'I don't do this because I enjoy it.'

'Lie to yourself all you want, doll. Because you do. It's no accident that people keep dying around you. That you dispose of the evidence. That you do it all over again every time. Once is an accident. Twice is maybe even careless . . . But three times? Four?'

He's baiting me.

Just shoot him, Jen.

Do it.

Do it.

'Then just kill me,' he says. 'Kill me and your name will be known all over the city. They'll say *there's the bitch that killed Glasgow's gangster number one*. People might even forget that you killed your boyfriend, your best friend . . .even a couple of their own. Worth it to see me out the picture.'

I steady myself. Steady the gun.

Look him in the eyes.

He doesn't look at me. Only at the gun.

'Do it, then,' he says. 'Do it.'

Fifty

I lower the gun.

Put it down on the ground. Carefully. Like I'm handling a small animal.

'What the fuck . . .?'

I deliberately plant my foot on the inside of Buchan's right leg, where the bleeding looks to be at its worst. He gives a high-pitched squeal and squirms beneath me. It's satisfying.

He's more scared of this than he is of dying.

Good.

This isn't about mercy. Or being the good person. This is about not giving him what he wants. Not letting him win.

I lift my foot, bend down and put my free hand inside his coat.

'The fuck?'

I take his phone and stand up. Swipe the screen. No password. Of course. Fine by me.

999.

'What the fuck're you doing?'

'*Which service do you require?*'

'*Police.*'

'Little fucking bit–'

I raise the gun with my free hand. Not really aiming anywhere other than his general direction. He shuts up. He knows by now that I'm probably not going to kill him, but he's not sure what else I might try to do.

I could shoot his balls off.

'*Please state the nature of the emergency.*'

'Three men dead. Another seriously injured with a gunshot to the leg.'

'*Can I have your name?*'

'My name doesn't matter.' I rattle off the address. 'Please tell Detective Inspector Crawford with the Glasgow Major Investigations Unit that he needs to respond.'

'*Officers will be with you shortly. But I need you to—*'

I clear the line. Drop the phone. Kick it into the dark.

'You'll pay, you wee fucking . . .' He trails off, all that bluster disappearing, like he knows it's useless.

'Did you bring the cash?'

'What do you think?'

'Did you bring it?'

'Fuck you.'

I step past him. No time to waste.

Outside, I see a car parked near the one I came with. It doesn't belong here. I take a brick and smash the window. The alarm goes off. There's a duffel bag in the back. I pull it out, check the contents. All as advertised.

Runt's greed was what got the better of him. If he'd stuck to his guns and delivered me to Buchan as promise, I've no doubt he'd have been paid as soon as I was dead. Buchan was a man of his word, in an odd way. Long as you weren't in his way. Even what he did to Mum, I kind of understand. He knew I was going to screw him one way or another. Why keep any promise he made?

Runt also knew that if I killed Buchan, we'd have had a fifty-fifty split. Maybe it seemed like a bad deal to him. After all, who was I? Buchan was one of those men you'd think could

266

survive the apocalypse, so maybe he seemed the right person to back.

Ah, well. Runt's loss.

* * *

I take the early morning train to Edinburgh. Once I arrive at Haymarket, I take the bus out to the airport and use one of the internet terminals to book a ticket to New York in the name of Dorothy Rose Harrow. The ESTA takes a bit to fill in, and I create a fake last known employment. Not that anyone really checks. The application is fast-tracked through.

Everything works. Runt had been playing both sides against the middle, maybe not entirely sure who was going to come out on top. Everything I'd asked him for, he'd delivered. Hedging his bets in case I really did kill Buchan.

Dorothy Rose Harrow is real. Which means Jen Carter can stay dead.

I'm not sure how that feels.

I still don't believe I am Dorothy. *Dot.*

I go to the airport's chapel and sit down near the front. Take deep breaths and look up at Jesus on the cross. I've never been much for religion, but same as everyone else, I took my indoctrination at school, and in times of need I still turn to Him in an odd way. Maybe just because I figure I might get lucky: there might really be someone up there, even if I know the truth in my heart.

Jesus looks down at me from the cross.

I don't know what I see in his face.

His suffering? Or his distaste for me?

I didn't mean to kill anyone. I don't want to do it again. That's not who I am. I killed to protect myself. And those around me.

Except Ed.

Always except Ed.

267

He was an accident. What happened with him was beyond my control. Jesus, in His infinite wisdom, being one and the same as God and the Holy Spirit – however that works – has got to understand that and be able to forgive me. But I can't read his expression.

A man in a dog collar enters the room. He looks at me. I look back. We're alone. He walks over. 'Excuse me,' he says. 'I don't mean to interrupt, but you look troubled.'

'No,' I say.

I look back at Jesus. And then at the man in the black shirt and white dog collar. Of course I don't believe in signs from God. But sometimes it pays to hedge your bets.

'I'm sorry,' I say. 'That was rude.'

'We all need peace,' he says. He has a kindly face. Although he's not old, his face is lined, but not with pain or hardship. Laughter around his eyes. There's an odd serenity to his expression. I'm both reassured and nervous to be in the same room as him.

'That's what I'm looking for.'

'In general?'

'It's been a rough few weeks.'

'Oh?'

'People I know have died. I feel responsible.'

'Did you kill them?'

I hesitate. He's being glib. Exaggerating to show me how things could be worse. If only he knew the truth. 'I feel like what happened was my fault.'

'But you did not intentionally kill these people?'

'No.'

'You have to let go of the guilt,' he says. 'We all do or say foolish things. Sometimes we see connections between our actions and what happens to others that aren't really there, but because we care for those people, we feel we have to make that connection, to share the burden in some way. If we're happy and they're unhappy, or if we're healthy and they're unwell, then that seems somehow unfair. Our happiness makes us feel guilty.' He pauses. 'Does that make sense?'

'Maybe,' I say. I stand.

'Stay,' he says. 'For a while.'

'I have to go.'

I can feel his eyes on me as I leave the room, walking just a touch too fast, as though running from something that only I can see.

Fifty One

'Passport?'

I hand it over, along with the boarding pass. The girl checks it and nods. She looks up at me.

'Did you pack your bags yourself?'

'Uh-huh.'

'First time going to New York?'

'Oh, aye.'

'Great city.' She tags my luggage and I watch it wheel through. She passes me my tickets. 'Thank you very much, Miss Harrow. Have a good flight.'

I tell her I will.

I head upstairs but I don't go for security. Instead I stop in at one of the food places, a glorified Wetherspoons. On the screens, they're showing BBC news. Right now, there's an aerial shot of the building where I killed Runt and left old man Buchan rolling around in his own piss and blood.

And the two other men, Jen. Don't forget them. The ones whose names you never knew. But you killed them anyway.

At the bottom of the screen, the subtitles flash up:

. . .led to the detention of suspected gangland boss, Solomon Buchan . . .

I have to smile at that. For years, they've danced around the topic, but now they have free rein to say what they like. There's no coming back from this for him. He can't explain how he came to be there, surrounded by the dead and the dying.

And then there's the little matter of the emails I uploaded to the police: the ones that explained where the money was, and urged professional standards to look closer at the accounts of some of their officers. Of course, I mention Michael by name. Although given how he died, maybe they've already worked out some of his secrets.

I drink a Coke and watch the news.

...events unfolded dramatically over the last twenty-four hours ...

More than that.

...In other news, Police Scotland are still refusing to formally identify a woman's body recovered from the Clyde two days ago. The body is suspected to be that of alleged murderer Jennifer Carter, who they believe is connected to the deaths of at least four men ...

My picture flashes up. The old one. My hair is different. My clothes. Maybe I really am Dorothy. Dot. I don't resemble the girl I used to be.

Maybe in the right light.

I resist the urge to look round and check if anyone's noticed me. But I'm the only one watching the screen.

I take a deep breath.

Someone sits down at the table across from me.

'I'm sorry,' I say. 'But–'

I stop speaking. I can't say anything else. Words evaporate in my brain.

Crawford.

'Miss Carter,' he says. 'Or maybe not. You won't be using that name, I guess. I mean, you're not stupid.'

'It was worth a try,' I say.

'Where are you going?'

'Away.'

271

I don't think I have the energy to run. What would be the point?

'A good answer,' he says. 'I just wanted to see you.'

'Before you put me away?'

'Did you kill your boyfriend?'

'An accident.'

'Your friend, Caroline?'

'No.' I take a deep breath. 'I didn't kill that police officer, either.' I feel my cheeks overheat. I've forgotten her name. She's barely a drop in the bloodbath that my life has become.

I don't know that I feel bad about that, either. Embarrassed, maybe, that I forgot her name, but not ashamed or horrified.

'There was a police officer, too. They just called him Michael. Young guy. I watched him get his throat ripped out by a dog after Buchan decided to show me just how serious he was.'

'You really are . . . You really . . . This just happened to you?' he says.

I nod. 'And now it's over.' One way or the other. 'How'd you find me?'

He smiles. 'Funny what a person can do, with time on their hands. I've been put on gardening leave following the debacle with Buchan, and my little stunt in the interview room. Guess they're trying to work out just how hard they'll throw the book at me. Second time in three years I've fucked up something big time related to the Glasgow gangland.' He smiles. 'Being off duty, though, it didn't stop me from finding a friend of yours and having a nice little chat.

'Aye?'

'Chris. When Runt was found dead at that massacre, I made the connection. Don't know how you knew him. Don't think that it matters.'

'Oh?'

'He told me everything. After I knew enough, it wasn't too

tough to track down Dorothy Harrow's credit cards.' He tilts his head to the side. 'I don't know that the name Dorothy really suits you, though.'

'My friends call me Dot.'

'You have friends already?'

So this is it. The end. I keep expecting to feel a heavy hand on shoulder, Crawford producing the cuffs.

'That's all well and good, except . . .I don't think you're who I'm looking for. You're not the girl who killed all those people.'

I don't trust him. 'Why? Why would you say that?'

'She's dead, for one thing.' He leans in across the table. 'Call it a judgement call,' he says. 'Maybe an error of judgement call, but we're all entitled to those.'

'What if anyone finds out?'

'You don't look the same as you did. I tell anyone who asks that you convinced me. If those papers are good enough to fool passport control, they're good enough to fool me.'

'I didn't know what else to do.'

'I know. And then I went and tried to use you. Which was stupid. Really stupid.'

'Aye, it was.'

'I have a habit of making bad decisions. What got me demoted in the first place, you know.'

'You told me.'

'The investigation that messed up your friend Kat's life . . . I always wondered what happened to her. I wanted to apologise. Sincerely. Not in the line of duty. As one human being to another.'

I shrug. 'So I can go?'

'Yes.'

'This isn't a trick?'

'I could change my mind.'

But he's not going to.

For a moment, I almost feel for him, sitting across the other side of the table with his salt and pepper hair, and his face that could be handsome if it wasn't permanently hangdog. Those grey eyes too. The kind of eyes that speak of a sadness he can't really express.

I stand. Walk away, not quite turning my back. I don't believe he's doing this. Or maybe he'll change his mind.

But I join the queue. Pass through security.

Make it to the other side.

* * *

Final boarding call.

Walking the umbilical beside everyone else. Thinking everyone can see how subdued I am. Even the Americans seem upbeat, as though the lure of their country is so vast that it doesn't matter their holiday is over.

I grab my seat – next to the window – and close my eyes.

'Long wait, hun,' a voice says. I open my eyes, and a woman with dark hair who could be an old forty or a well-made up fifty, sits down next to me. 'I hate airports myself.'

I smile, not desperate to engage in conversation. But she doesn't take the hint.

'You from Scotland?'

I nod.

'Ever been to New York before?'

I shake my head.

'You're going to love it.'

I close my eyes.

'You really have had a long day.'

'I'm sorry,' I say. 'You know how it is before you go away.'

'Hun, I was burning the midnight oil before I left. You don't want anything to interrupt a vacation, am I right?'

'Uh-huh.'

'You just rest. I figure there's gotta be a few films I can watch on the way back. Maybe that *Braveheart*'ll be on. I so love that movie. The way you guys handed it to the English.'

I say nothing. Just keep my eyes closed.

* * *

My dreams are calm.

I'm out in the middle of the sea in a rowing boat. I assume it's the sea, anyway, because I can't see any land. Just me and my boat in the middle of all this water.

There are no storms brewing, no signs of danger. All I can hear is the lap of the water against the side of the boat. The sound is gentle and soothing.

The water is still, save for tiny ripples.

I should feel afraid to be here, all alone.

But I'm not afraid. I welcome the silence and the solitude.

* * *

When I wake up, my arm has remained asleep. I try to shake it out, and as I do so, I look out the window.

'Welcome back,' my neighbour says. 'And just in time, too.'

New York shouldn't be real. That's what I'm thinking. It's a place of dreams to me. It exists only on the TV or in movies. I shouldn't see it flying in like this, as the plane banks to start making its final descent. I see the familiar buildings, and then I see the water and then . . .

'It's a hell of a town, right?' the woman says, her voice filled with a certain kind of awe I know has to be genuine. 'You get a chance, no matter what else you do, you want to go down to Battery Park, just get a peek of Lady Liberty. Never tire of the sight. Seeing her makes me think I'm home.'

'Aye?'

'What she represents. She's the dream of this country, the real dream, I mean. That everyone who comes here can make a fresh start, can be free to be who they are and if they can't have that, then to discover who they can be.'

I must be smiling a little, because she bristles and says, 'I'm serious, hun. When I talk about these things, they're what I believe. My great, great, great, or maybe just great, great – whatever – my great-something Grandfather, he came across on the boat and he sailed past her. He used to tell my grandad, when he was a boy, he would say how he looked up at the statue and he knew that she was a promise. Anyone could come to this country and find their true self. See, back home he'd been something of a vagabond, but when he came here he decided to remake himself, become someone better. And he did. He really did.'

The statue is gone now. All I can see are buildings and the flatter land of New Jersey on the other side of the water. But just that glimpse, that moment, I think I get it, what this woman is talking about.

A new start. Freedom.

Jennifer Carter is dead.

She died with Ed.

And I think that, for the first time since it happened, I'm fine with forgetting her.

END

About the Author

Russel D McLean is the author of six previous novels, including *And When I Die* (2016) and the five J McNee novels, which have been published in several countries. For two years, he wrote a crime fiction column in the *Herald*. He spent ten years as a bookseller in Dundee and Glasgow, and now works as a freelance editor when not writing his own fiction.

Acknowledgements

Ed's Dead started with a single joke based on a somewhat terrifying anecdote told to me by someone I know. With thanks to them for letting me embellish it for fictional purposes (all names have been changed to protect the innocent).

Like Jen, I was a bookseller for a long time. This book is of course dedicated to booksellers everywhere, but especially those long-suffering souls who were forced to work alongside me.

Specific thanks are due to:

Sara Hunt at Saraband/Contraband, who might just be one of the hardest-working people in publishing. And one of the nicest.

Louise Hutcheson, for helping me figure out that there was one plot twist too many, and then gently easing me through the process of eliminating it from existence. An editor *par excellence*.

Al Guthrie for his consistent support, and for reassuring me during early drafts that this was going to work.

Jay Stringer and Dave White, for all those emails still sending me down rabbit holes of distraction when I really should be working.

Helen Fitzgerald, for kindly allowing me to quote *that* opening line from her brilliant novel, *Viral* (go buy it, folks!)

Lesley McDowell, who always makes it all worthwhile (and brings the prosecco).

Moriarty, Mycroft and Magwitch – because if you don't thank your cats, you're some kind of monster.

Mum and Dad, who must be getting more worried with each book about the kind of people their son is associating with . . .

The Contrabandistas – a more wretched crew of miscreants one could not possibly hope to be associated with.

The Noir at the Bar Crew – across the world, and maybe even beyond . . .

All my enablers out there – far too many of you to mention, but if you think you're one of them, you most definitely are, and you are absolutely incredible! I wouldn't be here without you.

And you. Yes. You. The person reading this now. Without you, the reader, there is no point to any of this. So thank you.